Dead Man Who Walks Away

The entrance to Massacre Ground

Dead Man Who Walks Away

Part II

The Survivor / The Dutchman's Gold

Herbert Dean Ely

MILFORD HOUSE

an imprint of Sunbury Press, Inc.
Mechanicsburg, PA USA

MILFORD HOUSE

an imprint of Sunbury Press, Inc.
Mechanicsburg, PA USA

For information about special discounts for bulk purchases, please contact Sunbury Press Orders Dept. at (855) 338-8359 or orders@sunburypress.com.

To request one of our authors for speaking engagements or book signings, please contact Sunbury Press Publicity Dept. at publicity@sunburypress.com.

FIRST MILFORD HOUSE PRESS EDITION: November 2023

Set in Adobe Garamond Pro | Interior design by Crystal Devine | Cover by Lawrence Knorr | Edited by Taylor Berger-Knorr.

Publisher's Cataloging-in-Publication Data
Names: Ely, Herbert Dean, author.
Title: Dead man who walks away part II / the survivor / the Dutchman's gold / Herbert Dean Ely.
Description: First trade paperback edition. | Mechanicsburg, PA : Milford House Press, 2023.
Summary: Dead Man Who Walks Away, II is the continuing story of the legend concerning the origin of the gold of the Lost Dutchman Mine of Arizona. It is the only legend that is actually physically possible as opposed to the many accounts involving superstition, religious innuendo, or mysticism.
Identifiers: ISBN : 979-8-88819-151-4 (paperback) | ISBN : 979-8-88819-152-1 (ePub).
Subjects: FICTION / Historical / General | FICTION / Fairy Tales, Folk Tales, Legends & Mythology.

Product of the United States of America
0 1 1 2 3 5 8 13 21 34 55

For the Love of Books!

To my lovely wife, JoAnn, who has suffered through the long period of my research and efforts get this book right; my sons—Jon, Jeff, and daughter Jacqui; grandkids—Brian, Chris, Lauren, Katie, Megan, Bradley, Jake, and Dana—all who were probably wondering "Is he serious?"

Acknowledgments

My thanks go out to my longtime friend, Mr. Jim Davia, who walked, climbed, and jumped the rocks and ravines, dodged rattlesnakes, and searched the desert locales of this story to find and visit the "Lost Dutchman Mine." The origin of the gold of the Lost Dutchman Mine is the subject of this legend. Many thanks! For the use of the Spanish version of his name, Diego DaVia, muchas gracias!

My thanks to my friend Mr. Bruce Johnson, retired educator from Illinois, for his time and interest in *Dead Man Who Walks Away*. His effort is especially appreciated for having accompanied me to Massacre Ground as well as other pertinent locales important to this story.

Preface

In what is now the state of Arizona there exists a box canyon. The canyon's entrance faces the setting sun, sloping somewhat gently eastward and upward until it reaches the far wall. Now strewn with boulders and cacti and overgrown with bristly brush, it hides the grisly beginning of a golden legend.

Bones of horses, mules, and of men at one time littered the floor of this bleak, unforgiving canyon. Among the bleaching bones, here and there, filling the small crevices in the rocks or making small piles of glittering dust on the granite floor... gold! Some of it had washed away. Some of it had merely settled into the dirt and gravel. Some had been picked up by prospectors or wandering drifters. Each one thought that he had found "El Dorado," the fabulous wealth each of them dreamed would change his life.

Unfortunately, what they had found was merely float gold—gold that was there, not by nature, but dropped there at the same time as the living bones had dropped there, in the canyon that is now called "Massacre Ground."

With no written language of their own, the story was told only by the old ones of the Yavapai and the Apache.

The breeze plays among the thorny branches of the canyon's brush. Mesquite, ocotillo, saguaro, and many other forms of cacti abound. During the day, the blinding white-hot sun of summer bakes every inch of the canyon floor too hot for man or beast to walk upon. Yet now and then, usually during the cool winter months, a wanderer ventures into the canyon. Having taken his fill of its stark desert beauty, the wanderer begins to feel uneasy and hurries to find a trail out of the canyon. Something in this canyon, unseen, perhaps the spirits of those who cannot leave, warn him of danger. Wisely, without turning back, he departs, leaving the canyon to only the sun and the breeze and the shadows of the past.

Introduction

Peralta!

Even now, the name Peralta stirs the imagination of people in the southwestern deserts of Arizona and New Mexico. The aristocratic Peralta family of northern Sonora, who ruled their empire of mining, cattle, and lumber from Sonora to California, left their mark on the early history of the Southwest. But then, and even to this day, the only item of genuine interest to Sonoran Desert dwellers was the mining: gold mining. For a hundred years after the Jesuit and Franciscan padres forced Indian laborers to work their mines, the Peraltas continued to reap the gold from the land of the Yavapai and Apache tribes. Before being driven out by the Yavapai, the Peralta family had been the controlling economic force in what is now Arizona.

Then, during the period of 1848 to 1854, after the Mexican American war, events led to the Gadsden Purchase of what is now the southern portion of the state of Arizona. Prior to that purchase, Don Miguel Peralta, with financing and military support from Antonio de Lopez de Santa Anna, president of Mexico, embarked on a large expedition to the old mines in what is now Arizona to retrieve as much gold as possible before that Gadsden Purchase became fact. That endeavor was almost successful.

Realizing that the Yavapai and their allies, the Apache, were about to attack in retaliation for their mistreatment and lack of due respect, the Peralta expedition made a desperate run to save their lives and their gold.

The Yavapai and the Apache trapped them a bit northwest of Superstition Mountain in a box canyon now known as "Massacre Ground." The Peralta miners and their Mexican cavalry all died, all save one, Lieutenant Diego DaVia. Somehow, a day or so after the slaughter, an injured Lieutenant Diego DaVia pulled himself from under his dead horse and, with his mind reeling from the horror of what he had just survived, walked away.

High on a hillside overlooking the tragic scene, the great Yavapai warrior O hi Cama and a young shaman of the Apache watched DaVia make his way out of that canyon. They marveled at his survival and feared his medicine. O hi Cama remembered him well as the very capable and brave soldier. He referred to Lieutenant DaVia as "Dead Man Who Walks Away." Thus, would Lieutenant Diego DaVia be forever known among the Yavapai and Apache and avoided by those warriors who knew his story. Lieutenant Diego DaVia became "Dead Man Who Walks Away."

This is the continuing story of the Peraltas, the massacre, the survivor, and the Dutchman's gold.

1

The nightmare of what had happened to him over the past forty-eight hours played over and over in the unconscious mind of Lieutenant Diego DaVia. He was unaware of his writhing in agony, as images of the slaughter of his comrades in arms continuously plagued his pain-wracked mind.

Startled, he awakened. He knew not what had awakened him. Perhaps the pain in his head, perhaps the overpowering smell of dead men and animals alike, or perhaps the deafening silence in place of that incredible din as he had left consciousness. He lay there, smashed back into a hole in the canyon wall, partly covered by the dirt and small stones that fell on him when he struck the wall. The dead body of his horse lay in front and partially upon him. The Apache and Yavapai had evidently overlooked him because of this.

Lieutenant DaVia waited patiently for several minutes before even trying to move. He had no way of knowing whether he had been in that hole for a few hours or several days. He waited for any sound, any shadow that would indicate that the Apache and Yavapai were still about. At last, sensing nothing moving, he tried to get a better view of his surroundings. What he saw, looking from behind his dead horse's neck, made him reach for his neck bandana to tie around his nose and mouth to lessen the nausea. The late evening sun had bathed the whole slope of the box canyon in what would normally be a beautiful orange hue. That evening, the hue in the waning light accentuated the horror of it all.

After much effort, the lieutenant freed himself from under the neck and shoulders of his horse and crept out into the open. The sight was

revolting. The dead were everywhere: in the cactus, in underbrush of every sort, draped over the numerous rock formations that had made for a beautiful scene the previous visit, but that evening added a macabre aspect to the entire canyon.

The dead and already bloating bodies of the men had been stripped of everything the Apache and Yavapai thought to be useful to them. Wounded horses and mules had been killed and left where they had fallen. Many were simply gone. The horses were to be used by their new owners. The mules were to be eaten. The bodies of the men had been mutilated—hopefully after they were already dead. Lieutenant DaVia turned away to put the alternative out of his mind. The image of that alternative was too horrible to contemplate.

He soon found the bodies of Capitán Garces and Manuel Peralta lying near each other. Their swords and other weapons, as expected, were missing. However, it looked as though they had fought to the bitter end. There was evidence that dead warriors near them had been carried away by their fellow warriors. The only others in that canyon were dead Mexicans and one very much alive Lieutenant Diego DaVia.

DaVia's only thought at this point was to "get the hell out of this place!" But he needed food and water. Everything had been stripped from horses and mules and men by the warriors as their plunder. However, DaVia's water canteen and supply of jerky were still under his own dead horse. It took some time and a huge amount of work to dig under the horse to retrieve them, but he did it.

The horses and mules, those taken by the warriors, had been outfitted with packs containing the Peraltas' precious gold. Probably very few of the warriors realized the potential value of that gold in future trading with Mexicans or anyone else. It was commonly discarded in crevices or in the Rio Salado and disappeared, in most cases forever. Some of it became float gold left in that stark canyon. But, whether unseen by the warriors or thought not to be worth any effort to retrieve, the warriors missed the saddlebags of Lieutenant Diego DaVia.

Once past his initial revulsion, DaVia had collected his canteen and weapon from under his horse and was about ready to begin his journey away from the scene of carnage. Then, having regained his faculties, he dug the saddlebag filled with gold from the torn and broken saddle. He certainly did not want to forget that. All this had nearly drained him of physical strength, but his instinct to survive forced him onward.

Unknown to Diego DaVia, two mounted warriors, unseen from their vantage point near Green Rock on the western slope of Superstition Mountain, noted his survival and his walk from the massacre grounds. They marveled that he had survived that brutal onslaught. They were themselves both brave warriors, but marveled at the strong medicine of this man who walked away from the dead. Each would tell of him to their fellow warriors. He would be known as "Dead Man Who Walks Away" and, by those who would hear of him, be allowed to go in peace because of what he had done, and because of their fear of his powerful medicine.

As Dead Man Who Walks Away disappeared into the dusk, the young shaman of the Apache and O hi Cama, warrior of the Yavapai, rode off in different directions to their own people, each to tell of what he had seen but hoped never again to see—Dead Man Who Walks Away.

O hi Cama had recognized, even from that distance, the soldier whom he respected as a fellow warrior—Lieutenant Diego DaVia. He would be sure to honor him by telling of his identity and his powerful medicine throughout the tribes, and thus secure him safe passage.

2

As the sunset was turning to twilight, Mexican cavalry Lieutenant Diego DaVia, carrying only his jerky, a canteen of water, his Dragoon revolver, his saber, and a saddlebag full of gold—covered by a dirty shirt to camouflage it—began his long walk out of the box canyon, around the west end of Superstition Mountain, and toward the southwest and the Rio Gila. He hoped that he could follow the Rio Gila west by southwest until he could find civilized transportation west to California.

He had no idea as to whether he would be able to get word to the Peralta family about what had happened to their expedition, or to their son, Manuel.

He walked and walked and walked.

Aside from the Yavapai and Apache warriors involved, Lieutenant (former capitán of dragoons, Mexican army) Diego DaVia found himself the only survivor of the Peralta massacre. This lone survivor turned his face southwest and plodded away from that place of the dead and, hopefully, from the memory of the horror of that massacre. However, that memory would not be left behind. It would plague him and bend him in ways he would never imagine. But he had survived.

Diego DaVia walked on. He was exhausted. The running battle, which was unwinnable from the very beginning, had lasted from sunup to sundown that day . . . whichever day it had been. Yesterday, the day before, he did not know. He had lain unconscious for an undetermined amount of time. The effort of trying to extricate himself from that boulder hole and from under his horse left him all but unable to continue.

Then, once free from his confinement, the horror of the sights and smells that greeted him—the mostly naked, dead soldiers and miners, the dead horses and mules, bloating in the hot sun—had sent him frantically adjusting his bandana to reduce the nausea. He had turned his back and was walking away from . . . Hell!

Then, he faced the desert. The partial moon and stars made passage in the night a fairly easy walk. But DaVia had to force every step. It was the early part of autumn. The days were still hot and dry, but not as hot as they had been the week before. The nights were cooler by comparison and made traveling on foot more bearable. That night, in the silver light of an unfeeling moon, DaVia, despite his exhaustion, plodded on through the dark. His tired body called out for rest at each step. But this was not the first time he had dealt with hardship.

He had spent many years rising in rank within the Mexican army. He was the son of Italian nobility residing in Spain. However, his experiences were not the spit and polish of many military officers. His rank had been earned in the hardship of combat on many fronts, against many enemies. Lieutenant Diego DaVia had until recently been Capitán of Dragoons Diego DaVia. That rank had been earned against the Americans in the recent Mexican American war. It was much later, when attacked by a numerically superior force of Chiricahua Apaches in the province of Chihuahua, that his rank was reduced. His superiors had recommended promotion and decoration for Capitán DaVia but were reversed by political policy of the government in Mexico City. It seemed that the government had begun a new policy of pacification of the Apache. Therefore, because of the zeal demonstrated by DaVia in winning that battle, Capitán DaVia became Lieutenant DaVia. This reduction in rank, which at no time negatively affected the performance of his military orders, doubtless made him less inclined to follow them without question.

———

Morning arrived and with it the intense morning sun. His focus at this point was merely to find a safe, shaded place to get some rest. After first making sure that he would not be sharing it with rattlesnakes, he chose to rest under a north-facing ledge. He feasted upon a few bites of jerky, sipped his small ration of water, and slept until nearly sundown.

DaVia awoke to the sudden realization that the last vestige of the summer monsoon was making a show of it. The dust wave that preceded the actual shower from the thunderstorm just seemed to add insult to injury. After the dust, he relished the rain. He decided that walking in the rain was preferable to waiting it out. So, his journey continued toward the south, as the evening sky became the night sky. The rain did not bother him at all. The critters of the night were in their shelters, or looking for shelter, and presented no obstacle to his travel.

His earlier intention to make his way toward the southwest began to change in favor of the southeast. This would be very much a retracing of the trail that the Peralta expedition had followed to get into that country. The idea that finding civilized transportation to California might not be the thing to do, under the circumstances, began to bend his steps more toward the Rio Gila and then, possibly further east along its bank. There, he might follow that river to the Rio San Pedro. He was contemplating avoiding any real civilization for a time. After what he had been through, DaVia began to realize that he could not count on any support from anyone to relieve suspicion as to why he alone had survived. Someone would doubtless demand accountability for what had happened, and he, as the only survivor in all probability, would be a scapegoat. Based upon recent past history, he felt that he could count on that. Besides, the previous march northward had shown him many places where he could leave the Rio San Pedro and disappear into the wilderness, at least for a while.

He had been severely dehydrated since that whole running battle for their lives, the massacre, and for however long he had been unconscious. This rain proved to be a genuine blessing. He drank the raindrops as they fell. He made little reservoirs out of agave leaves, poured the small supply into his canteen, and walked and walked through mud puddles . . . whenever he found mud puddles. It was not much pleasure, but it was all he had, so he relished it.

—

The lieutenant had now walked for two nights, separated by one day of exhausted sleep. The horrors of the massacre would not long leave his mind. The saguaro cactus made him imagine they were soldiers and warriors. It would make him stop often, thinking he was hallucinating. The hallucinating stopped—cold. He was not sure what he was seeing. After a moment of staring at the convoluted shapes, he became convinced that he was looking at a real horse!

The horse was not moving, and neither was the lieutenant. DaVia was frozen where he stood. He knew the horse was real; he could hear it breathing. He feared that the horse would panic and run away if he made any move at all. DaVia, leaning forward, realized the horse was caught on something, or tied to something. DaVia froze again. The light from the now-visible moon made the lieutenant catch his breath. The horse's rein was held by an Indian! The Indian lay on the ground—not moving. He was also not breathing. Lieutenant DaVia, his saber drawn, approached. The Indian did not move. Upon prodding the prone figure a few times, DaVia was convinced that the Indian was, indeed, dead. The moonlight revealed the badly wounded Indian to be Apache. He must have been one of the few Apache warriors who did not survive. He had ridden his horse, or perhaps was carried by his horse, until falling there. His horse, too exhausted to move, remained with him. No doubt, considering the coming heat of the sun in the morning, the horse would then have broken free.

DaVia led the horse some distance farther away from the dead body. He gave the horse a drink of the limited water supply he had. After that, the horse would have followed DaVia anywhere. However, DaVia was taking no chances. He led the horse until the light of dawn. Then, when he mounted to ride, the horse gave him no trouble. Now, Lieutenant DaVia was mounted. Now, he was technically cavalry again.

Now that he was mounted again, DaVia realized he was not likely to die in the desert. Now he could begin to make some basic plans. No one knew of his survival. Probably no one knew, or might ever know, of the massacre. He, like everyone else, had merely disappeared. With the knowledge that Presidente Santa Anna had been forced into exile, he was not sure if his army still even existed. No matter. Shucking his uniform would be no problem. It wasn't presentable anyway. Well, maybe it was salvageable. Perhaps he would keep it. He had a horse. He had his pistol, his knife, and his saber. All he had to decide was where to disappear. Oh, yes, he also had a saddlebag full of gold, mostly dust and nuggets.

Mounted now, DaVia could make better time. He saw the Rio Gila by the end of the day. Another hour's ride put him into the low trees along the riverbank. Here he made a cold camp. Feasting on jerky and fresh water gave him a much needed feeling of satisfaction. But he was still so tired. He made sure that he and his horse would be unseen in the shadows throughout the night. Then he lay down for some overdue sleep.

If only he could stop those awful dreams. His tortured mind, remembering the sudden attack from both sides of Camp Creek Wash, the terror-filled running battle through the Rio Verde at Needle Rocks, the day-long race, losing man after man to the arrows of the Yavapai, awakened him often. The screams of the wounded men who had to be left to the butchery of the attackers also would not grant him sound sleep. They had raced under a shower of arrows all the way. DaVia had been in many battles before, so that screams of dying men were not new to him. But the realization that the Yavapai were already in place along the banks of the Rio Verde made it plain that they were being herded as part of a well-conceived plan. The single-shot muzzleloader rifles were useless after their first shot. It had proved to be impossible to reload on the dead run through the desert thorns and the shallow Rio Verde, all the while dodging the arrows of the Yavapai. The desperate run for their lives kept up all day, from sandbar to sandbar, in the water of the shallow Rio Verde. It stopped only at sunset at the convergence of the Rio Verde and the Rio Salado. There, across the Rio Salado on the south bank, cavalry, miners, horses, and mules stood gasping for breath, seemingly not taken since morning.

It had been a time to regroup and make some decisions. They were nothing like the force they had been. It was not known if the Yavapai would attack again in minutes, in the morning, or if ever. It had been decided then to make a night march, tired or not, toward Superstition Mountain and the box canyon that had rested and protected them on the trip northward. At some point when they were within range of the canyon, they had halted to make the final decision. The Yavapai did not have firearms; the Apache did. If the Yavapai only were involved, the Peraltas would head south toward Sonora, leaving the Yavapai behind. If gunfire occurred, it meant the Apache had arrived. The Peraltas would have to dash to the box canyon and hope to defend themselves there.

Minutes after starting to turn south, gunfire had opened on their right flank—Apaches! The Peraltas turned and in sheer panic raced for the canyon. Lieutenant DaVia saw immediately that Apache were on the right and Yavapai were on the left. DaVia's assertion that they were being herded toward a predetermined destination was verified. There had been no stopping the stampede into the canyon. When the Apache waiting at the far end and side walls attacked, it was all over in minutes.

The remembered screams of the wounded, the dying, the men being unceremoniously finished off; the horrible screams of animals in pain; the smoke, the dust, and the oblivion, as Lieutenant DaVia was crushed into a boulder hole under his dying horse, snapped DaVia's eyes open repeatedly, allowing sleep to come only in snatches.

Finally, having been able to sleep for only a few hours before dawn, the rising sun ruined even that.

The Rio Gila, rarely very deep except during freak thunderstorms upstream, was only knee deep that morning. Crossing was easy. DaVia began to appreciate the horse he had appropriated from the dead Apache warrior. It was a well-muscled stud, grey black in most places and seemed well trained by its former owner. The grey needed no guidance to pick its way through the rough terrain and vegetation. Then, on the south bank of the Rio Gila, DaVia made his way eastward. He was not sure how far he was from the Rio San Pedro, but he knew all he had to do was keep moving eastward. The Rio San Pedro flowed south to north, emptying into the Rio Gila. He could not miss it. The big grey was making his travel much easier.

Diego DaVia had a lot on his mind. Keeping his focus was difficult, considering what had been his lot these past few years. His focus did peak occasionally by necessity. He had become aware of being watched. Now and then, he would see an almost imperceptible shape in the distance. His travel had been noticed by the Apache. They were keeping track of his movement yet were not willing or daring to observe him within range of his firearm. It was just something else for DaVia to have on his mind. However, he was past worrying about being watched. His fatigue had reached the point that made him almost uncaring about what would happen next. If the Apache wished to start something, he would be more than willing to oblige. Anger was boiling within him beneath the weariness. Unmindful of that weariness and anger, Diego DaVia remained in control. He would do nothing foolish. If they wanted to watch, let them watch.

— —

No longer hindered by the heavy wagons that had so undermined the progress of the Peraltas on the trip north, Diego, with the big grey beneath him, moved with ease. That night he made another cold camp at the junction of the Rio Gila and the Rio San Pedro. His back to a rock ledge and the grey tethered in front of him, Diego DaVia slept at last.

3

The Rio San Pedro, still flowing with the remnants of the summer monsoon rains, provided Diego with a water source and cover for his now southward trip. He kept to the east side of the stream in the morning hours to take advantage of the shade, thus partially covering his movements. He did likewise on the west side in the afternoon. He proceeded at a walk yet still made good time. That night, in the cover of a small wash that intersected the Rio San Pedro from the west and made a slight turn, DaVia felt safe enough to camp with a small, almost smokeless fire. How strange that a small campfire can stimulate a man's thoughts—comforting, restful, and very necessary. He had plans to make.

His mind was still in a whirl over all that had happened. He was hoping for a remote, secluded, even isolated place to call his own to live his life in peace. No matter how long he gazed into the fire, the revelation would not come. He had known better than to make his way north. The north held no prospects for him. Yavapai and who knew what else lay in wait. Westward lay deserts even more desolate than what he had ever known. This he knew from his encounters over the years with those who had been to western Sonora and southern California. On the way to the coast, he was certain to meet Mexican troops who would identify him. Eastward held more deserts and the probability of also encountering Mexican military. He held no illusions of returning to Arizpe, that area of Sonora and the home of the Peraltas. There, he would have to face questions, the answers to which he could not prove. He had dealt with Mexican military justice before. Therefore, going that far south was not a good idea. He at last fell asleep with no good answer but to keep moving and hope for the best.

———

The next morning, Diego moved farther south along the Rio San Pedro. Every step was taken with great care as to not to be seen by the Apache or any wandering Mexican. The days had begun to look remarkably alike. Four days into the southward march along the Rio San Pedro, DaVia came upon an artesian spring making a small fountain-like spray. Cool, clear water! Here he decided to make camp and take advantage of this rare treat. He had just finished filling every conceivable container with this sweet water in anticipation of his continuing march, when the big grey threw back his head in startled warning. Dodging to his left, Diego avoided a very painful meeting with an Apache arrow. As DaVia whirled, his face and uniform became visible to the Apache warrior. The Apache realized he had attacked the one called Dead Man Who Walks Away. He raced away into the creosote and mesquite desert, thereby avoiding a hand-to-hand fight. Diego DaVia stood there somewhat perplexed. He had expected to fight for his life and could not help but wonder why the Apache ran away. However, that night he slept as the Apache would, his horse's rein tied to his left wrist.

He slept undisturbed and woke up terribly famished. A quick check of the snare trap he had set the previous evening produced a jackrabbit. Finally: some meat. Making a fire with as little smoke as possible, he was able to eat his fill. Marking the Apache's swift retreat and noting the obvious disregard of any attempt to cover the tracks caused Diego to wonder why the Apache had left so hurriedly. He thought about it often as he continued south along the Rio San Pedro.

———

The fifth day after leaving the Rio Gila found him a short distance east of the Santa Catalina Mountains, still on the bank of the Rio San Pedro. He was nearly due east of the presidio of Tucson. The military force stationed there would offer him no comfort. The probable few soldiers had deteriorated to no more than brigands, due to the possible order to withdraw in anticipation of the impending takeover by the North Americans but, more likely, to the discovery of gold in California. His uniform would be of no protection for him. Besides, he would have to offer up some sort of explanation for his presence.

Lieutenant DaVia was about to make camp in a wide-mouthed wash when he remembered exactly where he was. The white, chalky rock formation at the mouth of the wash identified the entrance to the camp where Mexican army deserters had held the captive Yavapai girl, U Day Ah, having abused her terribly. She had survived, but a second young girl had not. The Peralta party rescued U Day Ah and had taken her with them north. That place brought nothing but bad memories for Diego DaVia. His sleep was interrupted many times by those memories. Lieutenant DaVia knew that the Peralta expedition had no choice but to rescue her and bring her back to health; yet he immediately had seen the impending danger in having U Day Ah with them.

She was Yavapai. Her capture by renegade Apaches had led to her sale and abuse by half-breed Apache/Mexicans living upstream from that same wash. Returning her to that village would have—if she lived—continued her abuse. It would have also caused days of delay to the Peralta expedition. So, she was cared for and nurtured and returned to her young, beautiful self. Once she realized that the Peraltas were headed in the direction of the Yavapai, she made it a point to be friendly. Indeed, she developed a true friendship with many of the Peralta party. Realizing that she was as close as she felt the Peraltas would take her to her people, she ran off. After many days, U Day Ah was reunited with her Yavapai tribe. She became emotionally torn between her new Peralta friendships and the Yavapai and, unknown to the Peraltas, especially the young warrior O hi Cama. After a time, she became an interpreter and spy for the Yavapai and was instrumental in planning the coming massacre of the Peralta expedition. Lieutenant Diego DaVia would never forgive her for that.

—·—

After a fitful, interrupted sleep, a tired Diego DaVia continued his trek down the Rio San Pedro. He had progressed nearly five miles and was approaching the area of the village that had been U Day Ah's home in captivity, when a party of five mounted Apaches charged from the east side of the river, splashing water everywhere and shouting. They were nearly upon him when one of them raised his lance and, shouting a loud command, turned the entire party away from him in frantic retreat. DaVia had thought his time had come. Then there he was, his horse knee deep in the Rio San Pedro, all alone. *What the hell is going on?* he thought.

He would wonder about that the rest of the day. Whatever was going on, he was so far untouched.

The lieutenant remembered vividly the rank conditions in that village. The young U Day Ah without any doubt would have perished had Don Miguel Peralta ordered her return to that horrid place. No one could ever argue with Don Miguel's decision to save her and care for her on their expedition. After all, as he had said, "We are not barbarians!" Thus, the Peraltas trekked north, beyond Superstition Mountain toward the old mines. The don had put up with the antics of his son, Manuel, and Capitán Garces, each vying for the attentions of the young girl. It seemed even comical until U Day Ah sneaked off into the night looking for her Yavapai people. Then things became serious. Shaking his head to clear it of those thoughts, Diego DaVia resumed his march southward.

———

In the late afternoon, four days after the encounter with the Apaches, Diego DaVia set about finding a suitable campsite at the junction of the Rio Babocamari and the Rio San Pedro. There, he planned to veer westward following the Rio Babocamari into what seemed a vast wilderness on the horizon. He had gone only a few hundred yards away from the Rio San Pedro when he was confronted by a lone rider. The man sat very still for a moment or two before approaching the lieutenant. As the lone rider moved closer, DaVia first thought the rider to be an Apache. However, his clothes seemed to indicate a half-caste Apache/Mexican. The rider stopped, raised his right hand, and spoke. "Señor, I mean you no harm. May I get down?"

"Sí," said the lieutenant. Both dismounted and approached each other.

"I have seen no other for two days, señor," said the man.

"It has been four days since I have seen anyone," replied Diego.

"You have travelled from the north?" asked the Indian.

"Sí. And you?" asked Diego.

"I have come from the village of Fronteras. I am trying to get to the presidio of Tucson," answered the Indian.

"Why would anyone want to go to that hell hole!" exclaimed Diego. "I do not know if soldiers are still stationed there, but whoever is there cannot be worth much."

"It does not matter. I will try to make my way from the presidio to California," informed the Indian. "There is much trouble in Chihuahua and even in Sonora now. There is no law in those places. I am Mexican and Apache. I have no place there. Maybe I find a good place in California. I must try."

"I understand. But I cannot go to California. Perhaps there is no place for me either. But I, too, must try," said Diego. "*Buena suerte.* Good luck to you," said DaVia.

"Gracias, señor," said the Indian. Then he added, "Are you the one the Apache honor and fear?"

"The what?" DaVia asked in surprise.

"I think you are the one, the survivor. The one they call Dead Man Who Walks Away," replied the Indian.

"Never heard of him," denied Diego.

"I think you are that one. The Apache and the Yavapai honor you, but fear you and your medicine," relayed the Indian.

"I know nothing of it," said Diego.

"No Apache, Yavapai, or even Yaqui who has heard of you will attack you. Those who have not heard of you may try," warned the Indian.

"Gracias and buena suerte," said DaVia.

"Buena suerte to you," wished the Indian. With that, the Indian mounted, wheeled his horse around, and rode north up the Rio San Pedro.

Lieutenant Diego DaVia stood there, too struck by what he had just heard to move. Could it be that someone saw him leave that blood-stained canyon? Thoughts began racing through his mind. Who could have seen him walk out? Was he known to whomever saw him? No Apache would have known him, or even cared for that matter. To the Apache, a lone, unmounted soldier would have been just another victim to be killed. The Yavapai, too, would have no reason to just watch him walk away. He was dog tired and needed to find a secure campsite soon. He would worry about all that later, as if it even made any difference. "Buena suerte! Ha!"

—•—

About a mile west along the bank of the Rio Babocamari, Diego found a place to rest. A switchback to the right provided him with an almost invisible sanctuary. A curved ledge at his back even allowed for a semi-smokeless fire in the horseshoe-haped site. He had little left of his jerky, and so he finished that. The fire was burning merely because he wanted one.

The fire, that catalyst to a man's thoughts, allowed Diego's mind to wander once more to that horrible massacre. He never wanted to visualize that scenario again. But here it was, one out-of-sequence memory after another, plaguing him with unanswered questions. Why did he and Capitán Garces not simply take command and leave when the Yavapai chieftain, Nanni Chaddi, gave them the ultimatum, and a way out without disaster? He, through the lovely U Day Ah, had given them seven days to take their gold and leave . . . safely. But Manuel Peralta, in charge after Don Miguel had to hurriedly ride to California, would not see the obvious coming battle. He had deliberately, and with arrogance, delayed any departure until after Nanni Chaddi's deadline had passed. The tactic, obvious only to Lieutenant DaVia, was that the Yavapai, already in position along the Rio Verde, would force the running battle directly toward the box canyon at the northwest slope of Superstition Mountain. The Peraltas, armed with only muzzle-loading rifles, could not reload while crashing through the creosote, mesquite, chaparral, and cactus all the way to the Rio Salado. It had become a race of death.

Why, after the Peraltas had crossed the Rio Salado at sunset, did the Yavapai withdraw? It was a welcome breather at the time, but the answer came just after the dawn. With Yavapai, armed with arrows and lances behind and to their north and with Apache, armed with rifles on their south flank, they were herded into that box canyon. Apaches already at the east end of the canyon attacked. Within minutes it was all over, but not for Lieutenant Diego DaVia.

Then, in a flash, it came to him! Who else would have been there, able to recognize him? Who else would have known him well enough to single him out as worth saving? The realization that his fierce Yavapai warrior counterpart, O hi Cama, had to be the one brought him to his feet. But why would he do that?

U Day Ah!

Could that be why? Had U Day Ah told O hi Cama about that incident?

Some weeks before the massacre, U Day Ah had been searching her heart, caught between her loyalty to the Yavapai and the feelings of friendship for the Peraltas who had rescued her and nursed her back to health. She had ridden over the desert near the Peralta camp, not even knowing what she would do there. She had rested in the shade of a tree, unsure of herself or her motives, when she was attacked by Sebriano, a miner, intent upon raping her. Lieutenant DaVia happened by and, drawing his saber, ran Sebriano through twice, killing him. Even though Diego had saved her, they had had a very heated argument about the Yavapai and their plans for the Peraltas.

Could U Day Ah, at some time before the massacre, have spoken to O hi Cama about it? Could that have advanced at least some measure of respect on the part of O hi Cama? They had looked upon one another with deadly regard as to the other's prowess but had never been at all friendly. Could he have earned some small gratitude for sparing U Day Ah from Sebriano? Diego did not know. He probably would never know. But, at least after that thought, sleep came to Lieutenant Diego DaVia.

The Rio Babocamari—not much of a river—flowed with water from higher elevations from the west and southwest to the Rio San Pedro. Diego, astride the big grey, followed its course higher and higher toward the southwest. The daytime temperatures became noticeably cooler. The terrain began to show more grass and less cacti and other prickly growth.

The Rio Babocamari takes its name from the band of Indians who had lived in that area at the time of the conquistadores/missionaries. They had welcomed the strangers, learned to farm as the strangers wished, and, for the most part, converted to the missionaries' religion. Then, as time went by and the soldiers became more involved, the relationship cooled. The Babocamari managed to disappear into the mists of time. However, back in the hills overlooking the Rio Babocamari, a few bands did survive.

As Diego DaVia cautiously continued his way up the Rio Babocamari, he began to notice ruins of small, but in their time well-organized, villages. He took note that these ruins were not the scattered wooden wikiups of the Yavapai, or even of the Apache. At one time there were adobe homes, corrals for the livestock, and a small but obvious village square. In each village ruin, he would see a building curiously resembling a chapel. What he did not see were any people. But they saw him.

He stopped to make camp at one ruined village. One of the adobe buildings would serve as a very acceptable shelter for the night. His small, almost smoke-free fire was beginning to grow when Diego turned to give it another piece of wood. The sight of moccasins brought him up short with alarm. He lifted his gaze to look upon the three men standing before him. DaVia's instinct realized that a fight, or even flight, was not possible. All three were armed with drawn bows. However, one held out a small wooden cross.

"Señor, you look as if you have traveled far," said one who looked older than the others.

"Sí," acknowledged DaVia with some hesitancy.

"You come from el norte," said the Indian.

"Sí, I have not noted the days, but I have traveled far," said DaVia.

The older Indian asked, "Do you have food?"

DaVia thought, at first, that he was asking for food. "I have none," he said.

"Put out your fire and come with us. We have food. We will talk," said the older-looking Indian.

Darkness had fallen by the time the small party entered a small but well-kept village square. They had traveled nearly a quarter mile inland and southward from the river. A small fire was burning in the stone ring under the ramada. Twenty or so men and women were sitting by the fire enjoying the evening air. They rose at once when they saw the stranger. The Indian who had spoken to DaVia asked that food and drink be provided to their guest. Lieutenant DaVia was impressed by the village and the friendly atmosphere of the villagers. But regardless of the outward friendliness, DaVia could not help but be suspicious. His recent experience with the Apache and Yavapai prevented him from letting down his guard. The memory of that most recent experience with Indians kept his eyes ricocheting from one Indian to the next.

After eating a meal of corn and tortillas, with a meat that seemed to be rabbit, he saw that the women and a few children had disappeared into their respective dwellings. The man who had shown him the cross and invited him to the village began to speak. He spoke his Indian name, but DaVia could not pronounce it. The Indian grinned at DaVia's attempt and said DaVia could call him Romero. It was the name the Mexicans had been calling him. He referred to his band as Babocamari. Others referred to them as Huachuca. There were other bands, but they were scattered over the area. They had been pleased to become civilized, or Christian, as the missionaries called it. The Babocamari had already been farmers in their own way but learned much from the missionaries. When the Spanish conquistadores came, things turned for the worse for the Babocamari. They were forced to scatter into the desert and nearby hills. Now, they simply did their best to avoid the Mexicans and the Apache, even to the point of placing their small villages at a distance from the river.

After telling some of their tribal history, Romero paused and simply said, "You are he, aren't you?"

"Who do you mean?" asked DaVia.

"You are the one the Apache and Yavapai warriors call Dead Man Who Walks Away," said Romero. "The Yaqui, when last they were here, spoke of a Mexican soldier who rose from a place of death and walked away. It was far to the north, but you came from the north," Romero continued. "Your blood-stained uniform is that of a Mexican soldier. You are alone and seem to be wandering. We think you are he," added Romero.

"I was a soldier," stated DaVia, his eyes avoiding those of Romero.

"The Yaqui say the Apache fear your medicine. They say that 'a man who does not die, when he should be dead, is to be feared.' They fear you, and yet they honor you," continued Romero. "The Apache say you are a great warrior and must be allowed to go your way unmolested."

"I have fought the Apache and the Yavapai," DaVia said, more to seem agreeable than accepting of Romero's assertion.

Romero spoke again, making a more personal observation. "Your eyes tell more than your words. There is sadness in them that even a child might see. You are looking for a place to live but also a place to hide from your sadness."

Lieutenant Diego DaVia said slowly, "Any warrior, Mexican or Indian, would like a place of peace for a while."

Romero nodded and then said softly, "The women have made you a place to sleep. We will talk in the morning. You are safe here with us. Sleep well."

After all he had been through, Diego DaVia could use the sleep. Soon, with the exception of some fleeting memories of the massacre, sleep came to Diego.

———

With the first light of dawn, Lieutenant Diego DaVia was awake and preparing to continue his trek up the Rio Babocamari. He made his way past the morning fires to the big grey horse. He was surprised to find him already watered, even groomed, and quietly grazing. He turned to see Romero offering him some tortillas and a coffee-like drink.

"There is no reason for you to continue toward the west," said Romero. "The Rio will make a turn toward the south and soon become only one of many small streams that begin it. You will enter a wide canyon that proceeds for a three-day ride to the southern end. Mountains come together there. Make your way over many ridges, for two or more days. Then, a great valley will open to you. It is a beautiful, high grassy place. It is large, with rolling hills. There, the Rio Santa Cruz begins its way to the south. It is a dangerous place. Mexicans and Indians spend some time there. They can be bad. But" Romero then added, "a man can lose himself there. It is my prayer that you find yourself there."

Diego was without words to speak his gratitude.

"You are welcome to stay with us until you are more ready to travel," offered Romero.

DaVia did not wish to seem an ungrateful guest. So, when the tortillas were finished and the amenities were through, he climbed aboard the big grey. He managed to thank Romero for his hospitality and started to leave. As DaVia turned his horse toward the river, Romero offered one more comment: "Travel safely, with the knowledge that the Babocamari will never tell of the visit by Dead Man Who Walks Away." With that, Lieutenant Diego DaVia turned and slowly rode back toward the Rio Babocamari.

5

Diego DaVia followed Romero's advice, and the directions were easy to follow. The Rio Babocamari became as described, a maze of small tributaries, that together formed the headwaters. At that point, Diego turned south through a long, wide canyon. That took every bit of three days. When he, at last, saw the mountain ridges ahead, he smiled. There he would be able to find cover. There he would, at that higher elevation, leave the desert behind.

After two more days of riding between ridges and ravines and over the ever-higher mountain foothills, he looked down on the northern end of the San Rafael Valley. The beauty of it momentarily took his breath away. He was looking down on a valley, set at about five thousand feet in elevation—a high grassland surrounded by high mountains. Here and there, scattered across the grassland, were stands of both pine and deciduous trees. He could not even see the entire length of the valley to the south. Beginning as a small creek below him and swelling as it flowed southward, the Rio Santa Cruz provided water to the whole valley.

To this man—this soldier—this battle-weary lieutenant, the valley spreading out before him seemed like a bit of heaven. Trancelike, he gazed at the tranquil beauty of it. However, he was still Lieutenant Diego DaVia, and his senses returned to him. He was, once again, on the alert. The words of warning from Romero kept his eyes moving everywhere, as he slowly rode down to the edge of the grassland. The sun was now moving toward evening. Diego looked for a secure place to camp. He found a small *U*-shaped indentation in the trees and proceeded to make camp. A cold camp with no fire was necessary this first night in the valley. Romero's warning of bad men, Mexican and/or Indian, was worth adhering to, until he knew what he was up against.

— ▪ —

The dawn brought a new, clearer vision of the San Rafael Valley. It was beautiful. The view was everything anyone could want. Looking south, he could see the beginning of the Rio Santa Cruz flowing straight south, deeper into Mexico. Waving grass, as far as he could see. Behind him, the mountains he had so recently traversed, while mountains on either side framed the immense valley before him. And, so far, he could see no sign of men, Mexican or Indian.

I will make my base camp here, at the north end of this valley, and explore the perimeter. I need to know what else is here, he thought. Realizing that his presence there might not be welcome and remembering the gold, still tucked away in his saddlebags, he began looking for a place to stash that gold—that massacre gold. He hated even to think of it. But Diego also knew that he would need it, eventually. Looking around, he could not imagine a safer place to hide the gold than in the rock ledge under which he had spent the night. He found a small opening behind a solid overhang and a larger opening behind that. He assured himself that the hole was not occupied by rattlesnakes and, with utmost care, stuffed the gold into the hole. Diego did not want to leave the saddlebags in the hole; he might have need of them. The hole was hidden by natural-looking rocks that camouflaged the hole very well. Other possible campers would never notice the cache.

Having stuffed what loose gear he had into the now-empty saddlebags, Lieutenant Diego DaVia, riding the big grey, set out to survey what he was hoping would be his hideout, his new home, his place to start a new life. With every step, DaVia became more impressed with his good fortune. The valley was rich in grass. He could see signs of wildlife everywhere. The Rio Santa Cruz began as a small streamlet, then was joined by other streams, and flowed continuously. The surrounding mountains gave the valley the look of isolation Diego so desperately desired. DaVia had been riding nearly to high noon when he stopped short. More signs. This time, the sign was of horses. Wild horses, perhaps. But then he saw the hoofprint of a horse, a shod hoofprint. It was obvious that horses were being grazed and herded in that valley. Bad news! He had hoped that the valley was uninhabited. No such luck.

No sense waiting, he thought. Diego began following the tracks. He must see who else occupied his valley. The tracks were not hard to follow. The herd was not a large one, perhaps no more than fifty horses. The tracks indicated that only two vaqueros were with it.

Diego followed with caution. The tracks were fresh. Just before sundown, he caught up with the herd. The two vaqueros were attempting to get their fire started. Diego, not wishing to cause any conversation about his military background, removed his uniform coat and placed it in one of the recently emptied saddlebags. Then, he guided the big grey toward the campfire.

"Hola! Amigos in the camp! I am alone and wish to venture closer. *Con permiso,* with your permission, may I enter your camp?" he requested. He did not wish in any way to surprise them.

"Sí. But come in at a walk," replied one of the vaqueros. In the half light of the sunset and the small fire, Diego approached the vaqueros. As he did so, the wary vaqueros stepped back a few steps to better view this incoming stranger. What they saw was a man of average size, lean and hard, whose expression seemed to be cut from stone. He sat upright and proud in the saddle. It was not until he said, "Buenas noches . . . good evening," that they saw a small smile under the wide-brimmed, Spanish-style cavalry hat. That smile seemed to relax them. The hands that had been white knuckling their weapons relaxed.

"Stand down, señor. Have some coffee and share our meal," offered the older of the two vaqueros. To Diego, he seemed about thirty-five years old. The younger looked to be not much more than a teenage boy. Still, with their hands held close to their pistols, they could have been a problem. Diego DaVia disarmed them with a much wider smile saying, "Gracias, amigos," and dismounted as if he had not noticed their weapons. He accepted the hot tin cup of coffee offered to him.

"I am very happy to have seen your fire," said DaVia. "It feels as though I have been riding forever."

"From where do you ride, señor?" asked the older vaquero.

"From the north," answered Diego.

"From where in the north, and for how long have you been riding?" questioned the older vaquero.

"It feels as though I have been riding for a thousand miles," Diego answered somewhat jokingly. He did not intend to give out many details.

His quip brought forth appreciative smiles from the vaqueros.

"My question to you is: where am I now?" Diego asked with another grin. "My name is Diego DaVia. To whom do I owe this hospitality?"

"Pardon me, Señor DaVia. My name is Francisco Ruiz. But I am referred to as 'Segundo, second in command.' My young vaquero is called Pancho," he replied. "As to your current whereabouts, you are in the San Rafael Valley. This is a large Spanish land grant, the San Rafael de la Zanja. It extends from the mountains in the north way south, deeper into Sonora."

"Gracias, Segundo. Meeting you both is my pleasure," said Diego. "Where are the owners of so large a grant?"

"They are many miles to the south, deep in Sonora," Segundo answered. "I am responsible for the few horses pastured in this valley. They are to be fattened up and driven south to the main rancho and then sold."

"Is the rancho a large operation? Is this all that is here, pasturing in this valley?" queried DaVia. "I ask only because I see so much land begging to be grazed."

"Yes," agreed Segundo. "It seems a waste not to have huge herds here. The patrón and his family have many other interests deeper in Mexico. The patrón has a few more herds like these scattered within this valley. We will gather them together before the snow comes. I think they run these horses merely to keep possession of the Zanja grant."

All the while Diego was talking to Segundo, the younger vaquero, Pancho, was preparing a simple but tasty supper. The conversation continued after they served themselves and began to eat.

"Have you heard anything about the Mexican government in Mexico City?" asked DaVia.

"Sí! It is a clustered mess!" exclaimed Segundo. "No one in Sonora has any idea who is really going to govern Mexico."

"I heard that Santa Anna is not even in Mexico anymore," ventured DaVia.

"*Quién sabe* . . . Who knows?! Someday someone will ride into Sonora with some soldiers and say, 'I am in charge!' And we will all say, 'Good for you! Now go govern this place!'" jibed Segundo. All three men laughed at that. That was probably a true statement, however.

"Do you think that the problems in Mexico are, partly at least, to blame for the lack of interest in this valley?" DaVia wondered out loud.

"Sí. If anyone cares about this land, these horses, or these vaqueros, I have not seen it," voiced Segundo. "I cannot remember the last time any of the patrón's family came here. What a waste."

"Who is the patrón of this land grant?" asked Diego.

Segundo's reply was somewhat slow in coming. But he said, "Don Ramón Ruiz holds this land."

Pancho spilled some of his coffee because he had looked up at Segundo. Diego made a mental note that *Ruiz* was also Segundo's name. He politely did not ask if there was a relationship.

Segundo said, "That family is from the area of Arizpe, Sonora, but most of them spend their time in Mexico City."

DaVia was not certain whether Segundo had seen him avert his eyes as Segundo spoke those words.

For a few moments, the conversation paused. Diego DaVia became noticeably deep in thought. Segundo was about to interrupt as to what was wrong. However, Diego began speaking again.

"I wonder if anyone would be upset if I built a small cabin here, maybe at the north end of this valley, and stayed a while," mused DaVia.

"We are letting these horses fatten up a bit more before the weather invites us to move them out of here," said Segundo. "We have a little time, I suppose. Pancho, would you like to quit riding around these horses for a week or so? We can let them graze around the north end for a time. We could take turns helping Señor DaVia build a cabin secure enough to shelter him through the winter. What do you think?" Segundo asked Pancho.

"The sores on my butt, from being in the saddle all the time, would thank you for this opportunity to do something else . . . anything else!" was Pancho's enthusiastic answer.

"Amigos, I am indeed the fortunate one to have found men like you. I saw a spot up at the north edge of this beautiful valley for just such a cabin. The thought came to me as I shared your wonderful fire. Muchas gracias, amigos!" exclaimed Diego DaVia.

"Then it is agreed. After the morning breakfast, vamonos! We go!" shouted all three men.

6

The morning sun found the three men after breakfast, bustling around to move the small herd north to the spot Diego had first camped. Moving the herd north allowed the two vaqueros to continue caring for the herd as employees of the Ruizes. The herd was en route northward due to the skill of the two vaqueros. Yet it still took most of the day to arrive at the site of Diego's former camp. Along the way, Segundo and Diego spoke often. The conversations kept pretty much to ideas for the cabin and immediate plans for the winter.

No more was said concerning the Ruiz family. Diego had immediately noted that the Ruiz family was from Arizpe, Sonora. The family of Don Miguel Peralta headquartered at the Peralta rancheria at Arizpe. Arizpe was the embarkation point for the ill-fated Peralta mission to the old mines. He hoped that the connection was mere coincidence. Diego hoped the Ruizes had nothing to do with that expedition. That possible family connection merely became one more thing for DaVia to ponder.

Segundo offered much encouragement when he saw the place where DaVia wanted to build the cabin. The prospective cabin would be built on a small knoll and face southward, down the San Rafael Valley. It would be somewhat sheltered by the hills and woods behind it. Segundo, who had been there before, located a spring that flowed a short distance from the cabin. Fresh water! To Diego DaVia, a man who had spent so much time in the desert, this was a luxury. The woods offered numerous straight-trunked pines within easy carrying distance to be used for logs. The knoll presented no problems for digging a foundation. The work began.

Diego DaVia was no novice at working with his hands. However, Segundo and Pancho soon proved themselves to be genuine craftsmen. The vaqueros' small chuck wagon contained all the tools they would need. Those two men knew what they were doing. DaVia had expected a simple, primitive shelter. Segundo would have none of that. He elevated himself to the position of working supervisor. Good judgment prevailed. Diego gave way and followed instructions. That cabin looked more like a finished ranch house. A rancho hacienda had sprung up on that little knoll.

Segundo and Pancho looked upon it with pride when, after three weeks, two more than planned of steady labor, they laid down their tools. DaVia would finish it to his wishes after the two vaqueros left, but what a start! Made almost entirely of pine logs and stone, it had a fireplace for heat and cooking, windows that could be shuttered and defended against attack, and a ramada-like porch for relaxing and taking in the beauty of the San Rafael Valley. A three-walled shelter for the big grey was attached at the northeast corner.

Segundo told DaVia, "We must leave you tomorrow. However, before we depart, there is one more thing. Your horse is a magnificent animal, but he has no shoes. It is none of my business where you came upon him. Obviously, he had once been an Indian pony. I was looking at his hooves. The grey has been shod before. It is possible he had been stolen."

"Sí," agreed DaVia.

"We have horseshoes in the supply packs. Before we go, Pancho will shoe your horse," said Segundo.

"I am even deeper in your debt, Segundo," replied DaVia.

"Favors are delivered back and forth between friends," said Segundo quietly.

Morning came. The big grey shod and the vaqueros having mounted, they stood ready to move the herd south along with other stragglers they had located. However, as they were leaving, Segundo said, "Care well for yourself, Diego. Be wary of everyone. I will return in the spring with supplies, and together we will discuss what may come. *Vaya con Dios*. Adiós."

"Vaya con Dios, amigos!" shouted Diego. "Adiós!"

Watching the vaqueros move the herd down the valley nearer the Rio Santa Cruz, Diego could not but wonder what Segundo meant by "what may come." He would wait and see what Segundo had in mind. Diego had not formulated exactly what he, himself, wanted to come. But he knew he could do about anything he wished, due to the gold cached in the stone ledge near the cabin.

As if to announce the change of season, the air became chill. DaVia had not thought much about it, but November had arrived. At five thousand feet elevation, winter can come without warning with dramatic results. He needed to get wood cut for his fireplace. That wood was going to be his only heat for this upcoming winter. The nearby hillsides provided much deadwood to be cut into fireplace logs and kindling. Diego surely would not freeze in that cozy cabin. The cabin was a single-floor structure with ceilings of ten feet at the center, sloping gently to five feet at the outer walls. The roof sloped well past the outer walls, providing a protected area all around from wind, hail, rain, and/or snow. Should he be attacked, windows were cut into the narrow shape of a cross on the outside, angling inward to an area one foot wide. This was designed, as in all good fortresses, so that a defender had a good line of fire from inside, while an attacker had to try to hit a very small outer opening.

It had taken many days to lay in enough—what he hoped to be enough—firewood to last through the upcoming winter. There had already been a small dusting of snow flurries. He had dug a small fruit cellar to house whatever fruits or nuts he could find in the woods. There was no fruit at that time of the year, but Diego had learned to be quite competitive with the squirrels for nuts. When ice would be available from the Rio Santa Cruz, it would be stored in that cellar. Meat could also be kept refrigerated for a time in there. Segundo had left an older muzzle-loader rifle for him. His pistol and that rifle were all he had with which to kill game. Lieutenant DaVia, because he had been crushed out of sight under his horse at the massacre, had been able to retain possession of his Colt model 1848 Dragoon revolver. This made DaVia a formidable enemy to men as well as game. After loading up with firewood, that Colt Dragoon began providing game.

———

Winters, as a rule, were not severe in that region known as the San Rafael Valley. Snow fell, but not to any great depth. However, Diego Da-Via's first winter seemed particularly harsh. One snowfall after another would melt away, and another would follow. Then, early in February, it snowed hard for two days. Then the clouds cleared, and the wind from the northeast roared into his valley. The temperature dropped below zero for three days. DaVia kept close to the cabin. He ventured out only to care for the big grey. The high, ungrazed grassland provided well for the grey. But there was no sense hunting for game. Any animal was hunkered down in any shelter it could find.

———

When the weather relaxed its hold, Diego stepped out to take advantage of it. It was still crisp, and the snow was still covering the grassland, but he found it pleasant enough. The big grey was eager to leave the confines of the lean-to stall and kick up in the snowfall. DaVia rode the perimeter of the valley at the base of the hills to the north, to make sure he was still alone in his pristine paradise. He had not gone far when he saw the tracks of two horses. He thought, at first, they could be wild horses. He had followed for a short way only when he saw what he did not want to see. The tracks stopped. The horses had milled around the area trying to nibble some bark from an aspen tree. The tracks of two men, wearing moccasins, demanded his attention.

Who were these Indians? Why were they here? Were they hunting? Did they have something else in mind? They had remounted and turned their horses toward DaVia's cabin. A few hundred yards away they halted behind a couple of pines where they could observe the cabin. From the indications, they had spent more than a few minutes there. Then, they turned their mounts eastward toward the mountains that bordered Da-Via's end of the valley. Diego was about to follow them but thought better of it. Those Indians could double back at any point on their snow trail and ambush him from cover.

Was this a random chance encounter? Was their departure, without confrontation, due to their knowledge of Dead Man Who Walks Away? Or were they just unwilling to chance any kind of meeting? The weather, and the related inactivity, had evidently lured him into a false sense of security. This encounter would ensure that would not happen again. It was clear; he could not live a hermit's life there. After all, he never actually wanted to, anyway.

—

Another near encounter gave him more cause for wonder. The snow had gone. Spring had begun in that semi-high country. Early one morning, he spotted four mounted Indians loping swiftly out of his field of vision. Their clothing was obviously Apache. Again, they had chosen to leave rather than initiate either a conversation or attack. That morning, Diego began work on re-enforcing the door and windows from the inside. He did not wish to be surprised in his sleep. Deep sleep had not been his for a long time anyway. Now, being a light sleeper would be an advantage. Even then, the old story that "Indians did not attack at night" was well known. He knew the truth of it: that "Apaches did not attack at night . . . unless they wanted to." He would be alert. He needed something else, but he wasn't sure what.

7

It was late March. The weather had been particularly mild for two weeks. So, it was no great surprise when DaVia saw the small herd moving up the valley toward his new cabin. As they moved closer, he could see that the vaqueros were the same two amigos, Segundo and Pancho. He saddled the big grey and rode out to greet them. Segundo instructed Pancho to settle the herd while he and Diego rode back to the cabin. After the warm greetings were delivered and the herd was settled, the three men sat on the front porch to talk.

Segundo observed, "You have done well, Diego. This place looks very well kept and organized. Your military discipline has served you well."

"Military tactics or not, I'm still here. I am still enjoying this valley, thanks to you both," said Diego.

"Have you seen any others during the winter?" asked Segundo.

"Seen a few Indians now and then," answered Diego.

"They caused you no harm?" Segundo asked.

"No. They came in close enough to look and left," asserted DaVia. "Why?"

"It seems strange. Others, farther south in Sonora, have not fared so well. There have been many attacks—many dead," related Segundo. "The Apache know you are here, alone, and have not attacked?"

"Just lucky, I suppose," said Diego.

"Maybe," said Segundo. "The war with the Apache in Chihuahua has been over for some eight months perhaps. The Apache fought the Mexican army to a standstill there. Many concessions were made to end that war. They have become very bold now. The Chiricahua Apache have been raiding in Sonora. It has been a bad time for many."

"Where have the Chiricahua attacked?" asked Diego, showing great concern.

"Battles have been fought at Fronteras, Agua Prieta, Cananea, and even Arizpe. Many are left dead in those towns," said Segundo.

"I have been to each of them," said DaVia, not letting on that the Peralta expedition originated in Arizpe at the Peralta rancheria.

"I have lost a number of friends; some worked with Pancho and me for our patrón." Segundo raised his eyes to meet Diego's gaze and said, "Things are different now, even from how they were when we last met."

Diego rose to pour coffee for each of them and asked, "How different, amigo?"

Segundo drank some coffee and paused a moment before speaking to Diego. "Amigo, I must tell you what I hesitated to say to you last autumn. Our patrón was my father, Don Ramón Ruiz. We never did agree much on anything. He was more than willing to exile me out here in this valley, away from him. That suited me just fine."

"I suspected the relationship from the *Ruiz* name," said DaVia.

"The Chiricahua raid on Arizpe, with the loss of so many friends, caused my father to suffer some kind of heart problem, and he died," Segundo said.

"*Lo siento.* I am sorry," offered Diego.

"Because we argued about so many things, my father left most of his estate to my brother, Raoul. Some of it he left to my sister. My sister and I now share ownership of this beautiful valley," continued Segundo.

"Still, that does not sound too bad to me," said Diego.

"It leaves me with something I cannot control. My sister is my father's daughter. She has always followed his lead. She will make our shared ownership of this land most difficult for me. She will try to squeeze me out and then sell it," Segundo answered in a loud tone.

"Why do you think that?" asked Diego.

Segundo, calming himself, explained, "She has never been to this valley. She cares nothing for it. She and Raoul prefer to live in Mexico City and act like aristocrats, the darlings of the Mexican social scene. And she does not approve of my enjoyment of ranching."

"Do you think she is in a hurry to sell it? Does she or your brother need the money? Is she already pressing you?" asked Diego.

"No. She and Raoul take great pride in ownership of the land. Owning great quantities of land, like everything else, makes her feel more prestigious. Working the land is below them both. In Monica's mind, working the land is for peones!" angrily said Segundo.

"Monica?" asked Diego.

"Monica is my sister. Forgive me for not saying her name before. I was upset," related Segundo.

Diego was about to say that he understood. But the look in Segundo's eyes told him that he wished not to speak of his sister anymore.

———

The next morning, Segundo, having had a good night's sleep under Diego's new roof, was his former active self. His horses had been allowed to graze nearby and showed no inclination to wander far. A good breakfast was in order. Pancho became the most important man there. He was the master cook. Segundo took it upon himself to speak more of his situation. "I love this place," he said, "and I love working with the horses. Most of these horses were born wild. These horses—as even the gringos call them, these mustangs—are beautiful to me."

It was then that Diego asked, "What do you do with these mustangs of yours?"

The answer was to the point. "I catch them, nearly tame them, and sell them to the military, or to other ranchers to grow their herds. Sometimes, I drive them all the way to Hermosillo."

"That is a long way, amigo!" exclaimed Diego. "Why drive them all that way? Surely, there are horses already in Hermosillo."

"Sí. But from there their new owners trail them west to the Sea of Cortez, to ships that take them to other parts of Mexico and even to California," Segundo told Diego.

"I suppose even old ladies need them to drive their fancy carriages," said Diego, laughing.

"I have been supplying horses for many people for many years," said Segundo. "My sister and that lazy brother of mine do not like that at all. But they will see."

"See what, Segundo?" asked Diego.

"Things are changing, maybe good . . . maybe bad. *Quién sabe?*" said Segundo.

"What is this change, as you see it?" asked DaVia, his interest growing.

"The nortemericanos, the gringos, are showing up all over," replied Segundo. "It is being rumored that el Presidente Santa Anna has begun bargaining with los Estados Unidos to sell much of northern Sonora. Even now, some very rough gringos, including many pistoleros, are moving into Sonora, north of Cananea. We will be on a frontier; maybe we will have to fight to keep what we have. Monica will be trying to sell this valley once she understands what keeping it could mean."

"Sí," agreed Diego. "When the americanos took over California, they made it very tough on the Mexicans in the area. Mexican landowners were under much pressure to be able to keep their land," said Diego, remembering the urgent call for Don Miguel Peralta to leave his expedition to fight for his rights in California.

Segundo added sadly, "With all that happening, I cannot imagine who she'd sell it to."

Diego sat very quietly for a few moments. He was envisioning a solution for Segundo's problem that could ultimately resolve his own situation as well.

As usual, Segundo had at least one eye on the horse herd. "Pancho! The herd is scattering too far. Move them closer to the west meadow and hold them there."

Pancho swiftly mounted and headed toward the herd.

Segundo sat leaning forward, his great, wide sombrero tipped a bit, covering his face. He was deep in thought. When Diego began speaking to him, he listened but did not move. "Amigo," said DaVia, "do you have enough money to buy your sister's share of this valley?"

"No," answered Segundo with sadness showing in his tone.

"If you had enough cash to buy it, would you?" asked Diego.

"Sí, amigo!" exclaimed Segundo. "I would buy it, build a hacienda like yours, and live here forever."

"That could be dangerous, considering all that you have told me," said Diego.

"Ah, but then I would find a beautiful young chica, marry her, and bring her here," voiced Segundo.

"Ha! That could be the most dangerous part," warned DaVia, laughing.

The laughter died down. Then Segundo said, the sadness still showing, "Dreaming. I am just dreaming. I do not have the money, so it is all a dream."

Diego DaVia became serious in his tone, saying, "I have the money, Segundo."

After a very deep breath, Segundo said, "You have the money? But how would this happen?"

"I have been thinking about it as you spoke, amigo mio," said Diego. "I do not want to own your land, Segundo. It means so much to you. But, from our first meeting, you have been a true friend to me. So, I hope you will like this idea." Diego began to say that, because of some recent events, he did not wish to have his whereabouts known to certain people. He said that, although he did not fear them, he did not want the trouble they could bring right now.

"Pancho has Yaqui relatives. He has heard of a warrior . . . a soldier who survived a massacre that should have left him dead." Segundo paused, then went on. "This warrior is called Dead Man Who Walks Away," he said. "Pancho believes you are that one. I, too, after hearing that the Apache have been giving you a wide berth, think that you are he," asserted Segundo. He then added, "I am proud to call you amigo mio. Please tell me your idea."

Diego DaVia cleared his throat and said, "I have much gold. I suggest we use whatever it takes to buy this beautiful valley. You will be the full owner of this valley. We will agree that I will be your partner in making this a prime horse ranch. That way, you have what you want, and I have what I want. The money will not be wasted, and I will not need to be listed as an owner on a public record."

"Dios mio!" exclaimed Segundo.

"Do you think this would work for you?" asked Diego.

"Of course!" exclaimed Segundo. "You must have been sent from Above!"

Choking from laughter as Segundo danced all over the cabin porch, Diego DaVia replied, "*No, no, no,* not hardly!"

8

Within a few days, Diego and Segundo, leaving Pancho to watch the herd, began the long ride to Cananea. There they would board a coach for the long journey to Mexico City. While in Cananea, Lieutenant Diego DaVia purchased some new civilian clothes. Once transformed from his military-uniformed identity, he was able to move less conspicuously and with ease among the people of the area. He became the very image of a dapper and affluent gentleman. He even wore a tan colored duster to ward off the dust of trail coach travel.

En route to Mexico City, Diego DaVia was able to learn more about Segundo's family. Segundo's brother, Raoul, was five years older than Segundo. His sister, Monica, was three years older. Neither had ever been married. According to Segundo, "Neither has found anyone as good as they think they are."

Raoul was something of a snob. He would have been a much better man if he had ever initiated anything on his own. Instead, he had always deferred to his father and also to his sister, Monica. Segundo referred to him as a "lazy leech."

Monica was much like her father: headstrong, domineering, and intolerant of any way other than her own. She had always been a spoiled brat as a child. Her growing up into a beautiful young woman changed nothing. Like her father, she made no requests; she merely gave orders.

Don Ramón Ruiz, like Don Miguel Peralta, brought his style of aristocracy from Spain itself. The difference between them was dramatic. Don Miguel Peralta had involved himself in every facet of his family's operations from his early youth. He understood firsthand the procedures and the hard work necessary to accomplish anything in the new land of Mexico. He, therefore, was better able to manage those individuals necessary to complete any project. He had friends and employees who were not made to feel inferior. However, Don Ramón Ruiz considered himself superior to any of the people of Mexico. He still regarded Mexico as a colony of Spain and the Mexicans themselves as subservient. Even his own family members who disagreed with any of his orders were punished, sometimes with unnecessary severity. As time went by and his children grew older, Francisco—Segundo—was the one receiving most of that negative attention.

The revelations concerning the personalities of Segundo's family made it obvious to Diego that his identity as a Mexican soldier survivor must not be revealed. That revelation could be dangerous to him. He did not need problems with a military in transition. Segundo's family could well jeopardize his very existence. He had been through that before over much less serious incidents.

—•—

The trip by coach was long and grueling. By the time they reached Mexico City, they were exhausted. Not wishing to cause undo notice, they procured separate rooms at a hotel. The next day, Diego accompanied Segundo to the Bank of Mexico to evaluate the portion of Diego's stash of gold for the transaction and deposit of that amount in the bank in Segundo's account.

There was more than enough gold to purchase the property, plus a lot more for anything else. Having secured the excess gold in a special account, Segundo and Diego rode by carriage to the Ruiz family home. The Ruiz family, Monica and Raoul, had no idea that their brother, Francisco, was on his way. Diego decided to exit the carriage some distance from the estate, not wishing to be noticed by the Ruiz family. He did not wish to be identified in any way as the potential partner. As far as the Ruiz family was concerned, Segundo was to be the sole principle in the transaction.

Segundo did not wait to be welcomed. He did not announce himself. He opened the gate and walked right inside. The surprise was complete. Monica and Raoul were enjoying a late breakfast with a few friends and acquaintances when Segundo strode into the courtyard. The polite laughter over coffee stopped when Segundo curtly asked that he and the other two Ruizes be excused from their presence. Comments of "Well, I never!" came from all concerned. Segundo's reply of "Until now!" silenced all. The Ruizes hurriedly moved to an adjacent room for privacy.

At that point, the charade of cordiality ended. "What the hell do you think you are doing, Segundo?!" shouted Raoul.

"Indeed!" exclaimed Monica.

"Shut your mouth, Raoul, and sit down. You are not part of this today," Segundo ordered. Raoul, having contested other things with Segundo at other times, sat down.

"What is the meaning of this intrusion? We have friends here!" voiced Monica, her voice rising.

"I do not think you have any real friends anywhere!" was Segundo's swift retort. "Quiet yourself, and you will find out." Segundo continued, "I'm sure you'll be pleased. Remember how you worried and berated me over having to retain ownership of that, as you so delicately described it, 'damnable San Rafael Valley'? Remember how you said you hated to have to share such a remote place, especially with me?"

"I do," replied Monica, remembering her anger at the reading of their father's will. "Imagine me having to share that with you, of all people. What about it?" she demanded.

"You will not have to share that with me much longer," said Segundo.

"Well, you can be sure I am not going to buy your share of that desolate place!" she retorted angrily. "And I will not share ownership with anyone you have chosen to buy it! You will get no money from me, either! Will he, Raoul?"

Raoul started to say something, but the fire in Segundo's eyes would not let the words form. He sat there, dumbfounded at what was transpiring in front of him.

"I, beloved sister, have a buyer for that land," calmly said Segundo.

"I do not believe that! Who would buy that godforsaken piece of the world?" she asked loudly.

"I will," said Segundo, controlling his voice. His assertiveness left everyone silent for a moment.

"With what?" scornfully asked Monica. "You've never had enough money to buy more than some cerveza in one of those cantinas you visit!"

"The Bank of Mexico says I have the money to buy that land. After what you have just said, do not tell me that you find it so precious," answered Segundo, remaining very collected. "I will offer you a fair price, and you will sell it to me for that price. Having said what you just said, and considering today's economic and political uncertainty, you will gladly sell that valley to me."

"How can you d—" started Raoul.

"You are not part of this, Raoul! Go kiss up to your so-called friends," Segundo ordered. He then added "while you can!" Raoul was already on his way.

"But I . . . I . . ." began Monica.

"Here is the offer. It is fair, all things considered. Even the banker thinks you would be a fool not to accept it. Sign here," ordered Segundo. Monica looked at the offer, swallowed once, and signed it.

"Bueno. Now we will go to the government office and record it," directed Segundo.

"Now?" said the surprised Monica.

"Now! I do not have all week for the social amenities," assured Segundo.

And so, it was done . . . as if by surgical procedure.

As Segundo and Monica left in their carriage, they passed Diego Da-Via on the street. The wide smile on Segundo's face said it all to Diego. He would wait in the area for Segundo's return.

———

The signatures affixed, the transfer of ownership accomplished, Segundo met Diego DaVia on the street down the way from the Ruiz family house. Segundo was beaming. "I cannot wait to return to our San Rafael Valley!" he nearly yelled.

"You are going to wait," said Diego with a smile huge as all outdoors. "I am hungry. While you were becoming a Spanish landowner again, I was walking all over town without eating."

"There is a cantina ahead of us. There we will eat," Segundo offered.

"We will find a different cantina and eat as we leave this over-populated pueblo," said Diego. "This one is too close to your family."

"No one knows you in Mexico City," said Segundo.

"No, but there are people here who know you. Seeing us together might compromise the idea that you are alone in this endeavor," said Diego. "Let's get out of this place."

The meal still had to be eaten within Mexico City. There was no coach going north until the next day. But another cantina was located, and both men ate their fill. Never did two men enjoy their dinner as much as those two.

———

The next day's coach ride northward found both men exhausted. They would have to endure more uncomfortable travel. Ten days in that spring-less, dusty, drafty old coach deposited them in Cananea feeling as though they would never be able to walk again. They were able to find accommodations, eat, and go to sleep. The next day, they went to the office of the alcalde—mayor—to have the partnership agreement legalized. Don Enrique Vasquez, the alcalde of Cananea, did not verify the transfer papers himself. His aide performed that task. Therefore, Don Enrique did not make the connection of Diego DaVia to the expedition of his old friend Don Miguel Peralta.

The men had left their horses at the local livery stable for the duration of the trip to and from Mexico City. With little or no ceremony, they paid the stableman and began the ride northward.

———

Four days later, saddle weary and hungry, the two travelers saw their horse herd grazing peacefully near the cabin in what they then called Meadow Valley. Diego DaVia had chosen this semi-secluded meadow at the far northern end of the San Rafael Valley. Seeing it, as they ended a very tiring ride, made each react with great pleasure. The sun was just beginning to sink in the west, bathing the entire valley with a very appropriate golden glow.

Pancho had been getting a fire started to prepare a meal when he saw the two riders approaching the cabin. With a loud war whoop, he leapt off the porch and ran to greet them. "Hola, Pancho!" yelled Segundo.

"What? No deer steaks ready yet?! What have you been doing?" chided Diego.

"I am lucky to be alive to cook anything!" exclaimed Pancho. "I have seen more Apaches in the last month than in my whole life!" he continued.

"What were they doing to you?" asked Segundo.

"Nothing! I could not believe it! They come close and then ride away," Pancho said, somewhat wild-eyed.

"Were they the same ones?" asked Diego, becoming rightfully concerned.

"I do not think so. They come in groups . . . three, ten, twenty warriors at one time. They look around, suddenly yell like coyotes, and ride away fast," told Pancho.

Segundo looked at Diego. Diego had remained sitting upright in the saddle, his look showing his thoughts. Segundo, trying hard not to seem worried, spoke. "It seems that many warriors know who you are or, at least, who you were."

Diego DaVia voiced his one thought: "I wonder what they would have done if they had seen me here."

"As many as I have seen here in this past month, you probably will not have long to wait to find out," said Pancho, his eyes very wide.

Segundo could not help a slow smile at seeing Pancho's face. The humor was contagious, and Diego had to laugh, too. Soon they were all laughing as if the whole thing meant nothing. Except that, to Diego DaVia, it could mean plenty.

—•—

With the dawn, all three men were in the saddle. Breakfast had been good, albeit mostly coffee. While Diego and the new owner of the San Rafael Valley were making their purchase in Mexico City, Pancho had been almost, but not quite, able to contain the herd of horses where they were supposed to be. They had scattered over most of the northern half of the valley. Diego, Segundo, and Pancho, whether they wanted to or not, had to become vaqueros—mounted herdsmen—to return the herd to the area of the cabin. For Pancho and Segundo, this amounted to doing what they had been doing for years, but to Diego DaVia, this was very new. He had been cavalry, but controlling a herd this size was grueling work. All three were exhausted at the end of the day, but Diego could not get horizontal fast enough.

That evening, at the fire outside the cabin, decisions were made. Horses were going to be allowed to graze at will within a specified area dependent upon the grass available. Beginning immediately, large corrals were to be built to contain and care for those horses that needed it for injuries, foaling, and preparing for sale. After all, this ranching endeavor was not for entertainment. Expenses had to be paid, and profit must be attained. The herd would be increased. Extra vaqueros must be hired. Plans had to be made to make this endeavor a bonified business.

Thank goodness there was still money, namely Diego's gold, to do just that.

9

The summer came and went. The San Rafael Valley had burst into all the reds, yellows, and browns imaginable. All this, against the backdrop of the deep green of the pines, made the view from the cabin porch nothing short of breathtaking.

Many foals had been born. The herd was growing on its own. This herd had originally been made up of horses purchased by Segundo. Over time, wild horses had become integrated with the others. Horses having wandered from herds south of the valley had been assimilated into this herd. A good many of these horses bore the brands of some very prominent ranching organizations. Diego DaVia, while not interfering with Segundo, could not help noticing a brand he thought might be that of the Peralta rancheria. As Segundo put it, "Brands can be changed. It is not for us to return every stray horse to its far-away owner." Whatever the reasons, the horse herd was growing.

Hiring vaqueros in most cases came down to whether a man had some experience with either cattle or horses and whether he was able to ride well enough to get the job done. At the San Rafael Valley ranch, Diego DaVia had to wonder—he dared not ask—whether this Indian or that Mexican vaquero had ever heard of Dead Man Who Walks Away. Diego wondered, in his own private thoughts, if one of these men would try to do him harm because of some knowledge of what had happened at Massacre Ground. However, well into the autumn, nothing like that occurred.

What did occur, thanks to the sharp eye of Pancho, was that a surprising number of horses that had once belonged to various Indian tribes were noticed to have found their place in the herd. Neither Segundo nor Diego felt it wise to try to find those individual owners. Those ponies could not be turned loose, because they would just return to the herd. Pancho's opinion was "just wait a while; the owners will show up."

It was not long after the Indian ponies had been seen in the horse herd that some small groups of Apache, and some Yaqui Indians, had been seen observing the herd. The vaqueros were understandably nervous. Segundo had given orders that no vaquero would initiate hostilities with the Indians observing the herd. Most, if not all, the vaqueros had experience with hostile Apaches and/or Yaquis in the past. They could not understand why the order to just go about one's business had been given. The Indians, Apaches or Yaquis, kept out of range but stayed close to the herd.

After a few days, one lone Apache, dressed in finery that identified him as a kind of shaman or holy man of the tribe, approached one of the vaqueros some distance down the valley from the cabin. He made a sign that he wished to talk to the vaquero. Within minutes after he left to rejoin the other Indians, three vaqueros rode up to the cabin. They spoke with Segundo. Segundo bade them wait on the porch. "Diego, you'd better come out here a minute," said Segundo.

Diego stepped out and asked, "What is it, Segundo?"

"Listen to this. *Dígame* . . . speak up," ordered Segundo to one of the vaqueros.

"Patrón," said the vaquero with respect, "that Apache told me that we have a few of their ponies. He said he had seen them. They want the ponies, but they do not want to offend Dead Man Who Walks Away. I asked who they meant. He said, 'the man with the iron eyes who rides the big grey horse.' I did not know what to say."

Diego DaVia could hardly believe his ears. It was clear that they were afraid of him, or his medicine. He had to think about that for a minute. Then he said, "Vaqueros, we do not wish to have a war with these Apaches. We will try to make the best of this situation. Go to him. Tell him your patrón does not wish to keep ponies belonging to the Apache that have wandered into his herd. Tell him that if they had been stolen honorably, I would fight for them. Tell him to take the ponies as a gift, one warrior to another warrior."

"Sí, Patrón!" answered the vaquero and galloped off down the valley. The vaquero returned within a matter of minutes to report.

"Patrón! I have never heard of such a thing. The Apache insisted that we ride along with them to be sure that they took only the ponies that belonged to them. They did not wish to anger you," spoke the vaquero in amazement. "Madre de Dios! Surely you must be that one that they fear!" he exclaimed as he rode away.

Diego looked at Segundo. "So much for your secret, amigo," said Segundo at almost a whisper. "This will be known all over this valley and even deeper into Sonora by morning."

"Things could start getting interesting, amigo mio," agreed Diego.

"What do you think will happen?" asked Segundo.

"I think we need to keep control of our horses and make ready to sell them in the spring," answered Diego, avoiding the question. "Have the outriders move them to the north end of the valley every sundown. Let them graze at will during the day."

———

Winter had arrived, yet no snow had hampered the activities of the ranch. Diego DaVia and Segundo were enjoying a comparatively peaceful day-to-day operation. Soon, an attempt to sell part of the herd to recoup the expenses of operating the ranch had to be made. Diego had no direct experience in that regard, so the marketing of the herd fell to Segundo. There was a military presence in Cananea that controlled most of the Sonoran Desert up to and including the San Rafael Valley. However, due to the uncertainty of whatever government was currently in power, Segundo would have to work hard to find a potential buyer. His best chance would be to consign part of the herd to the Mexican army. Getting a fair price could be difficult. Therefore, a trip to test the waters was inevitable.

Segundo made ready and planned to leave a week before Christmas. His journey began as the first snow began to frost the grasses of the San Rafael Valley. While he was gone, Diego, Pancho, and the vaqueros made the best of his absence with fresh venison, small cakes dreamed up by Pancho, and some tequila. Activities by hostile Apaches were not likely due to the weather. It seemed evident the word was out about Dead Man Who Walks Away, and so no Indians of any tribe had been seen for many weeks.

Things settled down soon after the little Christmas celebration. Aside from a little commotion over the occasional card game in the vaqueros' bunkhouse, not much was going on. Diego DaVia had begun to think, "Ah! This is the good life!"

— —

Two weeks after Christmas, Segundo returned.

"Welcome, amigo," greeted Diego. "You were gone so long we all thought you had found some young chica."

"I did!" proclaimed Segundo. "But that was not what kept me the extra few days. There is much happening in civilized Mexico," he said.

"Like what, for instance?" asked Diego, becoming serious.

"Revolution!" replied Segundo. "Or the talk of revolution is being heard all over the northern villages. The faction keeping Santa Anna from returning to power, la Reforma, has already been fighting some skirmishes with the forces wanting to keep the Church and the old military in charge."

"How bad is it, Segundo?" asked Diego. "Do you see it spilling over into this valley?"

"Not yet, amigo mio," said Segundo. "But I think the changes will affect us."

"You know this business, Segundo. I am still new at it," offered Diego. "But militarily, I see a different market for our horses."

"Sí, amigo. Evidently you see it as I do," agreed Segundo.

Diego sat down, paused in his speaking momentarily, and then said, "We now have more than one market for our horses. We have the existing military, and we have a possible revolutionary army market. We can sell to both . . . at top prices!"

"Mexico will always be Mexico. The power swings first one way, and then the other. Always too far and back again! These fools will never work together . . . sad," said Segundo.

"It is true," said Diego. "Those with money and power love to tread roughly on the less fortunate, until those poor ones have had enough and retaliate hard against their oppressors. Neither side seems to know when to stop before going too far. Thus, the hate and the fighting continue until they both lose."

"Sí, but with death and destruction on all sides, who really wins?" said Segundo.

"Neither the combatants nor their families, to be sure, but we could well profit by it," Diego said hesitatingly. "If these fools decide to fight each other, why should we not profit from their stupidity?"

"The army of Mexico will be needing horses. El Ejército de la Reforma Revolucionaria will be needing horses. And that means we will be needing horses . . . to sell," stated Segundo.

"We will change our plans now, amigo. We will hold our horses here in our remote valley. We will add any wild horses to the herd. Any horses that we come across, not being supervised by an owner, will be our horses," proclaimed Diego DaVia. "We must begin branding our horses, so that we can control their sale. But we need to design a brand."

"I have been thinking about that," offered Segundo.

"Too much time in the saddle, huh, Segundo?" kidded Diego.

"Sí, way too much," was Segundo's comeback. "It seems the talk about Dead Man Who Walks Away has made it to Cananea. The vaqueros in the cantinas call this ranch 'la Rancheria Fantasma'— 'Ghost Ranch.' Our horse herd is referred to as 'la mañada de fantasma'—the 'ghost herd'."

"Damn!" exclaimed Diego DaVia. "Will I never get away from that?"

"Make it pay, then, amigo," stated Segundo. "Use it to your advantage."

"All right, then," asserted Diego. "Have you also thought of a brand for these ghost horses, Segundo?"

"Two leg bones crossed in the form of an *X*," stated Segundo.

"Very well, then. So it is. Have Mendoza, the blacksmith, make the branding irons. But be sure that the crossed leg bones do not look like an *X*. Put the round bone ends on each. We will begin branding la mañada de fantasma as soon as they are ready," ordered Diego DaVia.

And so, it was done.

Activity began in earnest on la Rancheria Fantasma. Corrals that had been built merely to hold horses having special care needs were expanded and converted with chute ways to accommodate counting for shipment. Grazing areas were more diligently patrolled to keep strays from wandering too far. Theft had become a distinct possibility now. The vaqueros' bunkhouse had to be expanded to make life more acceptable for the men. Good vaqueros were going to be hard to find; therefore, keeping the ones already on the payroll became even more important. The cook shack had become a mess hall, capable of serving an entire crew of vaqueros as they came off duty. They deserved all this and more. After all, these vaqueros were the best riders and herdsmen in the north of Mexico. It was decided to make the quality of the vaqueros known to all who would see them . . . especially themselves. They were special. They would wear colorful clothing: bright red neck scarves and bright yellow sashes around the waist to identify each of them as a Vaquero of la Rancheria Fantasma. And each Vaquero wore these items proudly!

There began an intensive push to recruit more and more horses into la mañada de fantasma. Right or wrong, the various Indian tribes—including the Apache—had to begin guarding their own horses from wandering off. No more helping Mexican ranchers' herds wander off for a while. La Rancheria Fantasma was earning a name for herself. All this occurred during the rest of that winter and well into the spring.

In June, Segundo made another sales trip into Cananea. The local military commander, Major Sanchez, at first did not even wish to speak of purchasing horses. However, within three days, he sent for Segundo at the small boardinghouse where Segundo had rented a room. Segundo was warmly greeted upon entering the small compound that served as a military headquarters.

The commander, Major Sanchez, after each had been seated said, "I am pleased that you chose to stay in Cananea for these past few days."

"I was hoping to visit some friends before finishing my other business interests," said Segundo.

"Well, in that case, I hope those interests turned out well for you," said Major Sanchez.

"That is yet to be seen," returned Segundo.

"I hope that you will forgive me for not immediately recognizing the name *Francisco Ruiz* when we last met," said the major. "I mentioned your visit to my lieutenant, and he told me of your family."

"How would that make a difference in the result of my visit to you?" asked Segundo.

"At that time, as to any purchase of horses, perhaps none. But knowing that you are the son of the late Don Ramón Ruiz, and of the dispatches that arrived this morning, I think we may be able to purchase some horses," admitted Major Sanchez.

"I must convey my appreciation to your lieutenant," responded Segundo.

"Tell me, Don Francisco. How many horses do you have to sell?" inquired Major Sanchez with new respect.

"I have many horses. How many do you think your cavalry will need?" returned Segundo, not wishing at this time to give more information than necessary. "How is it that the dispatches you mentioned changed your mind about buying horses?"

"You are of a highly regarded aristocratic family and, as such, are to be trusted, I am sure. But not everyone must know," cautioned the major. "We have been notified that la Reforma sympathizers in the area are arming themselves. There may be fighting soon to put down these traitors."

"I had not heard. But, in any case, you feel you need how many horses?" again asked Segundo.

"I think fifty quality stock would be sufficient. But understand, I will not pay for inferior horses," cautioned Major Sanchez.

Segundo remained calm and showing no emotion said, "There will be no culls at this price." Calmly he wrote the figure and handed it to the major. The major stiffened a moment and said, "This is a trifle steep, is it not?"

"This price is for fifty quality mounts, no culls, delivered to this post in three weeks," stated Segundo. He then added, "Payment to be in gold, here, at the time of delivery."

"From where do these fifty horses come?" asked Major Sanchez.

"They come from my rancheria, la Rancheria Fantasma," replied Segundo.

"La Rancheria Fantasma—Ghost Ranch! That is quite a name for a rancho. Where is it?" asked the major again.

Segundo, not wishing to give this major any ideas, simply answered, "It is where the horses are, amigo."

The major put his signature on a purchase order and handed it to Segundo.

"In three weeks then." With that, Major Sanchez returned to his paper-strewn desk, and Segundo, with a wide sweep of his sombrero, turned and walked out of the building.

10

"The major changed his mind about ordering our horses?" wondered Diego DaVia, after Segundo returned.

"Sí, amigo," said Segundo. "The major told me that the prestige of the Ruiz family caused him to rethink his hesitancy. He had received dispatches from somewhere. He said that possible insurrection in the area would necessitate increasing the cavalry mounts."

"Segundo, amigo mio, there may be more to it than that," said Diego. "You know some of the Vaqueros are part Yaqui and visit family now and then."

"Sí, Diego. Have you heard something?" asked Segundo.

Diego tried to pick his words with care. He did not wish to alarm Segundo with what could be just rumor. "Pancho told me yesterday that the Yaquis are saying that americanos have been slipping into northern Sonora."

Segundo stood up straight hearing that. "What are they doing?" he asked.

"The Yaquis are accusing them of stealing horses, some cattle, and starting fights and even shootings," answered Diego.

"Are they settlers, immigrants with families?" Segundo asked.

"No," came the reply. Diego stayed calm and let it sink in. Segundo sat back down, a frown on his face. After a few moments, he said, "The rumored sale of this part of Sonora to the americanos must be it. They come to raise hell to accelerate the sale by making the Mexican government, whatever government that is, glad to get rid of it."

"Unbelievable, but so it would seem," agreed Diego. "But many of these americanos are here just to raise hell."

"We could be in for much trouble," said Segundo.

"Sí, amigo mio. I believe that once our presence in this isolated valley is known, we will have to defend it and ourselves," ventured Diego DaVia. The memory of his last battle was still a nightly occurrence in his fitful sleep, but despite that, he was not afraid of another fight. He had survived before and felt that every breath he took was a bonus of life anyway. He was, however, afraid for Segundo, Pancho, and the Vaqueros he had grown to like and admire.

Segundo, looking deeply into the iron eyes of Diego DaVia, seemed to read his thoughts. "We are not afraid, Diego. All these men have been in one fight or another all their lives. This Rancheria Fantasma, which you have made for us, has put dignity into their lives and has been the best hope that they have ever had for themselves. We will all fight for it. This is our Rancheria Fantasma. It is also theirs. Lead us, Diego DaVia, and we will make it great."

"Gather all the Fantasma Vaqueros tonight outside the cook shack. We will graze the herd near our corrals for this meeting. We will not lead the Vaqueros into this blindly. This battle we will all fight together. But we will offer them the honorable choice," ordered Diego DaVia, the first real order he had given for a long, long time.

Sundown saw the horse herd grazing near the cook shack as planned. The Vaqueros were finishing their meal. They had not all eaten at the same place, at the same time, since joining la Rancheria Fantasma.

Francisco Ruiz, walking with Diego DaVia, left the cabin porch, and together they walked swiftly and with purpose directly to the informal meeting place. The Vaqueros rose as one and stood with respect to greet them.

Segundo spoke to them. "As you know, la Rancheria Fantasma has contracted to sell fifty of our horses to the Mexican cavalry in Cananea. We leave to do that in the morning. This is a good thing, and it is the beginning of why we all are working so hard."

At that, there were smiles all around and murmurs of gladness among the Vaqueros. "We are all happy about that," assured Segundo. "But there is more to discuss. Diego DaVia has information for you as well."

"Vaqueros of la Rancheria Fantasma! First thing, allow me to congratulate you on your efforts to make this place into the fine rancheria that it is. It could not be so without your hard work and dedication. Segundo Ruiz and I sincerely thank you." There was much applause after the words of Diego DaVia.

"You have succeeded here because you are fighters. Each of you, every day, fight the wind, the rain, the snow, the heat, the cold, the horses, and we know even each other now and then. But you have all fought your way as la Rancheria Fantasma Vaqueros. There are no others like you," praised Diego.

Diego continued. "Some of you may know of events that will, in all probability, force us to have to fight for our place in this world. We, as la Rancheria Fantasma, are going to have to face a changing world around us. Our government in Mexico City is in trouble. We do not know how that will end and so affect us all. La Reforma Revolución is firing up again. We do not know how that will affect us all. The sale of a large part of northern Sonora seems to be a reality, and we do not know how that will affect us all. For us to survive, la Rancheria Fantasma may, at various times, have to fight Mexican cavalry, la Reforma revolucionarios, norteamericanos— now raising hell around Cananea—as well as the usual Apache raids. After all, we have something they all want: our horses and our ability to acquire and provide them to each of these factions. I do not know if we are eventually going to be Mexican, American, or what. This I can tell you: we will not be Apache!"

After listening to the first part of Diego's comments, the part about not becoming Apache caused loud laughter. When all had quieted down, Diego then added, "Segundo and I have decided that we will fight anyone and anything that threatens our existence, our horses, and our Rancheria Fantasma Vaqueros. I offer you this: any Vaquero wishing to leave our ranks may do so without any ill feeling on our part. Segundo and I both respect your actions. However, those Vaqueros who decide to remain with la Rancheria Fantasma will receive added pay. You will also be trained to be both great Vaqueros and excellent cavalry. Some of you may know that I have experience in that area. If we must, for whatever time it takes, we will be a country unto ourselves. We will owe allegiance to none, until the time when such allegiance favors la Rancheria Fantasma and all who are a part of it. This is my promise to you all. Please accept my gratitude to all of you."

Diego DaVia then left to walk to the cabin amidst the loud cheers of the Vaqueros of la Rancheria Fantasma. Segundo then asked the Vaqueros to search their hearts and notify him of their decisions in the morning.

———

The next morning, breakfast was served to the unanimously committed crew of la Rancheria Fantasma Vaqueros. Any Rancheria Fantasma fight was to become their fight.

The fifty horses were on their way to Cananea, and the military unit stationed there. Normally four or five Vaqueros would be able to manage the horse herd for such a trip, even a long one as was this. But Diego ordered fifteen men to make the trip. Whether the major knew where la Rancheria Fantasma was located or not, a show of strength was required. That left the remaining crew somewhat shorthanded, but Diego was convinced that it was worth the gamble. It was. No strangers found their way to la Rancheria Fantasma.

The trip to Cananea would have taken a few days longer than it did, thanks to the extra Vaqueros assigned to it.

The Mexican military major was extremely happy to accept them. Segundo, on orders from his partner, Diego DaVia, would not allow the horses to be placed in the military corrals until the contracted price in gold was delivered to Segundo. Once that occurred, the horses had a new home. Francisco Segundo Ruiz was welcomed as "Don" Francisco Ruiz because of his obvious position as an owner of a sizeable enterprise. Major Sanchez made numerous attempts to ascertain the location of la Rancheria Fantasma, but Don Ruiz avoided all of them. However, although he could not hide the tracks of the herd as it entered Cananea, the circuitous route taken back might possibly have deterred discovery of the rancheria's actual location. The Fantasma Vaqueros were happy to be returning without the horse herd but with the contracted gold. Their future seemed better for that.

For the rancheria to function without unnecessary stress to the Vaqueros' personal lives, those men with families were permitted to bring them to the rancheria. This necessitated the building of some small, private family cabins in addition to the bunkhouse for the single men. Supplies were always difficult to obtain, but what the rancheria could not provide itself, various Yaqui cousins of a few Vaqueros were contracted to bring to the rancheria. La Rancheria Fantasma was becoming a small colony within itself.

The Fantasma Vaqueros began calling Segundo "Don Ruiz" after hearing the major address him as such.

"So," said Diego, "you are now Don Francisco Ruiz, Segundo. And why not? You have earned the title, amigo mio. Welcome home, Don Francisco!"

"Gracias, gracias," returned Segundo. "I admit to feeling somewhat uncomfortable hearing it spoken. 'Don Ruiz' has always been my father."

"Ha! But you will get used to it, and you will wear the title honorably," commended Diego.

"I have to say, Diego, that I do not mind the Vaqueros calling me Don Ruiz. But they sure are having great fun sweeping off their sombreros and bowing low as I pass by," admitted Segundo.

"Once you start barking orders to them again, that practice will probably stop . . . probably," Diego said, trying to be serious. "Now to business," he continued. "You did a fine job in Cananea. The sale of those horses benefited us in many ways. Now we must make some new plans. Let us go outside on the porch and think about what we must do."

The two men retired to the porch with a fresh pot of hot coffee. They looked over all that was visible from the porch, and both men were well pleased. "No one would ever believe that we have built this Rancheria Fantasma in so short a time," said Don Ruiz.

"We have not only created a new horse rancheria, but we have also created a new 'don,'" quipped Diego.

"Oh, stop it! Get serious," said Segundo.

"All right . . . for now," agreed Diego. "We need to ration the sale of horses to no more than fifty at any one time."

"Why? We have many horses on la Rancheria Fantasma," questioned Segundo.

Diego was careful not to offend his friend. "This is not a normal business cycle of raise horses, sell them, raise more, sell them . . . and keep doing it. Thanks to the likely high demand for horses from many buyers, we can sell horses at a higher price to cover our costs and profit; however, others who have horses to sell will do the same."

"The price of horses will go up. So, what is wrong with that?" asked Segundo.

"True. But where are we going to replace those horses that we sell?" added Diego.

"I see," said Segundo. "We could maybe sell ourselves right out of business."

"I suppose that could happen, but I fear that as our herd becomes smaller by selling off too many, that we might have to become horse thieves ourselves in order to stay in business," said Diego.

"Could something like that actually happen?" worried Segundo.

"I mean that we must maintain a balance between what we sell and what we are able to keep, regarding the size of our herd," explained Diego. "I fear that, once our location becomes well known, and they realize how many horses we may have here, we will be a target for horse thieves."

"No doubt about it!" exclaimed Segundo. "The military training of the Vaqueros, as you mentioned, must begin soon."

"I'm afraid so," said Diego. "In that regard, I must ask you and Pancho to select possible squad leaders and set up a chain of command. Something else, Segundo," added Diego. "We must try not to become a one customer only supplier of horses. I am sure we will be approached by la Reforma revolucionarios, to provide them with horses. Treat them even-handedly. We sell horses as our business . . . for gold . . . whomever the buyer is. I do not know what will happen yet, whether or not we become a part of los Estados Unidos . . . the United States."

"I have very mixed feelings about that happening," said Segundo. "I am Mexican, but I live here in this San Rafael Valley. I . . . I just do not know."

"We will live our lives as honorable men, as best we can, no matter what political authority is involved," said Diego.

"Enough of this," said an irritated Segundo. "What about selling horses to the presidio of Tucson?"

"We will wait and see if we are approached by them. At this point, I do not know on what side of the probable upcoming conflict they will fight," answered Diego DaVia, returning to his old military strategist self.

———

Diego DaVia, Dead Man Who Walks Away, still spent many nights sleeping in increments and waking from nightmares of the horror at Massacre Ground. He never winced from the prospect of battling to save la Rancheria Fantasma and his Vaqueros from the different factions of a political revolution. But the prospect of having to fight against the Apache again brought back too many memories. During the daylight hours, Diego DaVia was the strong leader he had always been. At night, however, he would wake up in a sweat. To his knowledge, he never cried out in his nightmares. His soldier's mind would not allow that. But, even in the daylight, he wondered what would happen if the Apache needed horses so much that they would attempt to steal them from la Rancheria Fantasma. He knew he would fight, but the prospect left him cold. On the other hand, what would he do if the Apache chose to trade, or even buy horses from him? Would he sell horses to the Apache? He would wait and see.

———

Work on the many improvements necessary for the day-to-day operation of la Rancheria Fantasma continued. More corrals had to be built to house the growing herd. As time went by, wild or semi-wild horses drawn by the natural need to herd seemed to wander into the rancheria. One or two at a time did not take long to increase the size of the Fantasma herd. Many of these, however, were formerly tame horses that had been lost to their previous owner. Thanks to the efficiency of la Rancheria Fantasma Vaqueros, those horses soon wore the Rancheria Fantasma brand.

The orders of Diego, which directed Vaqueros with families to be allowed to bring them to la Rancheria Fantasma, meant construction of small cabins to house them. This work took time. But these Vaqueros were more than eager to perform that work. Many rancherias did not provide for such amenities. These Vaqueros became fiercely loyal to their dual patrones.

All these persons—single Vaqueros and married Vaqueros with families—must be fed. In addition to the usual tortilla-based tasty fare of Sonora, the required addition of meat was necessary. They could not all eat venison. Venison was becoming hard to hunt so close to so many men. Chicken was good, but beef was better. And the children of the Vaqueros needed milk. All that meant cattle. Therefore, pens, buildings, and fencing to house all this were necessary.

—-—

Busy days were followed by more busy days. La Rancheria Fantasma grew. The herd grew. The population grew. Segundo put it thusly: "We have created a monster. We'd better sell some more of this herd to relieve the pressure on everything, or it is going to blow up."

"I know," said Diego. "I want to avoid any large sale to the military at Cananea for a while. We should spread the wealth so as not to favor any one political faction."

"When I spoke just now, I had a reason," added Segundo. "One of the Vaqueros told Pancho that a Reforma rider expressed interest in our horses."

"Was that rider talking of buying some or rustling some?" asked Diego.

"According to Pancho's Vaquero, he merely stated that la Reforma was aware that we have many horses."

"Segundo, bring the herd in closer and add more Vaqueros to watch over them," ordered Diego. "And, Segundo, make sure that they are armed. Las Reformas are probably getting desperate by now."

"Sí. We will be ready for them," agreed Segundo.

"Bueno. However, see if that rider can be contacted again. I am interested to see if they have gold and would rather actually buy some horses instead of rustling them," said Diego. "I would not object to a meeting with their commander. Perhaps convince them that buying a few horses at a time would be to their advantage."

11

Within a week after their discussion regarding talks with la Reforma revolucionarios, Pancho, along with five Vaqueros, escorted three of las Reformas through the herd of horses to the main cabin of Diego DaVia and Don Ruiz. All three of las Reformas were smiling and trying to seem as friendly as possible under the circumstances. The circumstances were that they had been stripped of their weapons and, until now, had to wear bandanas over their eyes. Diego and Segundo both looked at each other as if to say, "How can anyone trust someone who smiles after being disarmed and forced to travel blindfolded for many miles?"

Don Ruiz introduced himself and Diego DaVia and welcomed them to la Rancheria Fantasma. All three of las Reformas looked around in awe at the size and efficiency of la rancheria. The one who claimed leadership introduced himself as Colonel Narbona. Colonel Narbona merely stated, "We had heard that a rancheria existed somewhere in the wilds north of Cananea, but we never imagined anything like this!" As he spoke, he waved his sombrero in a sweeping motion in the direction of the herd and the many buildings and corrals.

Don Ruiz, after receiving a look from Diego DaVia, invited them to sit on the porch rather than enter the cabin to talk. The motion was noticed by Colonel Narbona for what it was. This was to be a face-to-face meeting in diplomatic terms, but with clear military overtones. The unsaid meaning was that we will discuss certain matters, but from a position of strength. It was then that Colonel Narbona noticed that every la Rancheria Fantasma Vaquero mounted or on foot was armed with a model 1848 Dragoon revolver. The negotiators were only too glad to sit down then and discuss horses.

Two of the young women who helped in the cook shack served fruit drinks to all on the porch.

Don Segundo Ruiz began. "It has come to our attention that you have an interest in horses."

Colonel Narbona answered, "Sí, but we had no idea that this rancheria had so large a herd as this."

"I take it that you are interested in acquiring some of them," stated Segundo.

"Sí," replied Colonel Narbona. "It is our wish that you may choose to donate some of them to help us further the cause of la Reforma."

"We do not donate horses to further any cause other than what is necessary to continue our business at a profit . . . a reasonable profit," explained Segundo.

The colonel shot a somewhat uncomfortable glance toward Diego. Diego maintained his stone-faced expression. The colonel became more uncomfortable because of that. Colonel Narbona then asked pointedly, "Do you not favor the cause of la Reforma?" His tone was as much threatening as indignant.

Don Segundo Ruiz replied by saying, "La Rancheria Fantasma prefers not to let favoritism toward or against any cause adversely affect our business."

"Have you no loyalty to your country?" asked the colonel, his voice rising.

It was at this point that Diego DaVia chose to enter the conversation. He had seen that Segundo had begun to redden somewhat at the combative tone of the colonel.

"Colonel Narbona, our loyalty to a country depends entirely upon what country shows up. So far it is not clear who is in control of Mexico," interjected Diego DaVia.

Now it was the colonel's turn to be a little red faced. "I can assure you that la Reforma is, and will be, the legitimate government of Mexico!"

Diego, not wishing for a fight at this time, but not shying away from one either, clarified his position. "We here in this valley, until we have good reason to be otherwise, are loyal only to la Rancheria Fantasma and to our people who make it what it is."

While Colonel Narbona was digesting that response from Diego DaVia, Diego added, "I have only met one other man with the Narbona name. He is Miguel Narbona, a highly capable war chief of the Chiricahua Apache. Are you related in some way to him?"

Noticeably flustered now, Colonel Narbona rasped, "My father's brother married an Apache woman. Miguel Narbona, that damn killer, is a cousin!"

Diego prodded him even further. "Is he part of the military forces of la Reforma?"

"No!" said Colonel Narbona in a much louder voice. "La Reforma does not need an Apache to help us fight, or to take horses if we want! We can handle that if need be!"

"I would not count on that," said Diego DaVia as he slowly and deliberately stood up and looked down on the Reforma colonel. The colonel stood up also, but as he did, he noticed that the number of Fantasma Vaqueros had tripled since the conversation began.

Diego asked, before the colonel could regain control, "When you decide how many horses you will want from us, will you be paying in gold or what?"

"La Reforma will pay in gold," slowly answered the colonel.

"Bueno! Good! Send your messenger with your order, and we will gladly do business," said Segundo, getting back into the conversation. "Pancho, our visitors are leaving to return to their headquarters. Please see that no harm comes to them by blindfolding them for their return and providing them with safe escort."

Although it was not the most cordial beginning of a relationship, the point was made that la Rancheria Fantasma would not be bullied into an arrangement which was not to its satisfaction, neither by coercion nor by force.

After their guests had gone, Segundo said, "Diego, these people have their own small army. You know that. Why did you try to provoke that colonel?"

"That blowhard needed someone to stand up to him. If he tries to attack us for these horses, he will lose too many men, and he knows it. Look at this beautiful valley, Segundo. You and I, Pancho, and Pancho's grandmother could defend it against anyone . . . all by ourselves!"

"Ha Ha!" laughed Segundo, stepping down from the porch.

"Where are you going, Segundo?" asked Diego, also laughing.

"I need to find Pancho's grandmother," came Segundo's reply.

———

Ten days later, when fifty, and fifty only, horses were delivered to la Reforma, the delivery team consisted of five working Fantasma Vaqueros and a squad of twenty additional Vaqueros, all riding in cavalry formation. When the two groups faced each other to transfer the horses for the gold, it looked like a formal truce signing. However, the Fantasma Vaqueros looked more like a military cavalry unit than did la Reforma troops.

Diego was extremely pleased by Segundo's report. He personally informed the Fantasma Vaqueros how pleased he was by their performance. Professionalism had begun to show. The reputation of la Rancheria Fantasma, and its Vaqueros, had now begun to spread.

12

That reputation had spread more rapidly than even Diego had imagined. Thirty days after the sale of horses to la Reforma, a sergeant in the uniform of Mexican cavalry entered the San Rafael Valley of la Rancheria Fantasma. He entered from the south end of the valley escorted by a Yaqui scout. The sergeant was carrying a white flag. The Fantasma Vaqueros spotted him from some distance and sent a rider to inform Diego and Segundo of his arrival. Three Vaqueros escorted the party of two to the porch, where both Diego DaVia and Don Segundo awaited. The Yaqui scout was known to the Vaqueros. From what the Yaqui had told the Vaqueros, while riding up the valley, he had deliberately guided the sergeant into the valley from the south end, not the quicker way through the mountains at the north end. It was he who made the introductions.

The sergeant dismounted and, at attention, handed a leather pouch to Diego. The papers in the pouch identified Sergeant Eduardo Vargas, emissary from the Mexican garrison stationed at the presidio of Tucson. Former Lieutenant Diego DaVia told the sergeant, "Stand easy, Sergeant, while I peruse these documents."

After giving the documents a quick once-over, Diego DaVia sat down to read them again in detail. After he was sure he had read them correctly, DaVia asked the sergeant, "Are you aware, Sergeant Vargas, of the contents of this dispatch?"

"Sí. I am ordered to await a reply and report as soon as possible to my commandant," replied Sergeant Vargas.

"It is getting late," said Diego. "I will need time to study this request with my partner, Don Ruiz. You are welcome to stay the night. Pancho, please make Sergeant Vargas comfortable in the guest quarters. Sergeant, I would be pleased if you would join Don Ruiz and me for supper after you have had a chance to rest."

"Gracias. I look forward to meeting you at supper," said Sergeant Vargas.

No sooner had Sergeant Vargas retired to his accommodations to rest and freshen up before meeting Diego and Segundo for supper than Diego and Segundo went inside the cabin, turned hacienda, to meet privately.

"*Que pasa?* What's going on, Diego?" asked Segundo.

"The sergeant's dispatches ask for a meeting," answered Diego.

"So?" queried Segundo.

"So, the meeting must be in the presidio of Tucson!" exclaimed Diego.

"Whoa! Does the commandant want horses? How many?" asked Segundo.

"With proper identification and orders, the sergeant could have done the negotiating and purchase without a meeting in Tucson. No. There is something more involved," said a very apprehensive Diego DaVia.

Don Segundo Ruiz, a look of genuine concern showing on his face, stated, "I can handle the major in Cananea, but I do not want to get into a discussion with the commandant of the presidio. We can contract and sell as many horses as we wish, at top prices, to nearly anyone. Why should we have to go to the presidio of Tucson?"

"I do not know," answered Diego. "Perhaps to find out what would even prompt the presidio commandant to request such a meeting."

Segundo ventured that, "It must be something political. Something has either just happened . . . or is about to happen. When I went to Cananea, Major Sanchez seemed to be very agitated about those rumors that the sale of land to the norteamericanos might soon happen. However, I did not pursue that, and he did not say more."

"Can it be that the commandant of the presidio has heard something about that? Even if that were happening, why would he need to confer with us?" Diego asked.

"Not us. You! I am not going to see that commandant. I am not military. If anyone goes, you go," he said to Diego.

"I understand, amigo," Diego replied somewhat slowly. "I would like your company, but I know that your place is here at la Rancheria Fantasma. I must think about this."

"Well, we meet with the sergeant in about an hour for supper. What will we tell him?" asked Segundo, more like an assertion than a question.

"We shall see. We shall see," said Diego standing, prior to taking a walk about the meadow north of the cabin.

An hour or so later, before the sun began its swift journey downward beyond the horizon, Cavalry Sergeant Eduardo Vargas sat down on the wide porch of the cabin with Don Francisco Segundo Ruiz and Diego DaVia. The amenities were observed, and supper was served. A very casual atmosphere prevailed. After all, the partners of la Rancheria Fantasma really could not help but admire the successful effort on the part of Sergeant Vargas in having made so difficult and dangerous a ride from the presidio of Tucson. Surely his mission in so doing involved more than merely a request to buy some horses.

"Now, Sergeant Vargas, what can we do for you to justify such an arduous journey?" asked Don Ruiz.

"I truly wish I knew, Don Ruiz," replied the sergeant. "My only mission is to tell you that the commandant of the presidio of Tucson regards a discussion with you as most important. He has ordered me to persuade you to accompany me back to the presidio to meet with him as soon as possible."

"I have read the documents in the dispatch. That was easy; there simply were not many to read," remarked Diego. "However, even after reading the documents, the meaning contained within is not clear to me."

"The commandant did not feel compelled to disclose that information to me, Patrón," offered the sergeant.

"The letter in the documents spoke highly of la Rancheria Fantasma and bespoke more knowledge of it than I would have thought," observed

Diego. "I am quite surprised by that fact. After all, we are not exactly located in what one would call a well-travelled area."

Sergeant Vargas then spoke up. "That may actually be one reason for the attempt to meet."

"I am not sure. I have no military background on which to base my thoughts. Yet perhaps the fact that we are in a veritably unknown area of Sonora may have some bearing on what your commandant feels is happening in Mexico," speculated Don Ruiz.

"You may be right, at least partly right," agreed Diego.

"And you know what that means . . ." said Don Ruiz, tipping back in his chair.

"Damn, Segundo! Yes. It means that I have to go to that damn presidio of Tucson!" exclaimed Diego.

"In that case you must have some security. Ten of our best trained Vaqueros will accompany you. You will deploy them as best you see fit to protect you at all times," said Don Ruiz, as if to assure Diego that all would be well at la rancheria also.

Diego DaVia stood and addressed the sergeant. "Sergeant Vargas, we will leave for the presidio of Tucson after breakfast. At least we will leave on a full stomach."

The sergeant stood, nodded his head, said "*Hasta mañana* . . . until tomorrow," and left the porch.

"Diego, I know you do not wish to identify yourself to other members of the military," spoke Don Ruiz.

"I see no choice, amigo," said Diego.

"I do not believe there is any need to disclose your former cavalry history. Certainly not what had happened at Massa— . . . uh . . . that place," said the Don.

"No. They should have no knowledge of what happened unless some Indians have been talking. Yet I doubt that. They would probably be pretty close-mouthed about something like that," voiced Diego.

"Dress as you are now, as a prominent owner of a great rancheria, and you will be so treated," assured Segundo.

"I will take only my Dragoon . . . and my saber." Diego hesitated even to speak of the saber. "Also, Pancho does some nice leather work.

Ask him to stay up a little later tonight to fit a leather piece for the hilt end. It will cover the emblem of capitán of dragoons. I will feel more comfortable with my saber."

"It will be done. Sleep well, amigo," wished Don Ruiz.

The night seemed long and dark to Diego DaVia. The mission he was to embark upon the next morning stirred up too many memories. The military, the battles, the Peralta expedition, the dead compadres, and the massacre all contributed to a very sleepless night. Yet morning found Diego DaVia dressed in all the traveling finery of a true Spanish don, saber at his left side. When Sergeant Vargas mounted, Diego waved farewell to Don Ruiz and, with his Vaqueros, led the procession north, away from la Rancheria Fantasma, which he had come to love dearly. But he knew that his beloved Rancheria Fantasma must be protected. Therefore, he must make this unwanted trek to find out from what.

Northward they rode through the wild country. Occasionally, an old Indian trail would lead in the proper direction, and the party would follow it for a while. They were understandably careful, of course, while following an Indian trail. Luck was with them, however, and they proceeded along without incident. Their route first led them through the Canelo Mountains, northward and westward passing south of the Mustang Mountains. They managed to follow a pass westward through the Santa Rita Mountains, then followed the Rio Santa Cruz on its northward flow to the presidio of Tucson. Despite not having to deal with wagons, livestock, or even Indian encounters, the journey still took five days.

After those five days, the Fantasma party arrived at the presidio of Tucson. All were very tired but still managed to present a very militaristic bearing upon entering the military complex. The Vaqueros honored their patrón by sitting straight in the saddle, moving as one unit, and, in so doing, looked more like military than the residing military. The commandant ordered supper to be served to the Rancheria Fantasma party.

Diego accepted but asked, with the commandant's permission, that any discussions be deferred to the following morning, when all were rested, and Diego, himself, was able to see to the wellbeing of his Vaqueros.

Diego's request was graciously granted, and the supper became a pleasurable meal with courteous and friendly conversation. Even so, Diego DaVia could not help conducting himself, as he always had, with precise military table bearing. The Vaqueros, following Diego's lead, looked as though they had once been a military unit as well. They presented a disciplined military presence at that long banquet table.

The following morning, after breakfast, Diego DaVia was invited into the commandant's office, which, for being essentially on the frontier, was very well furnished. Once seated, a short period of silence followed. Normal protocol required, in such military meetings, that the ranking officer would initiate the discussions. Diego waited about as long as he felt prudent and then said, "Sir, my Vaqueros and I have been in the saddle for five long days. We have made this journey without any kind of briefing as to the subject to be discussed."

"Please forgive me," responded the commandant. "I have been in command here for a very short time and was trying to choose my words carefully."

"Then I suggest you ease your mind and simply tell me what you have on it," said Diego.

"Yes, of course." The commandant took a deep breath and said, "Our position here is very fragile. I do not know even if this garrison is still mandated to remain here."

There was no response from Diego, so the commandant continued. "You know of the treaty with los Estados Unidos, the americanos, to sell to them much of the land up to the Gila River?"

"We are very isolated in our San Rafael Valley. There have been rumors. There have been wild-eyed reactionaries now and then. If you have any real information . . . official dispatches . . . I would perhaps be better able to help you with whatever you are about to ask of me," ventured DaVia.

"Sometime soon, I may have to relinquish possession of this presidio to the americanos. I am hoping that I can do this peacefully. That is, I do not want to be forced out of here by some North American rabble. I prefer to officially turn over this presidio to a garrison of the American army," explained the commandant.

"Why would you not be able to do that?" asked Diego.

"Because all around this presidio—even inside these walls—American rabble have already begun causing trouble. I fear that they may try to take over this presidio on their own. We, as authorized Mexican forces, cannot allow ourselves to be driven out before an official departure. If that happens, we must fight," the commandant explained.

"I understand your concern, but how do you think I can be of assistance?" asked Diego.

"You have many horses, Señor DaVia. In whatever manner we leave the presidio of Tucson, we will have to evacuate our families, plus other civilians who wish to leave, as well as our full garrison of men and supplies. It will be a long march back to Mexico," explained the commandant.

It was plain to Diego that the commandant had genuine concern for his people. He felt personally responsible for their welfare. Wishing not to disclose his most recent experience regarding a similar evacuation, Diego asked, "How many horses would you require, and how would you be able to pay for them?"

"I had hoped that, understanding our plight, you could donate one hundred horses to help us in our fight, and to help evacuate our noncombatants," responded the commandant.

"Your situation is not a new one to me. But, regardless of the humanitarian need for them, I cannot just donate the horses to you. I must have payment. La Rancheria Fantasma has been created at too great a cost to allow it to crumble because of this political situation," explained Diego.

The look of desperation and disappointment that came over the commandant's face was genuine and showed the level of concern he had for his people.

"Again, if I supply you with one hundred horses, how would I be paid?" asked Diego.

"There is no gold here," sadly spoke the commandant. He then added, "I know you have military experience. I have watched you yesterday and today. You have the bearing of an officer . . . perhaps cavalry."

"This . . . is . . . true," admitted Diego. He then added, without discussing his most recent experience, "I was, at one time, capitán of dragoons against the Chiricahua Apache in Chihuahua."

"How then, with your military background, do you think I could arrange payment to you for these horses?" pleaded the commandant.

Diego DaVia stood and began pacing, back and forth across the office of the commandant. His mind was trying to help the commandant and the personnel of the presidio. This whole operation could turn ugly with one stupid, drunken individual shooting his weapon in that small fort. Yet Diego DaVia wanted no part of another evacuation battle.

"Commandant, you will send a small party of six officers or sergeants who are known to your counterparts at the garrison in Cananea. These men will accompany me and my Vaqueros to la Rancheria Fantasma. The owner of la Rancheria Fantasma will then replace me and together with your men proceed to the garrison at Cananea. Your representatives will present your request for the necessary gold, in coin, to that garrison commander. We have dealt with him in the past. I would expect him to authorize the payment. Assuming this is so, we will begin driving the horses to you after the party returns to la Rancheria Fantasma," said Diego, dictating the terms of the sale.

"Gracias, Señor DaVia," said the commandant, full of emotion.

"We will leave early tomorrow morning. Prepare an early breakfast. We will move fast," ordered DaVia.

—•—

The next morning after breakfast, as the sun was beginning to lighten the eastern sky, the party was about to leave. The commandant looked up at the already mounted Diego DaVia and said, "I have heard stories. My Yaqui scouts tell me that you are he."

"He who?!" exclaimed Diego DaVia in exasperation.

"He, the survivor," said the commandant.

"Do you want the horses or not?" demanded DaVia.

"Sí! Yes!" exclaimed the commandant.

"Then damn it, who the hell cares what some Yaqui dreams? I am only me!" yelled Diego. "Vamonos! We are wasting valuable time!"

The party turned south at a quick pace. And, as they rode, Diego Da-Via wondered how he would explain the double-sized sale to the presidio at Tucson, after once telling Segundo that he would not do so.

13

Late evening, nine days after having left for the presidio of Tucson, Diego, and a very weary party of Vaqueros and Mexican cavalry slowly dismounted in front of the cabin at la Rancheria Fantasma. Outriders had seen them coming from the time they exited the last mountain pass into the San Rafael Valley and ridden ahead to alert Segundo. He then ordered supper to be prepared for the party immediately on their return. The Vaqueros of la Rancheria Fantasma cheered loudly to welcome home Diego and the returning Vaqueros. The very tired riders of the Mexican cavalry were celebrated, too.

"Diego, everyone, get down and rest and eat! Welcome! Welcome home!" shouted Segundo.

"Amigo, I have served in the Mexican cavalry for many, many years. I have never liked long rides. And now I remember why. Dios mio, I am sore and tired," croaked Diego. "I feel so . . . old."

"You are not old, Diego. But today you certainly look like it. Ha!" teased Segundo.

"Well, 'Ha!' yourself. Wait until you hear what I have planned for you," teased Diego right back.

"You'll have to give me the bad news after we eat. We are hungry, but you and your whole party look starved. Everyone, wash up, and then we all eat," relayed Segundo.

At that, everyone rushed to the wash basins.

After supper, and after all the men were properly quartered, Segundo and Diego sat on the long porch. Segundo had been waiting way too long to wait any longer. "What is going on, Diego? What is planned for me? Or were you fooling?"

"No fooling this time. After nine tough days in the saddle, including one very trying negotiation in the presidio of Tucson, I am going to have to pass the torch to you, compadre," said Diego, the smile slowly retreating from his face.

"I knew this trip would be very serious, but now tell me . . . how serious?" said Segundo.

"The commandant is in the middle of a potentially explosive situation. The rumors we have heard are true. The norteamericanos are coming. The treaty selling Sonoran land north to the Rio Gila is signed or will be signed soon. That includes the presidio of Tucson and la Rancheria Fantasma. All that will become a territory of the United States: los Estados Unidos . . . no longer a part of Mexico. The americanos already in the presidio area are becoming a problem for the commandant. He does not want the forces of Mexico to be run out by these lowlifes. He prefers to formally transfer authority to an authorized military force of the American army . . . honorably. And I fully agree with him on that," related Diego.

"Well, we have seen this coming, have we not, Diego? I do not understand how all this will affect us and la Rancheria Fantasma, but what does this commandant want us to do?" asked Segundo.

"I . . . must stay here and rest my weary, saddle-sore old butt," laughed Diego DaVia. "However, you must leave tomorrow for Cananea to visit your friend, the major. He is to authorize release of gold coins to properly purchase one hundred horses from la Rancheria Fantasma, for delivery as soon as possible to the presidio of Tucson."

Segundo nearly erupted from his seat. "We were not going to sell more than fifty horses . . . to anybody!"

"I know," replied Diego. "The commandant believes that there may be a fight with the civilian americanos near the presidio. If so, he will need these horses. If not, he will still need these horses to evacuate the families and others back to Mexico. Either way, he is in desperate need of these horses."

"Great! Just great!" exclaimed Segundo. "And I am the salesman to deliver this to Major Sanchez. Right?"

"Right," agreed Diego. "You will proceed, I hope, with fifteen Vaqueros and the Mexican cavalrymen who accompanied me. They are known to Major Sanchez, so there should be no problem satisfying any doubts he may have."

"I suppose this happens early tomorrow," guessed Segundo.

"Get some rest, Don Ruiz," said Diego with a slight grin.

"Now . . . Now I'm Don Ruiz!" griped Segundo, going to gather his gear. "Buenas noches," he quipped to Diego.

Bright and early the next morning, rested and with fresh horses under them, the combined expedition of Mexican cavalry and la Rancheria Fantasma Vaqueros rode off toward the southeast and toward Cananea. Don Francisco Ruiz paused a moment to say goodbye to Diego.

"Take care, amigo mio," said Diego. "If this goes badly, my main concern is the safety of the Vaqueros and yourself."

"It will get done, Diego. Your concern is well justified, but we will save the mexicanos at the presidio of Tucson. Adiós," promised Segundo.

The combined expedition of Vaqueros and Mexican cavalry had disappeared in the distance when Diego turned, summoned Pancho, and began to busy himself with the daily activities of la Rancheria Fantasma. Yet his mind kept churning, over and over, about what was happening to himself, to la Rancheria Fantasma, and to Mexico. And he frankly had to admit that he did not really care so much about Mexico. He had seen so much, had been through so much, that whatever popinjay deemed himself in command of Mexico did not matter. One was as corrupt and inept at governing so large a country as the other.

The selection of horses for the presidio of Tucson became important to him now. He did not want unbroken horses for civilian families to evacuate Tucson. Yet said horses must be able to carry cavalry troops in battle if need be. *This will take some time,* he thought. And it did. It took so much time and effort on his, and everyone else's part, that he was surprised and amazed to see the expedition returning from Cananea.

"Welcome back, Segundo!" exclaimed Diego. "You made good time."

"Gracias," replied Segundo. "But we need to move as soon as possible with the herd."

"I trust you have the gold to pay for it," questioned Diego.

"Of course. Delivered without any delay," replied Segundo. "The major at Cananea already had orders to assist the garrison at the presidio of Tucson but had no idea how to do it. We saved his butt," said Segundo. "But it is urgent that we hurry. They are very worried about the americanos, but they are more worried about the Apache."

"The Apache?" again questioned Diego.

"Sí! The major said Yaqui scouts have reported the Apache are planning an attack to make it seem to all that they, the Apache, drove the Mexicans from the presidio of Tucson," Segundo replied.

"Very well," said Diego. "We should be able to move the selected mounts early tomorrow. What do the Yaqui say is planned by the Apache?"

"The Yaqui do not know for certain. They believe the Apache intend to gather in the saguaro forest, at the west side of the Rincon Mountains— east of the presidio of Tucson. When the mexicanos start to leave, they will attack, kill as many as they can, and leave the rest to limp back to Mexico," answered Segundo.

"They can probably do it, too," agreed Diego.

"If the American military are there, what will they do?" asked Segundo.

"If they are already within the presidio, they will probably fort up," Diego speculated. "They will not attack a large war party outside the presidio."

"What should we do?" asked Segundo.

"I have no idea. But let us get these horses ready. You and I will dream up something on the way," said Diego.

"You are going along?" asked Segundo, somewhat surprised that both might go.

"Of course. What did you think I would do . . . sit here? Ha!" said Diego. He was already moving when he said that. And he was already planning how to get some measure of revenge against the Apache. After all, the massacre at Superstition Mountain was still fresh in his mind. Maybe some revenge would help him sleep better.

— —

The next morning found the Vaqueros of la Rancheria Fantasma and the few Mexican cavalry already on the way to the presidio of Tucson. Diego felt, for the first time in years, the thrill and anticipation of a possible battle. His mind was working overtime on terrain, movements, and related strategy. The representatives of the presidio of Tucson, not realizing the military background of this Diego DaVia—who was clearly running things—found themselves impressed with the results. The herd was moving northward at a crisp pace. The outriders were guiding the herd and keeping stragglers in close to facilitate a smooth, swift north-ward drive.

Still, this drive would take a few days to accomplish. After the first three days, the Mexican cavalry noticed some of the Vaqueros were missing. Diego had ordered them to the ridgetops and to keep a half day ahead. They would be able to warn of impending ambush well in advance of trouble—much as Capitán Garces and Don Miguel Peralta had done during the march up Camp Creek to the old mines many years ago.

Segundo had always had a working knowledge of the experience of Diego DaVia as related to military matters, but he was certainly impressed by the way Diego had taken charge. Within two days' march of arriving at the presidio of Tucson, Diego had ordered one third of the Vaqueros to ride ahead in a pattern that would take them to an area west of the presidio. They were ordered then to circle around to the north side of the presidio and wait without being seen until either they were ordered to do otherwise or saw that they should join in a possible fight.

— —

The morning of the day they would arrive at the presidio of Tucson, Segundo and the remaining Vaqueros were surprised to see Diego DaVia appear dressed in his old uniform. The Vaqueros and the Mexican cavalry applauded his appearance as what they all thought was a magnificent gesture of unity. However, Segundo guessed that Diego was using this as a ploy to possibly cause uncertainty in the ranks of any Apaches who knew of Dead Man Who Walks Away. The uniform was dirty and still bloodied from the massacre that he could not forget. It was a gamble, but so what!

The Apaches were intent upon watching the progress of the herd. They had not known of it until the night before the Rancheria Fantasma drive was to arrive. However, they were giving it rapt attention that morning. The small detachment of American cavalry, which had relieved the commandant of responsibility, was preparing for a fight only to send the evacuees on their way. The Apaches were said to be in the area but had not been confirmed as a real threat to the departing Mexicans. At that point, plans for the evacuation were proceeding forward.

The Mexican forces, under the commandant, had had no choice but to proceed, even without the hoped-for horses, which they did not know were on their way. The evacuees were making the best of it in crowded conveyances and with not enough horses. They had proceeded about a half mile out of the presidio complex when the Apaches attacked from the low saguaro forest east of the presidio. The Apaches, well hidden in the desert foliage of creosote, chaparral, and the huge saguaros, burst forward. They charged with abandon, believing the evacuees were virtually helpless. Screaming their war cries, the warriors shot terror into the fleeing Mexicans. They were almost upon the Mexican garrison when the Apache leader, whirling his signal blanket in the air, brought his horse to a dust-throwing stop. The wave of Apache warriors had no choice. They had to halt, also. Cries of "Dead Man Who Walks Away!" were heard among the ranks. For a moment, the warriors were confusedly milling around while their leaders tried to sort out what they wished to do.

Dead Man Who Walks Away had been seen and was, with saber flashing, leading a charge of Fantasma Vaqueros directly at them. In their confusion, they ran their horses into each other as they tried to retreat and regroup. All this took many seconds, and Dead Man Who Walks Away was, by then, even closer.

That is when Diego's ploy of having a third of his Vaqueros attack from the north, directly at the Apache flank, ended the attack. The Apaches turned and fled back into the rugged desert from which they had come.

The attack was over as swiftly as that. Diego shook hands with the still-trembling commandant and informed him that he and his Vaqueros would escort him back to la Rancheria Fantasma. From there, they would take their new horses and make an orderly march to Cananea and Sonora, Mexico.

The American detachment, from within the walls of the presidio, could not believe their eyes as to what had happened. However, they used their time wisely and refortified the presidio. They then settled down to await the influx of more military and the beginning of the arrival of American settlers.

However, in the wikiups of the Apache, the tale of Dead Man Who Walks Away would continue. Surely, his medicine was the reason they did not accomplish their goal of claiming to have driven the Mexicans out of the presidio.

As things had begun to wind down, the detachment captain of the American forces, then in the presidio, rode out to meet Diego DaVia and Segundo Ruiz. The gratitude of Captain McCoy was overwhelming. The action of la Rancheria Fantasma's Vaqueros also saved his operation. "Sir, I have not seen so well executed a maneuver since . . . well, when we were on opposing sides in the past war!" he exclaimed. "I am glad that we were not on the receiving end of that charge!"

"I, too, am glad that it all worked out well," agreed Diego.

"What unit are you with, if I might ask?" ventured Captain McCoy.

"None now," said Diego. "It's only my old uniform to throw the Apache off their plan."

"Well, it certainly worked," said Captain McCoy. "Where are you headquartered, and who are you?"

"I am Diego DaVia, and this fine gentleman is Don Francisco Ruiz, owner, and my partner of la Rancheria Fantasma. We operate in the San Rafael Valley south and east of here, about five day's ride."

"I hope to see more of you both," said Captain McCoy.

"You probably will," said Diego.

Segundo said, "It seems that we are located on the North American side of a new border. I hope that this is a good thing. We have had enough of everything else."

"It is my wish also," said Captain McCoy. "Especially having seen how well you fight," he joked.

"We will try not to have any more of that," laughed Diego. "I want to be sure that the incoming strangers respect our property and our rights. If you can see to that, we will have no trouble with each other."

All Segundo could say was, "We must go now. Adiós."

"Farewell," said Captain McCoy.

—•—

In the meantime, the Mexican evacuees, having at last received the horses they had been waiting for, began sorting them out and putting them to good use. People who had expected to have to walk to Cananea were going to ride. Belongings that had been on their backs were being loaded on the backs of the horses. Still there were more horses than were needed. No one worried about that. They now belonged to the Mexican commandant and were in route to Cananea.

Once riding along with the procession from the presidio, Segundo asked, "What in the hell did you think you were doing charging those Apaches and waving your saber all over the place?"

"I have been living with this Dead Man Who Walks Away too long. I thought I might as well use it to my advantage. If their worries are real, maybe I could scare them a bit," answered Diego.

"Well, you did! I have never seen Apaches act like that. Just so they stay scared until we can arrive safely to la Rancheria Fantasma," Segundo said hopefully.

"Any casualties, Segundo?" asked Diego.

"I don't think so. Not on our side anyway. Come to think of it, I saw no one fall on their side either."

"That will set the old chiefs to asking some embarrassing questions!" laughed Diego. "What kind of battle was that? Nobody hurt? Ha!" And so went an uneventful trek home.

14

News was travelling fast all over Mexico. El Presidente Santa Anna was obviously in exile. The Gadsden Purchase had been accomplished. No one knew with any certainty whatsoever who was in power in Mexico or for how long. Revolutionary military forces were springing up all over Mexico. American businessmen, settlers, and roughnecks were pouring into the former Mexican settlements north of the newly created Mexican border. Everything had come to the area except law and order. It seemed that every man was for himself, and that included women. And if times were not tough enough before the purchase, they were even tougher after. Times were tough for Americans looking for a new life, but tougher for Mexicans just trying to hold on to what little they had had before.

Regardless of the troubles elsewhere, la Rancheria Fantasma seemed to be a peaceful oasis of quiet prosperity. Horses were bringing the highest prices ever, due to the ever-warring factions of the so-called Mexican government. Now and then, Apaches would appear on the fringe of Diego's San Rafael Valley. They would verify that Dead Man Who Walks Away was still there and leave. They did not need to trade for horses. They were acquiring them by raiding all over Sonora and in what was then being called New Mexico Territory. They felt the need to be sure of the whereabouts of Dead Man Who Walks Away. One thing that non-Apache people in the desert Southwest learned by necessity was that the Apache never initiated an attack without believing that they had the advantage. In that regard, the Apache wanted to know where Dead Man

Who Walks Away was at any given time. No one had ever accused the Apache of being forgetful.

With the incursion of a large number of Americans into their newly acquired region, many Mexicans began to realize that a new market was being created. It offered Mexicans a chance to make some lucrative business arrangements. Monica and Raoul Ruiz placed themselves in that group. Realizing that their brother Segundo, now Don Francisco Ruiz, was a landowner of some prominence on the American side of the border, they felt that a connection should be made to elevate their own status. Therefore, it happened that the southernmost Rancheria Fantasma Vaqueros were the first to welcome Monica and Raoul Ruiz to la Rancheria Fantasma. One of the Vaqueros raced ahead to apprise Don Segundo and Diego of their arrival.

It was late in the day when the Ruiz party arrived at the cabin, by then having been improved many times over to the point that it had become a sizeable hacienda with a long, rambling, still ramada-like porch. The coach carrying Monica Ruiz and Raoul Ruiz had come to a complete halt. Inside, the occupants awaited the formal opening of the door. Segundo, with the slightest trace of a grin, waited a moment before waving two of the Vaqueros to open the door. The first Vaquero, with extreme care, assisted Monica to the ground. The second Vaquero was so astonished by the foppish finery worn by Raoul that he just stood there and allowed Raoul to make his own way out of the carriage. Diego had to turn his head away to avoid showing the uncontrolled smile that action brought. The Vaqueros then escorted both the visitors up the few stairs to the porch.

Segundo greeted his sister and brother without much emotion, after which he made the introduction of Diego. "Monica and Raoul Ruiz, may I present my partner in la Rancheria Fantasma, Diego DaVia. Diego, may I present my sister, Doña Monica Ruiz, and brother, Don Raoul Ruiz."

"*Servidor de ustedes* . . . Your servant, Doña Ruiz, and Don Ruiz," said Diego DaVia showing military graciousness.

"Buenas tardes," was the Ruizes' reply.

"Doña Ruiz," ventured Diego, "your arrival, with only the amount of notice provided by our southernmost Vaqueros, still allowed us to have your quarters readied for you. I trust you will find them comfortable."

Doña Monica Ruiz replied, "We could not have expected anything more than primitive accommodations here in your wilderness."

"Nonetheless, we hope your stay will be enjoyable," said Diego, noting her denigrating inference.

Segundo, after having made the required introductions, noticed the slight insult by his sister, and the very tactful Diego letting it slide by with a most diplomatic comment. He knew his sister never left her spiderweb society without justification. This would be no exception. Segundo had no illusions about this visit. Monica must be desperate to achieve something. One look at Diego told him Diego was thinking the same thing. Both men knew that they were holding all the aces. Time would show them what game Monica and Raoul wanted to play.

Dinner was somewhat relaxed. The Vaqueros' wives had for some time taken over la Rancheria Fantasma's kitchen. They had spent all their lives making meals for their families, so that when they revolted against the simple fare of la Rancheria Fantasma's early days, the Vaqueros' lives were made much more pleasant. There was nothing primitive about the meal served to the haughty visitors from Mexico City. Perhaps they were especially hungry from their long journey by coach. Perhaps any food would have looked good to them after such a journey. However, after the first picky little bites, the visiting Ruizes could not help themselves. They dug in with a relish, devouring almost everything set in front of them. The ladies who had prepared the meal, watching from a short distance, giggled with pleasure at how their meal was appreciated. Even if no verbal compliment was made, they knew.

Segundo, having noted how their supper had disappeared, quipped that, "I am glad you were not very hungry, or we might well have lost a horse or two."

At that, Raoul Ruiz, seeming to take offense at the joke, started to rise from his chair. Doña Monica restrained him with a feminine little laugh and a tug on the arm so that he sat right back down again. She did her best to be diplomatic by saying, "La Rancheria Fantasma may be set far back in the wilderness, but the supper served could not have been better had it been served in the finest halls in Mexico City."

Segundo could not believe he had heard an actual compliment from his sister. He was about to say something in that regard when he was interrupted by Diego DaVia, who had been enjoying this meeting of siblings. "I am happy to hear you say that Doña Monica, because, although enjoying some celebrity for the quality of our rancheria and our horses, the meals prepared here for our Vaqueros have become known far and wide."

"Well, I must say that such fame is well deserved," replied Monica. "Your staff is to be complimented."

"They have been, Doña Monica!" said Diego with a flourish of his hand toward the ladies of la Rancheria Fantasma. "Please, let us adjourn to the west veranda to enjoy the remaining sunset. Bring your wine glasses along."

Segundo, the Don Francisco Ruiz of this group, was slow to rise. He was asking himself *What is going on here?* He had expected the usual biting comments from his sister and brother, but Diego DaVia, with courtly skill, had them behaving civilized. There must be more to this DaVia fellow than he had noticed before.

Once seated on the west veranda, Diego asked, "Is there anything further I can do for you?"

Doña Monica's reply came as something of a surprise to Diego.

"Are you married?" she asked.

"No," was his curt answer.

"Please forgive me for so bold a question," said Monica. "I meant no intrusion."

Segundo reentered his state of shock at this line of conversation. *Was she flirting with Diego?*

Doña Monica continued. "I ask because there is a good deal of mystery concerning la Rancheria Fantasma. People are aware of it and are curious."

"Persons other than you, yourself?" asked Diego, a subtle yet noticeable note of irritation in his voice.

"Yes, to be sure," came the reply. "Not only those interested in procuring horses, but also political figures."

Segundo sat staring at his sister trying to pierce her mind as to what she was alluding to.

"Who would care, other than the natural curiosity of a sister regarding the dealings of her brother?" asked Diego. His mind had begun to see that there was more than curiosity going on there.

"For instance, the name 'la Rancheria Fantasma'; it means something like 'Ghost Ranch,' does it not?" she questioned.

Diego DaVia, not particularly liking the turn this conversation had taken, said, "It does."

"How did a name like that happen? Surely there must be some story behind it," Monica stated. The underlying question involved was unmistakable.

"Of course. But this fine lady waiting here has signaled that your quarters have been prepared for the night," flatly stated Diego, not pausing to allow any discussion of the issue. The Ruizes rose and followed their escort to their respective rooms for the night.

After the Ruizes had gone, Segundo shook his head and said, "Was she flirting with you? I've seen that before but could not believe I was seeing it again, now."

"You did not really see it this time either," said Diego. "I've seen flirting. Do you think I have not had such an experience? Her eyes gave her away. They had the look of a predator staring at its victim, hoping it will come a little bit closer."

"I see you have come to know my sister well already," acknowledged Segundo. "Secure in that knowledge, I am going to bed. Buenas noches."

"Buenas noches, amigo," replied Diego.

Diego DaVia sat up for a while before retiring to bed. The feeling that Doña Monica—and her silent brother, Raoul—already knew more than he wished bothered him. But whatever they thought they knew would come to light in the morning, he hoped. Yet sleep still came in increments. Diego could not forget her eyes. There was something more than the look of a predator in them. Or had it been too long since he had been with a woman? Segundo's sister was a physically beautiful woman.

Long, raven-black hair, eyes so deep brown they looked black, and slightly tanned skin only partially described this woman. She was slim, with a womanly figure only partially concealed by the riding clothes she had worn on her journey.

Diego DaVia at that moment came to the realization that it had been a long time, and he was still very much a man, and very human.

— —

Next morning's breakfast was another culinary feast. Meat, eggs, burritos, all kinds of breakfast enchiladas, sopapillas, and coffee made for an extended time at the table. The visitors, refreshed and pleasantly filled, were ready to tour la Rancheria Fantasma. To be sure, they had already wandered the interior of the cabin/hacienda before breakfast. However, they seemed to be most interested in the outbuildings and facilities. That took most of the morning and involved many questions. What amazed Segundo was the seeming interest in the horse herd, especially because neither Monica nor Raoul had ever shown any interest in such things.

The inspection of the horse herd, la mañada del Rancheria Fantasma, took all afternoon, and the visitors could not manage to see it all. Segundo and Diego, however, took note of their interest. Segundo made it a point of concern when he said to Diego, "Monica and Raoul have never shown any interest in ranching or horses before. Why this sudden fascination? We must beware of something we do not know."

"I just think that she likes me," Diego said feigning sincerity as he looked at Segundo. As Segundo snapped his head around at that remark, Diego's laugh resounded across the valley. Diego was not fooled, but in his mind, he would play this out for whatever it was worth.

— —

That evening after the supper meal, Diego DaVia stood in the shadows, taking in the beauty of the sunset over his beloved San Rafael Valley. His mind was slowly evaluating the events that had occurred over the past months. None was more unexpected though than the visit by Doña Monica Ruiz and brother Raoul. Diego was sure that Raoul had not spoken more than a dozen words since his arrival. Doña Monica had evidently been in control of all conversation. Yet her conversation had not really had any substance to it. Both she and Raoul voiced interest in the beauty and efficiency of la Rancheria Fantasma but did not speak of their actual reason for the visit. Segundo was still waiting for the lightning to strike. His sister and brother did not come all the way from Mexico City because they missed him. He had told Diego of his concern shortly after their arrival.

Diego was mulling all this over in his mind, when he felt a soft touch on his arm. Doña Monica had quietly moved over to him as he stood deep in thought. "What could you possibly be thinking about so deeply during this lovely sunset?" asked Monica.

"Is this a serious question requiring a serious answer?" asked Diego in return.

"But of course! I never mince words with such a serious looking man," she quipped.

"Serious questions could result in serious answers," replied Diego.

"Go ahead, Señor DaVia. Amaze me with the seriousness of your answer," Doña Monica responded with a teasing tone and look.

"All right then. Obviously, you had heard that I was a handsome, dashing, extremely manly individual whom you wished to see in person. Or perhaps I am flattering myself. And, probably, because I have some doubts that you came merely to visit your long-missing brother Segundo," said Diego feigning sincerity.

"Segundo! How I hate that name!" exclaimed Monica. "He began calling himself that when we were children. Segundo—second. He was the third. Francisco professed to be second only to our father. He did that to aggravate me and our father. Yes. I came to see him, but not because I missed him!"

"Whoa, señorita! I seem to have touched a nerve," said Diego. "Evidently, you did not come for a social visit. Why did you come all this way?"

Regaining her composure Doña Monica said, "I had heard of you."

"From Mexico City, all the way across the new border, and into los Estados Unidos, just to meet this, uh . . . horse rancher. I am flattered," said Diego, acting most impressed and pouring it on.

Doña Monica's eyes widened just before she very coquettishly slapped Diego's arm. "You are terrible! You put me in a position where I cannot answer 'yes' or 'no'!"

Diego, laughing in a low tone, placed his hand over the one that had been replaced on his arm. "That is too bad. Either answer would have been most interesting. But I ask you again: why did you come here?"

Monica looked up at Diego's stern eyes, the penetrating eyes of iron she had heard about and said, "It is not safe for us to remain long in Mexico City. La Reforma is solidly in control, and that commoner, Benito Juarez, is now calling himself el presidente!"

"So now all the aristocratic families must seek sanctuary elsewhere, like here at la Rancheria Fantasma?" replied Diego sarcastically. "Juarez needs these people to remain and rebuild Mexico, and he will try hard to convince them of that. Try again, Doña Monica."

"I have had enough of this conversation!" said Doña Monica, showing her emotion at Diego's words. "Does your comment mean that Raoul and I are not welcome here?" she then asked, reverting to her feminine voice.

"Doña Monica," said Diego, "you are welcome to stay here as long as you . . . and Segundo wish."

The implication that the welcome was up to her brother, alone, was obvious. Red faced, Doña Monica left the porch and retired to her quarters. In one way, Diego considered his comment a bit stern, but on the other hand, it established who was running this rancheria. Diego DaVia once again went to bed with much on his mind.

—·—

The next morning found the visitors and their hosts rested and ready for whatever the new day was to bring. Daytime relaxation, with some evening entertainment at supper by some of the Vaqueros and wives, had been planned. It turned out to be quite a night. The supper was splendid. The entertainment was superb. Vaqueros with guitars, singing all manner of songs, ballads, and romantic serenades, left everyone feeling in a grand mood. It was a great fiesta indeed. For many of the Vaqueros and their wives and girlfriends, romance was in the air. Segundo was himself visiting with a lovely young chica, walking off with her in the twilight.

Suddenly, although not surprisingly, Diego DaVia again found himself the object of Doña Monica's attention. Diego DaVia was a gentleman by birth and personal intent and graciously escorted Doña Monica past the celebration along the pines at the perimeter of the meadow. He had certainly been in such situations before, but not lately. Therefore, he was at least somewhat surprised when Doña Monica reached up, turned his face to hers, and kissed him tenderly, then with much more enthusiasm. Diego DaVia, holding her close, could see past her to the main area of the entertainment. They were alone in the twilight. Holding her close, he could feel the soft, yet firm contours of her body. She had not been wearing the very formal, heavy garments of a lady of her status during the day. Her dress was very casual. It seemed to Diego also deliberately easy to remove. It had been a long time, but he had not forgotten how.

Memory is a funny thing. All the foreboding thoughts as to why she was at la Rancheria Fantasma were forgotten somehow as he remembered the pleasures of the past with other women. Monica was the embodiment of the pleasures of femininity. She was slightly over medium height, slim, soft, yet firm. She was aristocratic in manner but sleek as a panther. Evidently, Monica had not been with a man recently and was taking every opportunity to make up for it. Monica was going to have her way, and Diego, after one last look for intruders, for the moment decided her way was his way. Besides, why should Segundo have all the fun? Segundo was missing, and so was a certain fine-looking chica.

That night was a most memorable night for Monica, Diego, Segundo, and probably for the still mysteriously unnamed chica.

———

The next morning at breakfast, Diego somehow found it difficult to look at Segundo. Segundo noticed and was wondering what was going on, when he saw Monica looking at Diego like a baby deer. He could not help himself. "What the hell! I do not believe it. You two? Madre de Dios!" He stood up and strode across the yard toward the corral. Diego rose to follow him.

"Ha, ha," laughed Monica. "Let him go. Who cares what he thinks?"

Diego, walking swiftly, caught up with Segundo. He did not say anything. Segundo beat him to it. "What were you thinking?"

"Thinking?" wondered Diego. "Who was thinking? I knew what you were up to with your little mystery chica. I had no idea where the hell Raoul was or what the hell he was doing, and I don't give a damn."

"Damn!" again voiced Segundo.

"Is this a brother protecting sister action, or what?" asked Diego.

"No! I have never cared at all who my sneaky sister was enjoying," yelled Segundo.

"So, you just object to me?" Diego asked, becoming a little wild-eyed. "Because she was certainly enjoying me!"

"I am scared to death over why she is after you. She wants something more than just a tryst in the woods," said Segundo.

"I know, but I could not help making her work a little for it," said Diego. "Besides, amigo mio, it has been a long time."

"Well, I hope you enjoyed yourself," said Segundo, with the hint of a smile showing.

"I did," said Diego. "I did."

Back at the breakfast table, the atmosphere consisted of both contentment and concern. Doña Monica was trying to act like an infatuated schoolgirl. Don Segundo looked like a father with a shotgun in his eyes. Raoul seemed confused, as usual. Diego DaVia sat there with a very slight smile and let his eyes observe the others. It was somewhat uncomfortable for a while. Once the food was gone and only coffee was left, none but Doña Monica and Diego DaVia were left at the table.

"Last night was very enjoyable," said Diego but then added, "Why?"

"Thank you. I enjoyed it too," said Monica, smiling coquettishly.

"Why?" repeated Diego.

"Why what?" asked Monica slowly.

"I asked you yesterday. Why are you here?" he repeated.

"I told you yesterday," she replied, the smiling flirtation leaving her tone.

"I did not buy your answer then and thought about it all night . . . well, most of the night," Diego said with a slight smile. "I still do not buy it."

Monica started toward him but stopped when Diego said, "It is full daylight now. It is not moonlight under the pines. It is time for straight talk and straight answers."

She backed away. The softness in her expression was gone. "I heard about 'Dead Man Who Walks Away'!"

Monica thought he would get defensive. He merely looked at her with those eyes of iron, waiting for her to continue. "I did!" she yelled loudly. "I do not know what battle that was, but the Yaquis tell of it!"

"So, what would Yaquis know of it? Or of me?" said Diego calmly.

"The Yaquis say you cannot be killed. They fear you as a kind of spirit. Well, I do not!" said Doña Monica, nearly screaming.

"You say you do not fear me or that you do not want to kill me?" asked Diego, still in that calm monotone.

Doña Monica was trembling in anger but could not get the words out. "Last night, I thought you might be just a man; but you are not. You are a kind of spirit . . . untouchable!" she managed to spit out.

"Oh, you proved that I was touchable all right," disagreed Diego, still reacting calmly to Monica's tirade. "But I ask again . . . why?"

"Because you own half of la Rancheria Fantasma!" she replied through clenched teeth. "This ranch is certainly aptly named 'Ghost Ranch.' You are a kind of ghost!"

"I do not, and I am not," answered Diego DaVia.

"Liar!" Monica screamed.

"No one, man or woman, calls me a liar twice and remains standing," warned DaVia. "I am a full partner in the operation of la Rancheria Fantasma. Your brother, Segundo, owns this rancheria."

"This rancheria should be rightfully mine and Raoul's. We were tricked into selling it," Monica declared.

"No, you were not, Monica," asserted Diego. "It was purchased for cash and the new deed properly recorded."

"The new government in Mexico City has agreed to open the right to ownership pending an investigation," stated Monica haughtily. "I found out what I needed to know. We'll see who owns the San Rafael Valley." So, speaking that bit of news like a thinly veiled threat, Doña Monica turned and walked swiftly to her quarters.

15

As soon as Doña Monica had made the turn toward her quarters, Diego DaVia called, "Pancho!"

Pancho came running before the sound had stopped, "Que pasa, Patrón?"

"Find Segundo for me, Pancho. Tell him I need him pronto!" ordered Diego. Diego rarely gave an order to Pancho, so Pancho wasted no time. Pancho found Segundo visiting in the Vaquero's family area. The look on Pancho's face told him that it was important. Segundo ran to the hacienda. Diego saw him coming and motioned him to come straight inside the cabin. In few words, "Segundo, your sister is planning to steal your property."

"No surprise to me. But how do you know?" queried Segundo. "How can she do that?"

Diego could hardly speak slowly. "She has a lawyer in Mexico working with a Mexican government official to investigate your deed to the San Rafael Valley."

"She must be trying to break my father's will. I might have known she would try," added Segundo. "But so much time has gone by; I thought she did not really want it anyway."

"Well, she and Raoul certainly want it now. I'd say it has to do with whatever is going on in Mexico," stated Diego.

"Their precious status is under scrutiny. They may be wanting out of Mexico," guessed Segundo. "It does not matter why now. I must stop them somehow," he said, his head down in perplexed thought.

Diego reached out, lifted Segundo's head, and said, "You have kept the original deed to this valley here. Right, Segundo?"

"Certainly," responded Segundo, wondering what Diego had in mind.

"Get it. Take your three most trusted Vaqueros . . . preferably who have not had anything to do with Raoul or your sister . . . and hightail it to Tucson. Register your deed in the United States courthouse there. That way you have an American title to land in the United States. That way the Mexican deed has no meaning. Now that Mexico has sold us to the United States, we might as well benefit by it. Agreed?" instructed Diego.

"I will pack some supplies and be gone quick," said Segundo.

"Go, but secretively. Sneak out without being seen. Have your Vaqueros do likewise, one at a time, so as not to arouse suspicion," Diego told Segundo. "I will let it be known, if asked where you are, that you had to locate some missing horses. Now go!"

Within thirty minutes, Don Francisco Ruiz and three trusted Vaqueros had silently vanished from the headquarters of la Rancheria Fantasma.

It was toward the supper hour that Diego saw Doña Monica and Raoul Ruiz approaching the hacienda. Diego gave them a friendly greeting. He was surprised to receive a friendly greeting in return. The Ruizes had climbed the few steps to the porch when Diego asked, "Can I have some drinks sent over? It is still a little while until supper is served."

"Oh, that would be wonderful. It has been such a dry day," said Doña Monica. Raoul, as usual, only smiled his pleasure at the offer.

The drinks were delivered, and all were relaxing on the low chairs on the long veranda. Surprisingly, it was Raoul who asked, "I do not see Segundo. In fact, we have not seen him since early this morning. Where is he?"

"Unfortunately, or perhaps fortunately, la Rancheria Fantasma is a working rancheria. Don Segundo is off with some Vaqueros to locate and return some fifty or so horses, which have wandered . . . I hope only wandered . . . away," said Diego.

"What do you mean 'I hope' only wandered away?" asked Raoul, showing some actual interest.

"Rustlers, Raoul," answered Diego. "Although we have the best Vaqueros anywhere, it is still possible that someone, or some group, might try to steal some of our horses."

"Has that been tried?" asked Raoul. Raoul's interest level had risen substantially concerning the subject of rustling. Diego noticed this immediately.

"Not successfully," answered Diego.

"Why not successfully?" asked Raoul, sitting a bit straighter in his seat.

"Realizing that la Rancheria Fantasma's location is in a most remote area from the more populated areas of either Mexico or the United States, Don Segundo and I decided to hire only the best riders, gun handlers, and fighters in the entire region. Those men we hired are extremely well trained and compensated for their work and, as importantly, for their loyalty. We believe that the excellence of our Vaqueros and their expertise in many areas has influenced many plans to attack us."

"They certainly are a splendid looking group," added Monica. "Those red scarves and yellow sashes are almost a uniform."

"We are not a military unit authorized to wear a uniform. However, la Rancheria Fantasma's Vaqueros can outperform any military unit I have ever seen," explained Diego proudly. "I oversee their training. They do look sharp, am I right?"

"They are also well armed . . . all wearing identical *pistolas,*" admired Raoul.

"The training shows itself there also. Each one of our Vaqueros can shoot out a man's eye at twenty paces," ventured Diego. "Another reason to steal horses elsewhere."

"How about Indians?" asked Raoul.

Diego replied, "We have not had any actual trouble here with any of the various tribes."

"What about that tale all Mexico has heard—about the rescue of the families of the presidio of Tucson?" asked Doña Monica slowly and with purpose.

"I do not know for sure what version of the story you have heard, but upon confronting our Vaqueros, the enemy . . . chose . . . to . . . go . . . home," said Diego, also slowly and with purpose.

"I heard the reason for the retreat was because Dead Man Who Walks Away was seen leading the Vaqueros," stated Monica boldly.

"In past years, I have fought the Apache often. I have come to respect them as warriors and as a race. I have learned the hard way that the Apache chooses when and where to fight, based upon their own opinion of their chances of victory," asserted Diego. "Why the Apache chose not to fight is probably more likely to involve that logic."

"I am not sure which story I believe as to how you came to be Dead Man Who Walks Away, but it all centers around the fact that when you should have been dead, you rose and walked away," stated Monica. "The Yaquis say that man cannot be killed."

"Could be that we speak of a different man," said Diego. "How does anyone know that man is me?"

"The Yaquis say that Dead Man Who Walks Away is you!" returned Monica, sounding a bit angry that Diego was admitting nothing.

"Ah! Dinner is being served. I was afraid I would be killed before I could enjoy it," joked Diego. "But it looks so good that I promise not to walk away."

16

Segundo felt a little strange having to sneak off from his own rancheria as he did. But what he was about to do was necessary to keep the greedy hands of his sister and brother from stealing la Rancheria Fantasma away from him. The whole San Rafael Valley was at stake. The three Vaqueros accompanying him were silent as they rode away from the rancheria. Without being told, they seemed to grasp the importance of Don Segundo's mission. As before, when they rode to the aid of the presidio of Tucson, it was an extremely dangerous ride. Unlike the area around la Rancheria Fantasma, Indians were very much a presence. Not all were Chiricahua Apache. Other bands were roaming the region. The odds of running into them were quite good. Using great care, they proceeded northward toward Tucson.

It was five days later when the exhausted riders slowly rode into what was the presidio of Tucson. It had certainly changed. What had been primarily a military outpost with a settlement of farmers and small ranchers had become a sprawling center of population. The noticeable difference was the nationality makeup of the citizens. Spanish was still the language most spoken, but English was rapidly becoming more prevalent. The San Rafael Valley, with its la Rancheria Fantasma, had certainly not changed, but everywhere else it was obvious that the United States had clearly taken over. The presidio of Tucson was now the city of Tucson. The presidio thereafter referred to the small old fort within the city.

Segundo and his Vaqueros were very tired and checked into a small hotel. It was late, and the Vaqueros were hungry. But, while the Vaqueros were eating, Segundo was talking to the captain of the U.S. Cavalry detachment, Captain McCoy. Captain McCoy was the captain of the U.S. forces that relieved the Mexican commandant of the presidio of Tucson. Captain McCoy recognized Segundo immediately. "Don Francisco Ruiz! Welcome to Tucson! Is Diego DaVia with you?"

As tired as he was, Segundo managed a broad smile at the captain's welcome. "No, Capitán. Diego had to stay home."

"May I pour you a drink?" asked the captain.

"Any other time, Capitán McCoy," answered Segundo. "I have some things to accomplish here in Tucson."

"How can I be of assistance to you?" questioned Captain McCoy.

"Diego and I need some legal help. I have some legal documents to record but wish to do it properly, according to the laws of the United States. Would you be able to refer me to a reputable lawyer?" requested Segundo.

"After what you, Diego, and those wonderful vaqueros did for all of us not too long ago, I will get you only the best," replied Captain McCoy.

"I would appreciate that," said Segundo and added, "the document is in Spanish, so I expect that might pose a problem now that we are part of the United States."

"I trust not, Don Francisco. My adjutant is an extremely fine lawyer. Lieutenant Fernandez has been doing similar work in getting legal matters in Spanish transferred to English," ventured Captain McCoy.

"I will need to have this document recorded in the United States court, as it was in the Mexican court," said Segundo.

"I am sure Lieutenant Fernandez will be happy to see to that," assured Captain McCoy.

It was already quite late, and Lieutenant Fernandez had left for the day. Segundo and the captain agreed to meet again in the morning with the lieutenant.

When Segundo returned to the hotel, he found his Vaqueros refreshed and ready to find some entertainment in the already noisy Tucson. Segundo, realizing they certainly deserved some recreation after the dangerous trek to Tucson, sent them on their way. He did, however, admonish them to be careful. "Stay out of harm's way," he told them. "These americanos all are carrying *pistolas*." Segundo then cleaned up and settled down to rest. "Dios mio! I must be getting old," he thought to himself.

— • —

The next morning, a refreshed Segundo rose, dressed, and met his Vaqueros for breakfast. Looking very much the Mexican "don," Segundo was surprised to see his Vaqueros with some bruises and scratches. Evidently, they had had quite an evening. Not a great fight, as fights go, but they enjoyed the whole action. When Segundo asked what started it, they all agreed that the red scarves and yellow sashes of la Rancheria Fantasma became a topic of some discussion. Some americanos made some comments but, before the Vaqueros could respond with any great force, some American cavalry came to their assistance. They remembered those red scarves and yellow sashes from the "almost fight" with the Apache and kept the Vaqueros from any real harm. Segundo could only laugh.

Shortly after breakfast, Segundo met with Captain McCoy and Lieutenant Fernandez. It did not take long for Lieutenant Fernandez to understand exactly what Segundo wished concerning the document. The lieutenant listened intently to what Segundo had in mind, all the while scanning the document closely. When he had finished, Lieutenant Fernandez asked that the corporal on duty outside the office go to the newly renovated courthouse to see when a meeting could be arranged with the presiding judge.

"This should be only a legal formality," assured the lieutenant.

The corporal returned quickly and informed the lieutenant that the judge was free now for about a half hour only. Hearing that, the lieutenant, the captain, and Segundo hurried the short way to the courthouse and the office of the judge.

Upon hearing the story of what Segundo, Diego, and the Vaqueros had done to save the old presidio of Tucson, the judge was only too happy to be of assistance. "In most cases, a simple thing like recording a deed to property would be something the court clerk could handle. Under the circumstances, I will be honored to assure this is done properly," said the judge, smiling.

"The addendum you wish to have as part of this deed will require witnesses," instructed the judge.

Captain McCoy and Lieutenant Fernandez both said without hesitation, "We will be proud to witness this."

"Does Señor DaVia know about this?" asked the judge.

"Not yet. But he will soon enough," said Segundo with a slight chuckle in his voice.

Within a very few minutes, the deed was recorded and witnessed with all signatures, including that of the judge. After Captain McCoy and Lieutenant Fernandez left to return to their respective duties, the judge said, "This Diego DaVia seems to be a singularly interesting man."

"How so?" asked Segundo, realizing where this conversation might be going.

The judge went on. "The confrontation with the Apache a while back left everyone in amazement. Why did the Apache turn and run when they saw DaVia? Oh, do not say they did not. Too many people have told of seeing that happen."

"I will not deny that it did happen," agreed Segundo.

"We always have many Indians here in Tucson, and many have told of a 'spirit' man, whom they fear and respect. They call him 'Dead Man Who Walks Away,'" stated the judge. "The few Apaches that have been in the city of Tucson have said that he rose from the dead after a great fight and walked away. From the various tales, I would wager that Señor DaVia could be that man."

"Could be," said Segundo.

"What battle would that have been?" asked the judge.

"It was a battle fought a long time ago. He would rather forget it. Therefore, because of the horrible memories and the pain that accompanies them, I choose not to pursue the issue," asserted Segundo.

"Having fought some battles myself, I can understand that pain and your concern," assured the judge somberly. "Give him my compliments."

"I will," said Segundo.

"Oh, I meant to ask, have the Apache caused you much trouble in your valley?" asked the judge.

"Not yet," answered Segundo as he started to leave to meet his Vaqueros.

The judge was left with the thought that if Diego DaVia truly was Dead Man Who Walks Away, the Apache probably would not bother him at his Rancheria Fantasma.

"Funny, though," he added, "that la Rancheria Fantasma means Ghost Ranch. I hope to see him whenever he is in Tucson. Have him ask for Judge Morales."

After a good noon meal, Segundo, and his sore and bruised Vaqueros, started back on the long trek to la Rancheria Fantasma. The Vaqueros were feeling like they had been in a good, fun fight, while Segundo felt that he had officially shut an open door to the San Rafael Valley. Now and then his Vaqueros saw him smile as he rode.

17

Don Francisco Ruiz and three very tired Vaqueros of la Rancheria Fantasma rode slowly to the hacienda as the sun was setting. They were dust-covered, tired, yet rode straight and tall in the saddle. They were Vaqueros but with a military pride in being la Rancheria Fantasma Vaqueros. They escorted their patrón, Don Ruiz, to the steps of the hacienda's south porch before being dismissed and returning to their quarters. Standing on the porch to greet them, Diego DaVia quietly welcomed the very tired Segundo Ruiz.

Diego DaVia had been about to offer the Ruiz visitors some wine before dining, when Don Segundo arrived. The Ruiz visitors, Doña Monica and Don Raoul, spoke somewhat subdued words of welcome. Diego simply looked deep into Don Segundo's eyes. When Segundo's eyes met Diego's, each understood the other. The welcome from Diego was genuine. The return look from Don Segundo told Diego that all had been accomplished. Diego said without fanfare, "Segundo, we will wait for you to refresh yourself and join us here before we sample the wine and begin our meal." Only mutual regard, respect, and admiration for a mission fulfilled.

Yet, after Segundo returned to the porch, before a sip of the wine occurred; Doña Monica spat out, "Just where have you been all these days?! You certainly were not retrieving horses!"

Diego, having entertained these people for those many days, decided to simply sit back and let Segundo respond. Segundo waited a moment, took a little breath, and replied, "I was tending to the business of la

Rancheria Fantasma. The business of la Rancheria Fantasma is none of your business. Therefore, my duties and travels are, also, none of your business."

The iron eyes of Diego DaVia never wavered from looking at the two, the brother and the sister, as the full meaning of the conversation became clear.

"This rancheria is most definitely my business, as you will soon see, dear brother. The best lawyer in Mexico City has assured me that your deed to this whole San Rafael Valley will be judged null and void. I will own this valley and la Rancheria Fantasma," said Doña Monica with her voice barely rising in tone.

At this point, Segundo looked over at Diego and asked, "Has anything changed while I was away that would change our perception regarding the length of our visitors' stay?"

"Not one damn thing, Segundo," Diego replied in his own low tone.

"In your haste to steal la Rancheria Fantasma, you have forgotten—" began Segundo.

"I have forgotten nothing, my upstart brother!" interrupted Monica.

"Ah, but you have. The whole San Rafael Valley, including la Rancheria Fantasma, is on American soil. It is part of the United States of America. The deed of ownership of all this has been adjudged and properly recorded in the United States Federal Court. Any document you have, or may procure, has no effect or legality outside of Mexico," related Segundo, holding his temper.

"You bastard!" shouted Monica, not very calmly.

"I must protest!" voiced Raoul.

"You can protest all the way to Mexico City," stated Segundo.

"You forget that I am a very good shot as a duelist, little brother," threatened Raoul, showing spirit, albeit misguided and uselessly late.

At this point Diego intervened. "I would not wish to see a brother shoot down a brother over anything. However, I have no such reservations regarding shooting you if you were to try." The iron eyes of Diego DaVia showed clearly that he was quite serious. "I might remind all here that the length of stay by our visitors is up to Don Francisco Ruiz, the owner of la Rancheria Fantasma."

"You will regret this, brother!" swore Doña Monica.

"I swear I will—" began Raoul.

"You will . . . shut your mouth! Both of you will be outfitted and equipped for your journey to Mexico City in the morning and be on your way by midday," asserted Segundo.

"What are you going to do about this?" Monica demanded of Diego.

"I will instruct our staff to be sure you are properly outfitted for travel," said Diego. His eyes met the fire of her eyes as he said, "Don Francisco Ruiz is the owner and patrón of this rancheria and the whole San Rafael Valley."

"You dirty—!" began Monica.

"If I happen to miss your departure . . . adiós," offered Diego with a sweeping motion of his sombrero.

"Adiós, hell!" screamed Doña Monica. "This is not over yet! You will pay and pay dearly! Watch your back!"

With that, Doña Monica Ruiz reached out, grabbed her over-dressed brother, and hurried to their quarters to make ready to depart la Rancheria Fantasma.

———

The Ruiz party departed from la Rancheria Fantasma at the crack of dawn. Their escorts had to rush to keep up with their charges as they whipped their carriage horses into action.

"I suppose we'll have to eat a few extra eggs and bacon this morning, Segundo," offered Diego.

"Definitely a shortage of guests at the table," answered Segundo. "Do you suppose I said something to upset them?"

"It just might have been something you did, Don Ruiz," returned Diego. "That thing you said about recording your deed in the American federal court seemed to irritate your sister."

"Yes. I thought it might," Segundo said as if wondering if that statement were true.

"Some coffee, Don Ruiz?" asked Diego.

"Gracias, Don Diego," accepted Segundo. Diego DaVia spilled some coffee upon hearing that remark.

"Do not look so offended," said Segundo, laughing.

"What the hell are you talking about?" pressured Diego.

"Diego, I know my sister better than anyone on this earth," began Segundo, as Diego hovered over him. "And I know she will try to invalidate the deed to la Rancheria Fantasma and the whole San Rafael Valley just as soon as she and that predator lawyer of hers can do it."

"So, what can she do, anyway? The deed is properly recorded in the United States Federal Court. Right?" asked Diego, awaiting assurance.

"Pour the coffee, only in my cup this time," said Segundo. "Yes, the deed is properly recorded. But—"

"But what?" returned Diego, feeling anxious at this new direction in the conversation.

"But this, amigo mio," explained Segundo. "Our deed is to land, first owned as a land grant, the San Rafael de la Zanja, from a Spanish king to a former government of Mexico, to Don Ramón Ruiz. We purchased that land in Mexico City and recorded the purchase and deed in Mexico City, Mexico. Our deed shows ownership of that land to a Mexican . . . me."

"So, what?!" exclaimed Diego.

"So, as I was riding to Tucson, I began to see what Monica and Raoul could do," related Segundo. "Their damn lawyer could probably make a pretty good case that the recording of a Mexican deed in the United States did nothing except to change the location of the registry. Do you see, Diego?"

"I am beginning to see," replied Diego, wondering where this logic would go next.

"Listen. If my sneaky sister and her shady lawyer claim that some fraud existed in the purchase in Mexico City, by a Mexican to a Mexican, she might get the United States court to rule that our purchase and, thus, the deed of ownership be null and void."

"Well, what the hell can we do about it?" questioned Diego.

"You remember Capitán McCoy in Tucson, right?" said Segundo. "His adjutant, Lieutenant Fernandez, took me to the federal judge. His advice, which I accepted, was that if an owner on the deed was an American, the deed would be a new deed, to an American, of American land, recorded in the American court. It would be untouchable!"

"What . . . did . . . you . . . do?" asked Diego.

Segundo, laughing so hard that he had to get out of his chair, said, "Diego, you are not only a partner in this rancheria; you are a half owner of the whole San Rafael Valley, including la Rancheria Fantasma!"

At first Diego was going to throw something at Segundo, but then he saw the master stroke in Segundo's action. He was so stunned by this turn of events that he was speechless.

Segundo realized what Diego's concern was and said, "Diego, much time has passed since there was need for you to isolate yourself in this secluded valley. Now, you . . . we . . . are Americans owning land in America. Neither Mexico nor Mexico's army can touch you. The purchase of our part of Sonora by the United States has set us both free. And, after all, it was your gold that bought our rancheria."

Diego DaVia, still speechless for another moment, said, "Don Diego DaVia! I may need a long time getting used to that."

Hearty laughter ensued after that, as the two owners of la Rancheria Fantasma walked all over the hacienda calling each other "Don." But the laughter stopped when Don Diego said, "We need to prepare ourselves for trouble from your lovely but deadly sister."

"My sister may be sneaky and very untrustworthy, but Raoul can be more than deadly. When their attempt fails in court, Raoul is not above hiring violence. We must, as Monica threatened, watch our backs," asserted Don Segundo.

"That coffee was not strong enough," said Don Diego. "I may require something a bit stronger."

The coffee was strong, but not as strong as the resolve in the heart of Don Diego DaVia to never allow anything to happen to his great friend Don Francisco Ruiz. Over the next few weeks, Don Diego had one recurring thought: what exactly was his status? Was he now an American citizen, thanks to the Gadsden Purchase of part of northern Sonora, or was he still a Mexican citizen living in the newest part of the United States? That question would have a great impact on any litigation by Doña Monica Ruiz over the purchase of the San Rafael Valley.

"Segundo, what makes me an American citizen? If I am, then so are you; if I am not, then you are not," stated Diego.

"You are right. I did not think that all out," admitted Segundo. "But introducing another owner, not on the original purchase, will confuse things for those idiots."

"Well, we need to think that all out," said Diego.

———

After three weeks, he told Don Segundo, "I am riding to Tucson to see Capitán McCoy and that federal judge." His explanation to Don Segundo was readily understood and approved by Don Segundo. Don Segundo realized that, if necessary, he might have to do likewise. However, the results of Don Diego's visit to Tucson would determine that.

It would take a couple of days for Don Diego to be ready to leave on his mission. One thing that Don Diego felt necessary was to make sure he was riding on the proper horse. The big grey mount that Diego had found that night as he made his way from Massacre Ground had been showing signs that he was growing old and should be retired to pasture. This saddened Diego because he had become so attached to that magnificent steed. Diego had no idea how old the big grey was because he had taken him from a dead Apache warrior. The big grey probably knew that he was not being ridden as often as in the past, but who really knows?

However, the big grey, over the years, had been busy with the many mares in the herd at la Rancheria Fantasma. Many colts had been born with his stamp clearly visible. One such offspring was very much like his sire. He was big, well-muscled, intelligent and was a dark iron-grey in color. It was that mount, which Diego called Hiero—Iron—that he rode out from la Rancheria Fantasma. Diego did not ride out alone. Three Fantasma Vaqueros rode with him. They were men most willing and able to protect Don Diego DaVia on this important mission.

Don Diego and his Vaqueros rode swiftly after they crossed the ridges north of the San Rafael Valley. They carried their supplies in saddlebags only, not requiring any pack animals. They made good time. Don Diego's thoughts were not hampered by concerns for his safety on this trip. The sight of his Vaqueros, with their tell-tale scarves and sashes, would identify them as from la Rancheria Fantasma. No one wished to tangle with these Vaqueros! The thought that he was riding a strong, nearly identical son of the big grey that would identify him as Dead Man Who Walks Away somehow never entered his mind. What did enter his mind was the possibility of trouble coming from two different females—Doña Monica Ruiz and the young, beautiful chica, Socorra, a dark-eyed, long-haired person of interest for Don Segundo. Socorra was the eldest daughter of one of the Vaqueros riding along with Diego.

The possible trouble coming from Doña Monica Ruiz had been analyzed to distraction over the past few weeks by both Don Diego and Don Segundo. The possible trouble coming because of Socorra was that morning's sudden surprise for Diego. When Don Diego was about to ride off, Segundo waved one hand at him in "goodbye" and had the other hand and arm securely around the slim waist of Socorra. Both wore smiles as wide as the hacienda. Don Diego DaVia knew that, if not actual trouble, change was certainly on its way.

—•—

Four days after leaving la Rancheria Fantasma, Don Diego DaVia and three Fantasma Vaqueros rode into Tucson just after noon. Diego thought he had prepared himself for the new Tucson, as compared to the small military outpost it had been at the time of the now famous non-battle. Tucson had become a melting pot of people from all over and everywhere else. He had mastered enough English to get along and was glad that he had; he would need it. He arranged rooms for himself and his Vaqueros, and, admonishing them to behave themselves as Fantasma Vaqueros in this strange new town, he set off to locate Captain McCoy. His Vaqueros, with orders from Don Segundo, followed his every step. They waited for him outside. Don Segundo's orders evidently were to "protect Diego at all times." They took those orders to heart.

Captain McCoy, after the warm greetings were accomplished, excused himself for a moment. When he returned, he said, "Don Diego, I have ordered a small detachment of my soldiers to stand by with your vaqueros. Many here remember those magnificent fighters, but some do not. Those red scarves and yellow sashes could start something. Although I would love to see it, protocol prevents me from allowing it." His wide smile showed how much it would have pleased him.

"Thank you for your concern, Capitán. Segundo obviously ordered them to protect me," offered Diego by way of explanation.

"There is no doubt in my mind that they will do just that. But now my soldiers may have the honor to join them," McCoy said, laughing. "What can I do for you, my friend?"

"Capitán McCoy, I wish to visit with the federal judge here in Tucson. I want to be sure of my status as to my citizenship following the purchase you call Gadsden," related Diego.

"I would be happy to do that. I know the answer to your question, but I know you wish to be certain from official sources. Let us go over to the courthouse immediately," replied Captain McCoy.

"Gracias," said Diego.

"I know how much Judge Morales liked Segundo and how much he was interested in you. I am certain he will be greatly pleased to meet you," said Captain McCoy.

———

In less than ten minutes, Judge Morales entered the room. "Don DaVia, I am most happy to meet you!" he exclaimed. "I had hoped someday to meet the mystery man of the Battle of Tucson."

"It was not much of a battle from where I stood. I, too, am pleased to meet you, Your Excellency," stated Diego.

"Please, Don Diego, I am not 'Excellency' here. Judges are referred to as 'Your Honor.' We just do a job. How can I help you?" asked Judge Morales.

"I wish to know my status, Your Honor. I would like to know if I am now an American citizen or a Mexican living on American soil," requested Diego.

"The answer is simple, Don Diego. Because your land became part of the United States of America, so did you. Mexican citizens in America, as part of the Gadsden Purchase, are now automatically citizens of the United States of America," stated Judge Morales. "And, because you were not named on the original Mexican document, ownership to an existing American citizen changes the jurisdiction of the document to the United States."

Having dealt at times with the Mexican government, this answer seemed altogether too simple. Judge Morales saw the uncertainty in Diego's eyes and said, "I will draw up a document with the official seal of this federal court district that will proclaim you as a citizen of the United States of America. We will all sign and witness this proclamation."

"My partner, Don Segundo . . . ?" started Diego.

"Don Segundo, like you, is a citizen of the United States of America. But to receive a similar proclamation, he will have to come to Tucson to sign it," assured Judge Morales. "I have left some other business hanging to see you, Don Diego. Therefore, I must return to it."

"Thank you, Your Honor. Please accept my invitation to visit la Rancheria Fantasma. Segundo and I would be genuinely happy to show it to you as our honored guest," offered Diego.

The business for which he had traveled so far had been accomplished within two hours. Don Diego and his three Vaqueros stayed the night and celebrated with, and under, the protective eyes of a detachment of United States cavalry. The ride home proved uneventful . . . with the exception of some concerned thoughts about Don Segundo and one dark-eyed Socorra.

18

Socorra!

Diego DaVia, upon his return to la Rancheria Fantasma, found it hard to believe that he had not paid any attention to what was going on right under his nose. Socorra, a young woman in her mid-twenties, had thoroughly captivated Don Francisco Ruiz. Evidently, this captivation had been going on for some time. Diego DaVia had no sooner stepped down from the saddle on Hiero when he found himself looking directly at both Segundo and Socorra. In the case of Socorra, that was not a bad thing. Diego found himself looking at a beautiful young woman. Socorra was wearing boots, along with a flowing full skirt, a turquoise-studded belt, and an off-the-shoulder white blouse, all of which could not hide the beautiful figure of a woman. Her hair was long and black as a raven's wing, her eyes black and shining, but her smile was the focus of her beauty. Wide and open, her smile told him that Segundo had found his treasure. Socorra embraced Diego, an embrace that had never happened before. Diego surmised that a plateau had been reached in Segundo's relationship with Socorra.

"Segundo, we have much to talk about," said Diego. "It is good news but will require some planning."

"Sí, Diego. We do have much to talk about," agreed Segundo, with a subtle enthusiasm noted immediately by Diego. The fact that Segundo was guiding Socorra up the stairs to the hacienda porch made that fact abundantly clear. Having seated themselves in the surprisingly comfortable chairs at one of the small porch tables, Diego said to Socorra, "I believe that this is the first time I have had the pleasure of your company here on the hacienda porch. Seeing Segundo looking as though he is about to burst tells me that my news is not nearly as interesting as his news. Am I correct, Socorra?"

"Oh, I hope you will feel that our news is good news!" Socorra replied.

"Socorra, your smile, and your eyes—together with that wide smile on Segundo's usually expressionless face—are telling me that things are about to change around la Rancheria Fantasma. I am certain that he will tell me all about it once he recovers his ability to speak," said Diego, laughing. "Speak, Segundo!"

"I can speak," asserted Segundo. "I wanted you to see how happy I am without making a lot of noise about it first."

"Nothing has stopped you from making noise about anything before now; therefore, I have received the message that you two are happy about something. Do I have to guess or will one of you actually tell me what is happening?" said Diego, trying to wring it out of them.

With the lovely Socorra sitting now with head slightly down and expressive eyes looking up at Segundo, waiting for him to say it, Segundo said, in a low, controlled tone, "Socorra has agreed to be my wife."

"Considering how happy you both look together, I certainly am pleased by that!" loudly exclaimed Diego.

Then followed a round of happy talking and planning—planning that included a wedding, to be accomplished as soon as all relatives could be notified and travel to la Rancheria Fantasma. La rancheria was still in pretty good shape after the visit by the now-infamous Ruizes. Socorra was outwardly saddened that the Ruiz family was not going to attend. However, under the circumstances, she would make the best of it. Eight weeks was all the time they allotted for guests to be notified and make their way to la rancheria. Socorra and Segundo were not willing to wait any longer than that.

But, before the happy announcement and subsequent planning meeting had adjourned, Diego DaVia made his own announcement. "Segundo, I have to report that the meeting in Tucson with Capitán McCoy resulted in a session with the United States federal judge, His Honor Judge Morales."

At that statement, all other talk ceased, and both Segundo and Socorra looked at Diego with full attention.

Diego smiled as he said, "Segundo, you, and I—and all who were living here at the time of the Gadsden Purchase—are, and have been, citizens of the United States of America. I have the official document, witnessed, and signed, with the official seal of the United States of America."

"Let me see it!" exclaimed Segundo. While Segundo and Socorra examined Diego's document, Diego said, "To have one just like it, Segundo, you will have to meet with Judge Morales. He is more than happy to do that for you, but the signature must be done and witnessed in his presence."

Segundo looked up. "Tucson?" he asked.

Diego laughingly said, "At your convenience, according to Judge Morales."

That comment led to having more refreshments and celebrating. It was not until after Socorra had left the porch that Diego asked, "Have you heard any more from your illustrious sister, Monica, Segundo?"

"No. But as hateful and vicious as she can be, I am more concerned about Raoul. He is a quiet coward, but he associates with some powerful and nasty friends. They have no conscience concerning the use of violence to a purpose, even if the purpose is only revenge," related Segundo.

"You believe that he is really that bad," said Diego.

"Yes. He is. I do not fear him, certainly not directly. But he could use his finances to organize some vicious people against us and la Rancheria Fantasma," said Segundo, worriedly.

"Do not allow your family's vindictiveness to taint your happy plans with Socorra," voiced Diego. "Together, as always, we will handle that kind of problem. Right now, you must assist your lovely Socorra and her family to create the most wonderful wedding day ever. And, although I have not said it before, I fully approve of your beautiful and wonderful choice of a wife. Salud, amigo mio!"

"Gracias, Diego!" responded Segundo.

"Segundo, if you keep that wonderful smile on her face, you will be a happy man," prophesied Diego.

At that comment, that wonderful smile was on Segundo's face. After a moment, the smile dimmed. "What about the threat from Raoul and Monica?" asked a worried Segundo.

"I will concern myself with that little problem. After all, did we not agree that you and I, Pancho, and Pancho's grandmother could defend this whole valley?" said Diego, laughing. "By the way, where the hell is Pancho's grandmother?"

The days and weeks had been flying by. There was so much to do regarding the upcoming wedding. There was no way to post a letter, or invitation, or any message whatsoever, other than a mounted courier. These couriers had left with their most important cargo during the first week of Diego's return from Tucson. They had no sooner left on their missions when Socorra and Segundo came to the hacienda looking for Diego.

"This must be important. You actually came to see me," quipped Diego.

"It is important," answered Socorra, not yet seeing the humor in his comment.

"Believe me, Socorra, Diego will surely agree," Segundo said smiling.

"Probably. But tell me. Agree to what?" asked Diego.

Socorra began, "That little clearing over there, a bit east of this hacienda: we would like to build our home there. Would that be all right with you? Could we have your permission?"

"My permission!" exclaimed Diego. "Segundo, did you not inform Socorra that you own this place?"

Segundo started to speak, but Socorra interrupted, "Yes, he did. But you own it, too, and I wanted to be sure you did not object."

"Neither of you need my permission to do anything, here or anywhere else, if it makes you happy," asserted Diego.

Construction began immediately. Time was short, but ready or not, they would move in on their wedding day . . . or night.

About a week before the wedding ceremony, relatives and friends of both began to arrive. Most of those calling themselves friends of Segundo were already at la Rancheria Fantasma. They called themselves Vaqueros. The classy people were friends and relatives of Socorra. Accommodations had been made ready so that all were comfortable. For most of a week, la Rancheria Fantasma was a genuine picnic ground. The food was incredible, and the guitar music never seemed to stop. With all this preliminary partying, Diego could but wonder what it would be like after the wedding.

But it was beautiful. A priest had been coerced into coming all the way from Cananea to officiate. He did not mind officiating, but that long, bumpy ride certainly pushed his civility almost to the breaking point. Don Diego DaVia had been chosen to stand as "best man" for his friend Don Francisco Ruiz. He did so . . . proudly.

Then, the ceremony over, the happy bride and groom made their way to their new home in the clearing east of the current hacienda. Diego was engrossed in conversation with some of Socorra's family when a Vaquero quietly asked to speak with him.

"Señor Don Diego, I have news," he said nervously.

"What news?" asked Diego quietly, noting the Vaquero's low tone.

"War!" related the Vaquero. "The United States of America is at war with itself. It is a 'civil' war."

"How can this be?" asked Diego incredulously.

"The courier said that some rebel Southern states had fired on a Fort Sumter somewhere, and that started a war with the Northern states, the United States. That is all I know, Patrón," the Vaquero said.

Diego told him, "You have told me much. Go and join the party for Segundo's wedding. Enjoy yourself."

Diego returned to the wedding party reception with the disturbing thoughts brought on by the news of actual civil war between the Southern states and the Northern states, the Union. His joy was diminished considerably by this awful news. Yet he put on a happy smile and joined in the revelry with his friends, and Segundo and Socorra's family. The party lasted late into the night.

———

The next morning found Diego awake with the dawn. He wanted to wish Socorra and Segundo god speed on their honeymoon journey to San Diego, California. They would be gone for at least a month. He was waiting for them on the hacienda porch. Their travel luggage had been loaded into a coach and was waiting. But first—breakfast! The Vaquero ladies were not about to let the honeymooners leave without a breakfast to last them all the way.

"Gracias, amigas! Ladies of la Rancheria Fantasma! I fear I will be belching, because of this marvelous breakfast, all the way to Tucson, at least!" Segundo declared.

The happy couple had barely seated themselves in the coach when Diego leaned forward and said, "You must hear this news now, because it is important. Things may be changing soon and not because of your wedding, Segundo."

Segundo then, leaning forward to here, asked, "What is it, Diego?"

Diego answered in a low tone, "There is war between the Southern United States and Northern United States. We do not know how it will affect us here. In Tucson and San Diego, keep your eyes and ears open for news. It will be important to know how to relate to the Americans in Tucson and other areas. We must know how the lands here in the Southwest will align themselves, with the North or the South. But, other than that, have a happy honeymoon in San Diego!"

By this time, many of the visitors and family had gathered near the coach to wish the honeymooners a safe, happy honeymoon. The cheers were loud and long.

"Gracias, familia and amigos! And gracias to you, Don Diego! I wondered what I would be thinking about other than my beautiful Socorra. Now, I know. Vamonos!"

Diego, smiling, noted that Segundo had made that last comment with a smile, and so he knew he was not angry. This was important to

Diego. Segundo had, over the years, become his only dear friend. He thought of him as his *hermano*—brother.

Unknown to Diego, among the many relatives and friends, soft eyes had looked upon him with unspoken admiration. Unable to capture the attention of Diego DaVia during the busy time of the festivities, Socorra's cousin JoAnna found herself departing with the various families returning to Sonora. She was lovingly happy for her cousin but leaving without knowing Diego DaVia made for JoAnna a long ride home to Sonora.

Now, Diego must put together a plan to keep la Rancheria Fantasma secure. There was much to worry him. The threats by Don Raoul and Doña Monica Ruiz still were something of concern. The ongoing condition of revolution in Mexico possibly spilling over the border into la Rancheria Fantasma worried him. The uncertainty of that American Civil War and its effect on the Southwest, including la Rancheria Fantasma, would certainly not allow him to relax for long.

Diego went about the business of la Rancheria Fantasma as usual for a few days. Then, he asked Pancho to join him for breakfast. Pancho was not much more than a teenager when Diego first met him and Segundo. He had matured into a strong, fine young man. Without any fanfare, Pancho had assumed the role of Segundo's assistant. Whatever his assigned duties were, he performed them very well. He had earned due respect from Diego, Segundo, and the Vaqueros of la Rancheria Fantasma. So, it was to Pancho that Diego turned.

"Pancho, it is good to have you here, on the porch, for breakfast," said Diego.

Pancho replied, "I am happy to be here, and not just because of the food, Patrón. I love this rancheria. From here on the porch, I can see far down the valley."

"You are very much a part of this rancheria, Pancho," Diego asserted. "With Segundo busy for a while, I must lean on you even more."

"I will always be here," said Pancho. "What do you wish me to do?"

Diego began, somewhat sarcastically, "As you know, the United States is at war with itself. We can do nothing about that. We are nowhere near any area that either side would think of as necessary to their cause.

Therefore, I do not anticipate trouble concerning that for some time, if even at all. However, Segundo's sister, Doña Monica, and that sneaky, weasel brother, Raoul, are due to show whatever they think they can do to us. That bothers me. I want none of our Vaqueros hurt by them if they try something violent. The state of the revolution in Mexico worries me; that can spill over to our valley easily. We have many horses to steal. They would call it 'commandeer,' but for us it is the same . . . adiós, goodbye, horses! Also, and by far no less a potential problem for us, is an Apache called Cochise. He has become the war chief, I suppose, of the Chiricahua Apache. He is improving on his reputation as a great tactical leader. I expect his actions will affect us at some point."

Pancho interrupted Diego's thought, "It sounds as though we will have some work to do. Do you wish me to organize the military patrols and begin the training again? You are aware that, with all the recent activity, we have slacked off on the training."

"Ha! Pancho, you are reading my mind. I believe that we will, at some point, have to actually fight to keep our Rancheria Fantasma intact . . . not a non-battle like that action in Tucson," said Diego. "Get them organized. We have the best Vaqueros anywhere; I want them to be the best Vaquero cavalry anywhere. When you have your squads in place, notify me. I will take charge of the training."

"Sí, Patrón. After I finish my breakfast," said Pancho, digging in with relish.

20

It was six weeks before the happy bride and groom returned to la Rancheria Fantasma. Segundo and his bride, Socorra, arrived just before the evening meal was to be served. The couple was treated to a rousing welcome. Everyone besieged them with unending questions of what they saw and did in the far away city of San Diego, California. It was hard for them to describe the combination of fine places to visit, the green mountains, and the Pacific Ocean. But they did the best they could to paint the picture of "beach" living. The desert-dwelling Vaqueros and their families loved hearing every word.

When things settled down after the meal, Socorra said, "Diego, something is different here. Could it be that something has happened?"

"Nothing drastic has happened . . . yet," answered Diego. "I imagine Segundo has mentioned and you have heard of the civil war brewing in the United States. We are preparing for whatever that brings, as well as some more local events that may or may not happen here."

"Diego," began Segundo, "this place looks like a military post. I see Vaqueros riding in formation. The red scarves and yellow sashes have been joined by brown sombreros and white shirts. The Vaqueros are in uniform. What the hell . . . ?"

"Our Yaqui friends tell us that a large force of, for lack of a more descriptive word, 'banditos' have been massing between our San Rafael Valley and Cananea," answered Diego. "Yesterday we were informed that the banditos have moved their base camp to the Rio Santa Cruz just south of the border, at the south end of the San Rafael Valley. We are preparing for trouble."

"We certainly are!" Segundo agreed, his eyes taking in all the changes. "Who are these banditos? Revolutionaries?"

"The Yaquis say that they are Mexican and gringo low-life pistoleros. We believe they are organized by your little weasel brother, Raoul," said Diego.

"Raoul! That dirty, no good—!" began Segundo.

"Segundo! No!" chided Socorra, at the foul language she believed would be voiced by Segundo.

"Do the Yaquis know if Raoul is with them?" asked Segundo.

"I do not think so," answered Diego. "However, one of our Vaqueros told me that he saw your sister, Doña Monica, in Cananea."

After taking a long, deep breath . . . "How soon? How soon, Diego?" asked Segundo.

"I believe they may try it any time now," Diego stated, matter of factly.

"What are you thinking?" asked Segundo.

"The Mexican government has no troops stationed in Cananea in any great numbers. They would be powerless to interfere in any action occurring in the area," said Diego. His military background was beginning to resurface. Segundo almost believed he could imagine a Capitán of Dragoons, Diego DaVia, as Diego spoke. "I believe that it is always better to be the attacker than the attacked. Therefore, I plan to attack these banditos where they are staging to attack us. That way we avoid having a battle fought here, where we have family."

"What about the men?" asked Segundo. "Are they ready for this?"

"We have been waiting for you, Segundo," said Diego. "We leave in the morning."

Socorra, who had been silent during this whole conversation, said, "I do not like any of this, but I will pray and wait for you to return."

———

The next morning, sixty la Rancheria Fantasma Vaqueros, heads held high and riding straight in the saddle in formation, rode out of the main compound. At the head of that colorful column of men rode Don Francisco

Ruiz and Don Diego DaVia. Both were wearing the same uniform as the rest of the Vaquero column. Yaqui relatives of some of the Fantasma Vaqueros were already on their way to scout the enemy position. As the Vaquero column moved southward along the Rio Santa Cruz, these Yaqui scouts would begin reporting any information they could about the enemy, their strength, and the location of their base camp.

The Vaqueros had been on the march for about five hours when Diego called a halt. It was a good time to rest the horses and men, to eat some of the jerky and whatever pastries the Vaquero ladies had smuggled into their saddlebags. It was here that Diego began to lay out strategy to Segundo for this preemptive strike against the banditos. Segundo had naturally expected a general ambush style attack—sort of sneak up on them and let them have it. He was not surprisingly impressed with the strategy laid out by Don Diego DaVia.

"Segundo, when we resume our ride, we will split up into three separate columns. One column will swing east to the mountain foothills at the perimeter of the valley and move southward along it toward the bandito camp. The other two columns will do likewise along the west perimeter foothills. When these columns meet at the center, south of the valley along the Rio Santa Cruz, one column will cross the border on the east bank. One of the other columns will do likewise on the west bank. These two columns will proceed southward until we are close to the banditos' camp. By then we should have accurate reports from our Yaqui scouts as to the exact whereabouts of the camp," instructed Diego.

"But what about the third column?" asked Segundo.

"The third column, the one made up of the best marksmen of our Vaquero cavalry, will seclude themselves on both sides of the Rio Santa Cruz. They will form a rough *V*-shaped position, the narrowest point where the forested cover ends, then opening back southeastward and southwestward, ending some distance away from the rio," continued Diego.

"I never heard of such a thing, amigo," said Segundo. "That forms a funnel-like shape with the narrow center point at the rio as . . ." Segundo paused for a moment, looking deep into the iron eyes of Diego DaVia. Then he understood. ". . . as a chute to force any escaping banditos to be squeezed into a small area!"

"Very good, Segundo," complimented Diego. "When we are ready, the two columns in a semicircle at the banditos' camp will attack. The only avenue of escape for the banditos will be northward, up the Rio Santa Cruz, into the waiting guns of our third column."

"Dios mio!" exclaimed Segundo.

"The banditos, because of the funnel, will be herded into a no-escape situation," explained Diego.

"Diego, is that what the Yavapai and Apache . . . did . . . to . . . your cavalry?" asked Segundo, concerned for his friend's feelings.

Diego DaVia paused for a moment before answering his friend's question and obvious concern for his feelings. "It has been a while since then, and I am stronger now. But I have learned a few things from that lousy experience. This strategy is only one of them, amigo."

Segundo stood up at that point and simply barked, "Squad leaders meet here . . . now!" Segundo relieved the mantle of responsibility from his friend's shoulders by explaining, in detail, the plan for this operation to the designated squad leaders. They were impressed with the plan. To be honest, they had been wondering for some time when they would be able to use their training. They were quietly eager to engage the enemy and to protect their two patrones and la Rancheria Fantasma.

"Now we will continue our march along the perimeter of our valley. As we get closer to where we must enter the wooded area at the south end, we will hide ourselves along the wooded edge. By that time, our Yaqui scouts should have reported the banditos' exact location. Vamonos!" ordered Diego DaVia.

With that order, the columns began their maneuver quietly and resolutely. The Fantasma Vaqueros separated and rode their assigned routes. By the time the sun was lowering on the horizon, each unit had arrived at the wooded edge of each side of the San Rafael Valley. Both units made a quiet, cold camp and rested until morning.

———•———

With the new day came another quiet march, heading along the wooded margin of the valley toward the convergence of both Vaquero units at the woods on each side of the slow-flowing Rio Santa Cruz. Then another quiet, cold camp as each man prepared himself for whatever the next day would bring. Every Vaquero on that mission was a fighter. Each man was trained by Diego DaVia and Segundo and knew that their mission was necessary. Each man was ready, able, and, most importantly, willing to do his job.

Before the night was totally dark, Diego called a meeting with all squad leaders. Thoughts were to be voiced and issues were to be raised to clarify the orders for the coming fight.

All day Diego DaVia had been wrestling with his own thoughts for this encounter. His plan of encirclement and compelling the enemy into a small area was going to happen as planned—no changes to that. However, that plan resembled closely what he had seen and survived before. The memory of that strategy, as used against himself and the Peralta expedition by the Yavapai and Apache, had kept his stomach in a constant state of nausea all day. Diego DaVia did not want to see that scene again. He called Segundo and all the squad leaders together and proceeded to further outline his wishes.

"Vaqueros of la Rancheria Fantasma, two separate parties of Yaqui scouts have reported to us that our enemy is camped about a mile downstream from our present position. They, unbelievably, are in a bowl-shaped clearing, half on each side of the Rio Santa Cruz. In the pre-dawn hours, just before the rising sun, we must be in place to start the attack. On my signal, we will charge from the south to the north, forcing them upstream into the waiting arms of our third column at the funnel," instructed Diego. All seemed to understand their orders.

"Understand me now," Diego continued. "Whatever their background before, these men are now employed by Don Raoul Ruiz, who is intent upon destroying what he cannot legally own . . . la Rancheria Fantasma! These men, without the training that you possess, must think that they are going to run off a bunch of peaceful herdsmen and ranchers. For pay! If they were to succeed, they would be paid. If not, Don Raoul Ruiz would probably not pay them."

"What are you trying to say, Diego?" interrupted Segundo.

"I have seen more than one slaughter in my life. I would prefer not to see another," said Diego. "Here are my orders. We will attack with much noise and shooting. We will terrorize them into flight upstream into the waiting funnel and our third column. There, we will capture them. If killing must be done, let them bring it on themselves. We will batter them and bruise them, then take them to Cananea and turn them over to the Mexican military there."

At that, there was some murmuring among the squad leaders. And then there was some low laughter. "I think we understand, Patrón," said one of the squad leaders, the father of Socorra. "You want to quash their attempt to attack la Rancheria Fantasma now and deter any return revenge attack by them again."

Segundo stood up and agreed. "I see it now: as little bloodshed as possible, send them possibly to a military prison, and send my brother Raoul home in shame. Do you think we can do it?"

"If our surprise charge works, they will not be prepared. We each fire a couple times at the ground at their feet to start them running, and then fire to kill only if they are firing back," said Diego. "Do you think our Vaqueros can pull off an attack like that?"

Segundo did not have a chance to answer. Socorra's father, standing, stated it plainly: "We are Fantasma Vaqueros. We can and will attack like that."

With that assertion, the meeting ended. Diego DaVia sat looking into the brightening moon. Segundo, for a few moments, was content to let Diego be alone with his thoughts. Then he moved over to Diego and said, "I understand your reluctance to kill, amigo. I believe I saw it at the non-battle of Tucson. But I understand how, if this works as you plan, it could be far better for all of us, including you, and including all at la Rancheria Fantasma."

"Thank you, Segundo," said Diego. "In you I have a true friend."

21

The half-light of pre-dawn found the Vaqueros of la Rancheria Fantasma already in position in the semicircle south of the bandito encampment. Half of the semicircle was hidden close to the ground on one side and the other half on the other side of the Rio Santa Cruz. The Vaqueros had hidden their horses halfway between their position and the position of the third column of Vaqueros at the funnel. Don Diego DaVia had given orders that the attack not occur until he fired the first shot. The Vaqueros were waiting until all enemies were awake and able to be maneuvered up the Rio Santa Cruz and into the waiting guns of the third column.

After holding their positions for what seemed an interminable time, they watched the enemy, one at a time, begin their morning routine. As the light had become brighter, it was noticed that the enemy, in their belief that their attack on la Rancheria Fantasma was unknown to anyone, had posted no guards. So, the shot by Diego DaVia, followed by the volley from the half-circle of Vaqueros, had the effect of a bolt of lightning on the banditos. The banditos, reacting in disbelief, splashed frantically northward up the Rio Santa Cruz. Many had left their weapons and even articles of clothing in their camp.

As the banditos fled northward up the Rio Santa Cruz, Diego DaVia charged, leading his Fantasma Vaqueros on foot, noisily behind the fleeing banditos. Splashing through the shallow water, crashing through the underbrush along the banks of the rio, triggered memories of another such race and was agonizing for Diego DaVia. The difference this time was that he was not racing for his life. This time the enemy was racing for their lives. Very few shots were being fired by the banditos. The shots by the Vaqueros, in the air and at the ground at the banditos' feet, kept them running wild-eyed in fear, closer and closer to the third column and the deadly funnel.

Don Segundo, standing on a high mound of dirt on the west bank of the Rio Santa Cruz, had a good view as the fleeing banditos neared the third column's position. As the panicking wave of nearly fifty men entered the wide opening of the funnel, the Fantasma Vaqueros began a withering hail of lead directed at the feet of the running banditos. The enemy felt both the bullets striking the ground at their feet and heard the crash of the gunshots. They saw the thick smoke from the fusillade of gunfire. They stopped as soon as they could. Over the din of the gunfire, they heard the repeated command to "Halt! Drop your weapons! Surrender or die!"

The first few enemy fighters saw the inevitable wisdom in surrender. Some at the rear of the panic began firing back. These were cut down immediately. Those using more wisdom were allowed to live.

As the rear two Vaquero columns caught up to the action at the closed end of the funnel, they herded the captives into a tight group and ordered them to sit facing each other. At that point, Don Segundo ordered them searched. Any weapons found were immediately confiscated. One at a time, the captives were blindfolded with bandanas. They would remain seated, blindfolded, until their horses were caught and available to ride. Among the captives, Don Segundo recognized his brother, Don Raoul Ruiz.

"Buenos días, hermano mio," greeted Segundo. "And what brings you to this delightful place?"

"There is nothing delightful about this place!" snarled Raoul, as he was being tied.

Segundo asked, "Then why did you organize this picnic? Surely you were looking forward to a grand time. Have the activities not measured up to your expectations?"

"Damn you, Segundo!" snarled Raoul again.

"Blindfold him!" ordered Segundo to one of the Vaqueros.

"*Con mucho gusto!* With much pleasure!" said the Vaquero.

At this point, Don Diego DaVia stepped up and asked the then-blindfolded Raoul, "We should welcome your lovely sister, Doña Monica Ruiz, to this picnic. Where do you suppose she might be?"

"She is not here!" snapped Raoul.

"Obviously, 'Don' Raoul," said Diego mockingly. "But I am sure you could tell us where we might find her. I, for one, would feel terrible if she were to miss this picnic."

"Damn you all!" shouted Raoul, to the laughter of the Vaqueros gathering around.

Don Francisco Ruiz stepped in and ordered, "Vaqueros, when you give the other captives water, give this individual water at every second serving. And, because he believes he is something special, shove this bandana in his mouth so we do not have to hear any more from him!" Segundo's anger was boiling. So much so that Diego ordered Raoul be taken away from them.

"I think we should keep him separated from us for a time," said Diego. "In fact, place three men to guard only Raoul. He will ride in the center of our little caravan, so that we all can keep an eye on him."

While all this was happening, each captive was placed on a horse, backwards, his hands tied behind his back and also to the saddle horn behind him. The Fantasma Vaqueros ate their cold breakfast; the captives did not. After that breakfast, the caravan, in a column of twos, moved out on their long ride to the Mexican military post at Cananea, Sonora. Once again, Segundo was impressed by the way this whole operation had been organized. Diego's orders had been given to the Vaquero squad leaders and were implemented without question and without flaw, at the highest level of military precision. He and Diego were riding in the long procession, about thirty yards well back from the rear of the column. From that point, they could watch every move. Behind them, ten Vaqueros formed a rear guard. Diego had ordered guards on the perimeter flanks and scouts riding about a half mile ahead to provide early warning of any kind of surprise attack. The column was impressive: captive riders looking ragtag, while the Fantasma Vaqueros in their uniforms, looking sharp and militarily very formidable, would make any potential attackers think twice.

Yet, when Segundo looked at Diego, he saw the outwardly strong, confident set of the jaw but also a look of distant memories in his normally iron-eyed friend. He leaned over from his saddle and said, "It is a different battle, amigo mio. It was won without the massacre it could have been. You made that happen. Rest easy within. Look at this fine column of Vaquero cavalry that you created. Peace to you, amigo mio."

"I am so proud of our Vaqueros! They were magnificent in this encounter. But I envision tough times ahead, and I am concerned. But they have shown their mettle. If we must fight again, they will do well. But I would rather they were caring for our horse herd," said Diego DaVia. "I do not want to ever see another massacre."

———

Over the long march to Cananea, the Vaqueros of la Rancheria Fantasma did their job without flaw. The long, colorful column of twos, approximately fifty pairs of horsemen in formation, entered the military post as citizens and Mexican military personnel watched in amazed silence.

Major Sanchez, after the long column halted, strode out slowly to greet Don Segundo. At this time, Major Sanchez was introduced to Don Diego DaVia. The two new acquaintances shook hands, and for a moment nothing was said until Major Sanchez was able to speak. "Don DaVia, I am honored to at last meet you. I have heard much about you, but as a man far away and, perhaps, imaginary . . . a fantasma."

Don Diego graciously returned his greeting but added, "I am no fantasma, Major Sanchez."

Major Sanchez, with a sweep of his hat, gestured to the column standing still in formation, quietly not even allowing a sound from the captives. "I am aware of la Rancheria Fantasma Vaqueros. But I have never seen such a well-disciplined fighting force, not even among regulars."

"Thank you, Major," said Diego. Then, addressing the column, "Don Segundo and I are very proud of la Rancheria Fantasma Vaqueros, as is Major Sanchez!" Major Sanchez bowed low as he swept his hat in appreciation. At that, the Vaquero column broke their silence and cheered!

Don Segundo, after the noise died down, said, "Major, we have arrested these men who had planned to attack la Rancheria Fantasma. They were hired to do so by my no-good brother, Don Raoul Ruiz. Will you take them into custody and offer them for trial as paid brigands?"

"I will place them before a judge, but I cannot guarantee his judgment," stated Major Sanchez.

"I understand. When can such a trial convene, Major?" asked Don Segundo.

"It might be weeks before a judge can try these men," apologized the major.

"We must incarcerate these men now," said Segundo. "We cannot keep them in the street."

"There is a guarded military compound, normally used for revolutionary prisoners," offered Major Sanchez.

"Will you hold them in custody there until a proper trial can be arranged?" asked Segundo.

"I will do so, but I do not know, legally, how long I can keep them," worried Major Sanchez.

At that, Don Diego DaVia, realizing a problem not foreseen, spoke to the major. "These men, acting as a Mexican civilian militia unit, conspired to raid across the new border into the United States of America. They were stopped by a defensive force of American civilian herdsmen from entering American soil before they were able to cross into America. Do you see the danger of what has now become an 'international incident' between the United States and Mexico?"

"Dios mio! I had not thought of that," said the major. "I . . . we do not want to be involved in such a grave matter. Is it possible to avoid all that, Señor DaVia?"

"I, in my own military career, have had to witness some creative interpretations of what actually occurred versus what was possibly right or wrong. Unfortunately, but truthfully, some problems are solved in that manner," advanced Diego.

Major Sanchez was frantically, in his own thinking, looking for a way out of what he felt could be a long, possibly career-ending situation. "But what can we do? You attacked them on Mexican soil."

"Very true," said Diego. "But often suspected revolucionarios are caught and incarcerated for a time for being armed and organized . . . ready to do harm. What happens to many of them?"

"They are put on labor gangs and made to do hard work. Sometimes they are released; sometimes they escape; sometimes they die," said the major.

"Major Sanchez, you have been a good friend of la Rancheria Fantasma, both before and after the Gadsden Purchase put a border between our lands. Therefore, I wish to make this easier for you. We are delivering these pistoleros to you. Perhaps you can use some of them as soldiers. Perhaps you see that they are dangerous criminals. Whatever you do, la Rancheria Fantasma Vaqueros are immediately returning to our San Rafael Valley. We have recorded the names of all these men. If they ever return to the San Rafael Valley, we will kill them. I will trust you to make all that crystal clear to them. Will you?"

"I most certainly will, Don DaVia," promised Major Sanchez.

"One more thing, however," said Don Diego. "Don Raoul Ruiz, the instigator of this foul plan to attack la Rancheria Fantasma, must come away with us, anonymously."

"Never heard of him!" stated Major Sanchez.

"Bueno!" said Diego. "Move your cavalry into position to relieve us of these low-life pistoleros, and we will be gone!"

"Gracias for your fine police work on the border. That is how this will be treated. Gracias, Fantasma Vaqueros!" shouted Major Sanchez, as the Fantasma Vaqueros wheeled their column with precision and, under the command of Don Diego DaVia, marched away toward the San Rafael Valley. In the center of the Vaquero column, Don Raoul Ruiz rode, facing backward, hands tied to the saddle horn behind him. The scenery through which he rode was beautiful, but since he was blindfolded, he did not see it.

Don Diego DaVia rode quietly for miles as the column moved north-ward toward the San Rafael Valley. The preemptive strike on the pisto-leros hired by Don Raoul Ruiz, as successful as it was, had left him with a most distressing problem. That problem was Don Raoul Ruiz. What could he do with him? Don Raoul continued to ride, facing backward in the middle of the Vaquero column. Don Segundo, riding alongside Don Diego, was silent also. However, now and again, he would break into a momentary smile. This went on for hours, Diego pondering how to solve this dilemma and Segundo seemingly being entertained by thoughts resulting in mirth until Diego asked, "What the hell are you grinning about?"

"Raoul," came the spoken answer from Segundo.

"I have been thinking of nothing else for miles, but it has not caused me to break out in giggles," responded Diego.

"There are so many things we would like to do to him, now that we have him all trussed up," said Segundo, chuckling.

"Well, killing him is out of the question. As much as I would love to, I cannot shoot your damn brother," stated Diego.

"No. We cannot turn him loose either," said Segundo.

"Hardly," agreed Diego. "If he were to return to the 'powers that be' in Mexico City, this small war would continue. We need to make sure he never enters the San Rafael Valley again. No idea of mine this morning would seem to be feasible."

"Socorra's father said something to me last night at supper, in camp. I thought it was so funny. But now I wonder if it could work," ventured Segundo.

"Try me," said Diego. "I'm open to about anything, including a good laugh."

"Socorra's father has some Yaqui friends. These friends are said to be real pranksters." Segundo began having trouble continuing due to sporadic giggling. "He suggested that we scare the hell out of him so badly that he would never have anything to do with us, or la Rancheria Fantasma, or anything in the United States again!"

"All right. I like what you are saying, and your giggles are becoming contagious. But I still do not know what the hell you are planning," said Diego. "Tell me!"

Between giggles and fits of laughter, Segundo related, "Raoul is my brother. But he is rotten to the core and well deserves this and more."

"Keep talking, Segundo," said Diego.

"Tomorrow, we leave Raoul tied up as he is now, with his horse tied to a tree. A band of Yaqui friends of Socorra's father, dressed and painted as if they were Apaches, find him. They take him to an encampment and, acting as if they were Apaches, scare the living hell out of him! After a few days of this, they turn him loose, naked, on the Mexican side of the border and make him survive his way home!" Segundo said with a relish.

Diego had to laugh at the thought of Raoul, terrified, walking naked into some Mexican saloon in Cananea and trying to convince everyone there that he was a big shot "don."

However, he said, "Segundo, you realize that once your Yaqui friends turn him loose like that, Raoul might get killed."

"I do. But I remember that he was trying to get you and me killed," answered Segundo. "Once we leave him tied to that tree, I consider him on his own."

"Do you really want to try it?" asked Diego.

"Socorra's father swears, once his Yaqui friends turn him loose, he'll be too scared to try anything like he did ever again. So, let us do it!" ordered Segundo. "I'm told that the Yaquis could be finding Raoul by noon tomorrow. Ha! Serves him right!"

"Segundo are you sure there is not a little Apache blood in you?" asked Diego. "I agree, it serves him right, and that is a fact. But . . . ?"

"But what, amigo?" asked Segundo, not sure he liked that comment about "Apache blood."

"I do not care what the hell happens to that little weasel brother of yours," stated Diego flatly. "I don't think he'll ever be able to mount the courage for another try at forcibly taking la Rancheria Fantasma again. But I remember one of our own Vaqueros saying that Doña Monica had been seen in Cananea."

"That worries me," said Segundo. "If Monica did not see us deliver those pistoleros to Major Sanchez, she surely must know about it by now."

"She is your sister . . . thank God not mine!" plainly stated Diego. "Let me think about this for a while. *Hmmh!* There . . . that is long enough. Segundo, since Raoul is your brother, you should see about arranging his capture by hostiles. Anytime tomorrow should work out fine."

"I will talk to Socorra's father now," agreed Segundo and promptly rode forward along the column to accomplish that purpose.

It was only half an hour later when Segundo returned to Diego at the rear of the Vaquero column. "It is set. Tomorrow we will be sure that Raoul is tied very securely on his horse as he now is. We will tie his horse to a tree and slowly ride off and leave him. Socorra's father will remain nearby and see to it that all is handled properly. The Yaquis will unmask him at sunset and begin making him think his end has come. When they believe that he has shrunk to a mere prune of a man, they will leave him, naked, to survive alone. If he survives, he will be no more a threat to us. If he does not survive, too bad! So sad! He never was much of a brother to me. Besides, he tried to kill us—all of us—including me! Tough!"

"You are right. You must get our Vaqueros home. From now on we must have extra Vaqueros patrolling la Rancheria Fantasma," ordered Don Diego.

"Uh oh! Sounds like you are up to something else," suspected Segundo.

"Your sister, if she has not escaped from Cananea, must be removed from a position of doing harm to us over this. Your brother was a loose cannon . . . well, maybe only a loose powder flash. But Monica can still do us great harm if she gets to certain corrupt Mexican authorities. I will ride back to Cananea now to find out and take care of that unfinished business."

"Are you going to shoot her?" asked Segundo, wondering how serious Diego was.

"I might just do that," replied Diego, laughing. "I have all that I need for the ride. I will leave now." Wheeling Hiero around, he started back toward Cananea.

The thought that Don Raoul Ruiz was in for some very rough times came up often as Diego rode southward toward Cananea, and each time he would nearly laugh aloud. Served him right, though. Don Diego Da-Via had no remorse in ordering Don Raoul Ruiz's punishment. If he survived the treatment doled out to him by the Yaquis masquerading as Apaches, and the naked trial in the high desert, he would never have the heart to conspire against his brother Segundo or la Rancheria Fantasma again. La Doña Monica Ruiz was another problem. Diego had no idea whatsoever how to handle that one, but he was on his way to try.

Following the Vaquero's trail back toward Cananea was no problem; a blind man could do it. But it was still nightfall when he arrived. Cananea was not a large village. It had a small courthouse, a church, an alcalde—Don Enrique Vasquez—and the small military stationed there under Major Sanchez. Some shops, a cantina and what went with it pretty much accounted for the village. There were a couple of facilities where one could rent a room, one of which accommodated Diego for the night. In the cantina, Don Diego heard the name "Doña Monica" in very unflattering terms. The men speaking of her were very much intoxicated and, therefore, unreliable. Before collapsing in much-needed sleep, he planned to speak to Major Sanchez about her.

———

The following morning found Diego hurrying along the short street to the military quarters of Major Sanchez. He did not even have to enter the building. Major Sanchez had just stepped out of the doorway.

"Don Diego, I am surprised. Did you not leave with your Vaqueros yesterday?" he asked.

"Sí, but I had to return. I must ask you about la Doña Monica Ruiz," he replied.

"Ah. She is one beautiful lady," the major said. "What do you wish to know?"

"Is she staying in Cananea?" asked Diego.

"The lady has been in Cananea more than a few times lately, Don Diego," answered the major. "She had been gone for a few days but returned a couple hours after you left with your Vaqueros and that someone of whom I, of course, have never heard or seen."

"Is she still here?" asked Diego.

"She was here a short time but must have heard what happened concerning your Vaqueros. She became loud and angry. Within an hour, she had procured a horse and with two, I suppose pistoleros, rode out. I tried to ask her where she was going, and she was very uncomplimentary to me, nearly ran her horse over me," said the major, with a wry smile forming.

"Did she say where she was riding?" asked Diego.

"Some men in the cantina where she procured the pistoleros said she wanted to go to the city of Tucson . . . pronto!" answered Major Sanchez.

Diego DaVia was already walking swiftly to get his horse, Hiero, even before the major could fully answer. Within minutes, Don Diego DaVia was riding northward. His only thought was to get to la Rancheria Fantasma, resupply, and intercept Doña Monica in Tucson. Hiero proved his mettle on that ride. The Vaquero column was just arriving at the rancheria as Diego caught up with them.

Diego explained the situation to Segundo. Segundo promised to have his horse and supplies ready for him to leave for Tucson. He did just that.

—·—

Diego rode out on Hiero before morning light for Tucson. Hiero was certainly the son of the big grey. This was a horse that loved to run and could go on for miles. The miles flew by on that great, grey steed.

—·—

Late in the evening of the third day, the sunset found Don Diego DaVia slowly riding into the growing city of Tucson. The recently created don was very tired, yet he was convinced that Hiero was not. The horse seemed to prance into town. Diego just shook his head. The exhausted Don Diego DaVia found quarters for the night.

The dreams that had for years made a habit of torturing the sleep of the former soldier made their customary appearance. But that night Diego had another nightmare on his mind: Doña Monica Ruiz. Would he find her in Tucson? What would he do about her if he did find her? The morning might tell.

23

The morning told Don Diego much more than he had wanted to know. He had eaten a small breakfast and, feeling only a portion of the exhaustion of the night before, stepped out into the streets of Tucson. What he saw made him catch his breath and step back into the shadows of the early morning sun. He had intended to make his way to the local military garrison of United States Cavalry and his friend Captain McCoy. What he saw down the street caused him to immediately change his plans. Instead of the Stars and Stripes of the United States of America, he saw the Stars and Bars of the Confederacy! Southern forces and sympathizers had taken possession of the city of Tucson.

What Diego saw of the Southern forces occupying the city reminded him little of a regular military unit. They were ragtag and riffraff. After observing all he could from his limited vantage point, he decided to try to ascertain what had happened to Captain McCoy and his Union garrison. He walked boldly into what had been Captain McCoy's office. The person seated at the desk was about as poor an example of a military officer as Diego could have ever imagined. He told the officer that, having once had business with Captain McCoy, he would like to know his whereabouts. The Confederate officer laughed and said, "So would I! When that outfit heard we were on the way, he and the others burned most of what was of value and scattered."

Diego said, "Do you think they retreated to California?"

"Probably. There is certainly no safe place for them here. If we catch them, those we do not shoot, we will imprison. Dirty Yankees!" the officer expounded.

"I don't suppose there is any reason for me to remain here," observed Diego. "Thank you for your time."

"If you kin' find him and his family, tell him we got a nice ol' prison cell for all of 'em!" the officer laughed.

"Capitán McCoy had family here?" asked Diego. "I did not know that."

"McCoy, his wife, and that daughter of his. Pretty, but uppity, if you know what I mean," snickered the officer.

"I did not know his family," said Diego. "I may as well go home."

"Where's home?" asked the officer, briefly showing a little interest.

"Sonora," answered Diego. "I'd best be heading home to my family."

Don Diego DaVia turned and left, but not quick enough to miss seeing the officer spit his tobacco juice right on the floor of what was once a militarily neat and tidy office. Once outside, he made his way to the livery stable to fetch Hiero. Wherever he was to go, he knew he had to do it right then. Stopping only to replenish his supplies, and once mounted on Hiero, he made sure he headed out of Tucson by the most populated route. He wanted to mix his horse's tracks with the hundreds already on the roadway. He was a few miles west of Tucson when he veered from the established trail. He moved into the creosote and chaparral and waited to see if he was being followed. After half an hour, he was convinced that the Confederate officer was, as he had seemed, too stupid to know he should have had more interest in Don Diego DaVia. No one was following, so he brushed his tracks where he left the roadway and proceeded to a point a few miles southwest of where he had left the road. There he set his course to ride parallel to the roadway going west toward California.

As he rode, he began to realize that Doña Monica Ruiz, even if she were in Tucson, was becoming less and less of a threat. She would get nowhere with these low-life soldiers and undercover outlaws calling themselves a government. They were not even decent soldiers. If she were lucky, she would make her way back to Cananea. If she found out about her brother, Raoul, so be it. After all, Diego did not know for sure what had happened to Raoul. Segundo would have to handle whatever that pair would do. If they tried something, with Segundo's current frame of mind . . . ! Diego smiled. That would be something to see.

But, for now, Captain McCoy and his family were of concern to Diego. He did not reason why he should be concerned, but the look on the Confederate officer's face, coupled with his whole attitude, made him worry as to the fate of Captain McCoy. After a while on the parallel trail, Diego could not help but wonder, *Here I am again, alone in the middle of the desert, riding toward something that is probably none of my damn business.*

Evidently, the Union garrison had pulled out of Tucson possibly a week or so earlier, but the comments of that riffraff officer had Diego wondering. The proprietor of the livery stable had told Diego that the Union garrison, at least some of them, may have simply gone into the hills. He also wondered if maybe most had indeed gone to California. Whatever they had done, it was dangerous. Even those who stayed in Tucson were afraid of what might happen. The reason was the Apache. With the Union military pulled out, and the overland mail no longer functioning because of the Confederate takeover in the New Mexico Territory, the Apache had free rein. Folks were plainly terrified.

Diego's thoughts wandered over all those possibilities, and probably even some more; but, when night began to fall, he needed a place to camp. As he had done many times before, when events seemed to require it, he made a cold camp. Even with no campfire, his thoughts went deep. The comment about Captain McCoy and his family weighed greatly upon him. This was a nasty place to have to bring a family anyway, but to have to do it in haste, driven by a riffraff military, seemed unimaginable.

—◆—

Daylight saw Don Diego DaVia riding southwest, paralleling the primitive roadway that evacuating personnel would have taken to California. That roadway, if a party were not well supplied, especially with water, would turn into a trail of death. It was mid-morning when Diego came upon a trail that seemed to wander, sometimes to the left, then to the right, evidently striving to keep a westerly path. The tracks seemed to indicate a party of six to eight individuals. One horse was dragging a two-pole travois, probably carrying a wounded or very weak individual. The horses were shod, so probably not Indian ponies. The tracks were at the least a few days old. Diego began to feel that this could be Captain Mc-Coy's party. Assessing the condition of the party from the tracks, Diego believed he could catch them within a couple of days. He turned Hiero into their trail and began to follow it.

The first day following that trail saw Diego making good time. Any effort to cover their tracks had ended some time back. Diego began to wonder if they had provisions, or even water. The horses were not even leaving droppings. Diego picked up the pace, fearing that he could even be too late.

———

Late in the second day, about twilight, Diego saw a very faint hint of a fire light. It was after dark when Diego DaVia quietly hailed the camp. "Hello in the camp! I am alone and a friend. May I enter your camp?"

A very weak yet authoritative voice replied, "Identify yourself. You are covered."

"Capitán McCoy, I am Diego DaVia of la Rancheria Fantasma," answered Diego.

"I could not ask to receive a greater friend! Please enter," answered Captain McCoy, greatly relieved.

"It is good to see you, Capitán McCoy. I have many questions. Obviously, your party needs water. Let us see to that and talk later," said Diego.

It turned out that the McCoy party needed not only water, but food. They were on extremely limited rations. The party consisted of Captain McCoy, Mrs. McCoy, a grown daughter—Constance—two sergeants, and a Yaqui scout. As good a scout as was the Yaqui, game killed with a bow in that desert can be very scarce. In the case of the McCoy party, it was almost nonexistent. The extra supplies carried in Diego's saddlebags raised spirits considerably. The water was most well received.

Later, after all had bedded down except Diego, Captain McCoy, and the Yaqui, Diego asked, "What happened, Capitán?"

"Some time back, I forget exactly, we began receiving dispatches indicating that the Gadsden Purchase area was probably undefendable against the Confederates . . . Texans . . . advancing toward us. People began to panic and tried to escape. Quite a few made it, I suppose. I don't know for sure. Communications were abruptly severed. My scouts came in saying they were almost on us, in large numbers. We grabbed what we could, burned materiel they could use, and left," said Captain McCoy.

"Where is everyone else?" asked Diego. "Your garrison must be nearby. Did they not evacuate with you?"

"Yes. A few miles out of Tucson, I ordered my subordinates to continue west, try to get our cavalry to California. I would remain in the area, with a small patrol, to verify what happened and see if we would be pursued. My wife and daughter remained behind with me. After the first night, the patrol left us to fend for ourselves. I have seen none of them since. My two sergeants and our Yaqui scout faithfully stayed behind for us. They have done their duty and then some for us. It has been extremely difficult, but they have saved our lives," Captain McCoy explained.

"How long have you been out here in this desert?" asked Diego.

"I really do not know for sure. I had been keeping a journal, but . . . I do not know," he stumbled with his words.

"What do you plan to do?" Diego asked quietly.

"I do not even know for sure where we are, much less where we are going, or if we can even survive," admitted Captain McCoy.

"Well, I do!" said Diego DaVia. "We will rest here tonight. Tomorrow we will head southeast to la Rancheria Fantasma. After a few days, we will reach the Rio Santa Cruz. There we will find water and some game. Get some sleep now. You must act strong for your family tomorrow."

With that, both men rolled out their blankets.

24

The next morning, Diego DaVia, while packing up to break camp, paid some attention to the members of the group. Captain McCoy was older than Diego had first thought. He seemed to be in his early fifties. He had been thinking of retirement when events changed his plans so drastically. Mrs. McCoy was probably not much younger than her husband. So far, she had not said much. She was likely in a mild form of shock due to her hardship. The daughter, Constance, looked to be about twenty-five, maybe even twenty-seven. Diego had a hard time keeping his eyes off her.

Considering the hardship she had suffered, Constance certainly was a handsome young woman. She stood an inch or so less than Diego. She had a delicate, slightly tanned face. She was quick to smile just by being noticed. Constance had discarded some of the petticoats deemed necessary by fashion but unsuitable and without pity for travel in the desert, especially under those conditions. Diego was impressed by the firm, rounded female body, even then only partially exposed. But her hair—long, lightly waved, and brilliantly blonde—kept drawing his eye. Constance was quite a beautiful young woman. But "Vamonos!" Diego ordered.

The sergeants, Riley and Fant, dutifully fell in behind. The Yaqui scout, Ansaro, took his position a few hundred yards ahead of the others. Diego had given him orders as to what direction to lead the party. Ansaro indicated he knew what was wanted of him. Earlier that morning, Ansaro spoke to Diego about a mission along the way toward la Rancheria Fantasma. It was closer to Tucson than Diego would have ventured. Ansaro said they could resupply and rest without notice; the friars would see to that. That seemed a good idea. Ansaro had said that he was honored to be riding with Dead Man Who Walks Away.

For Diego DaVia, this exercise had a pleasant twist. He had been stealing furtive glances at Constance, and, each time, she met his glance with her own embarrassed glance and that infectious smile. The miles were long, but Diego did not mind that long trip. He was somewhat disappointed to see the Mission de San Xavier del Bac come into view.

— —

Ansaro had known that the Confederate riffraff calling themselves soldiers were not about to be seen in a Spanish Catholic mission for the Indians—the Yaqui Indians. Ansaro was right. The McCoy party was well-cared for. They spent two days at the mission, but the third day found them again travelling south and east toward la Rancheria Fantasma. Diego could not help but think how things had changed. He had rushed to Tucson to confront and deter la Doña Monica Ruiz from ruining la Rancheria Fantasma. He never saw Doña Monica, but here he was riding home with a beautiful, blonde, young woman instead.

— —

With replenished supplies and fresh water, the McCoy party made good time. Four more days and three nights of making eyes with Constance found them entering the northern meadow of la Rancheria Fantasma. The Vaqueros made a grand welcome riding in circles around the waving, happy McCoys. One of the perimeter scouts had seen them coming for miles and sent word to Segundo. When the party dismounted in front of the hacienda, Segundo and Socorra greeted them warmly. Then they were all led to their quarters, and then to the food and the inevitable fiesta.

During the refreshments and the incredible meal served to them, Diego and Captain McCoy related the story of the takeover of Tucson by Confederate irregulars and the resulting march into, and rescue from, the desert. Then Segundo relayed his side of the past couple of weeks. "The Yaqui courier service informed us right after you left, Diego, about the takeover of Tucson. It was too late to stop your trip. It would have been a wild goose chase anyway, because my sister never made it to Tucson."

"What happened?" asked Diego.

"Wait, Diego. I must explain to these lovely people how this all came about, or they will think we are barbarians, or worse," said Segundo, laughing. Thus, Don Francisco Ruiz related the tale of Monica and Raoul, Diego, himself, Socorra, the attack and fight on the border, and the expected punishment of Raoul. Socorra had been watching Constance throughout the whole evening. With a look that only a woman could have given to another, Socorra let Constance know that, as bad as it sounded, these men were the best in the land . . . whatever this land was now. With Constance now reassured, Diego said again, "Well! What happened?"

Segundo continued. "Evidently, Monica and some pistoleros rode off toward Tucson. They did not get far. They were attacked and captured by Apaches . . . real Apaches. We do not know for sure exactly what happened, but the pistoleros have not been seen since. It also is not perfectly clear what happened to Monica, but she was sold, naked, to some Yaquis . . . our Yaquis. She was brought to the Yaqui village where Raoul was. They both were made to believe they were in the hands of Apaches."

At this point, Socorra leapt into the story. "Thank God my father was the one who arranged this farce. He was there to prevent any real violence, and he did."

Segundo continued. "Raoul had been given little rest in that village. He had been kept naked and chased around by the women of the village, all the while making believe they were Apaches. Once Monica arrived, naked, Socorra's father figured that it was time to get out of this. So, Monica was given the barest essential clothing. She was then tied onto a horse, facing forward, while Raoul was tied, naked, onto the same horse, facing backward."

Diego DaVia and Captain McCoy were both nearly rolling on the floor laughing by then. The McCoy women were doing their best not to join them. Socorra put some sense of justice into the story by closing it out with, "They were then delivered into the town of Cananea and into the waiting stockade of Major Sanchez. The major has by now sent them off to Mexico City on charges of trying to incite an international incident."

That did it. The men were now on the floor. The women were still seated but laughing uproariously! Yet, during the laughter, Socorra noticed that Constance never took her eyes from Diego DaVia.

After all the hardship suffered by the McCoy party, a deservedly good night's sleep was in order. But, after their guests had retired to their quarters, Diego and Segundo remained to discuss the matter of la Rancheria Fantasma. What was going to happen next? To whom were they going to sell their horses?

"I tell you, Segundo, I certainly do not want to deal with those Confederate irregulars in Tucson. Those men are no more than outlaws," said Diego, sounding very irritated.

"The Union cavalry has pulled back into California . . . too far for us to deliver. Who is left for us? The Mexicans are always in need of horses," offered Segundo.

"Which Mexicans?" asked Diego. "The French have invaded, and the Mexican army is trying to fight them. We must stay the course and sell a limited supply to whomever has the gold."

"But not to the Confederates in Tucson," reiterated Segundo.

"You are right, Segundo. Not to them," agreed Diego. "Until there is a victor in that war in Mexico, there will be a market for our horses. After the war is ended, rebel armies will spring up all over the place. We will be extremely busy."

"We must increase our efforts to keep a herd sizeable enough to satisfy all these buyers," announced Segundo sarcastically.

"Then there is always the Apache," said Diego.

"Always," agreed Segundo. "But put first things, first. What about that golden-haired Constance?"

"What about her?" came Diego's reply.

"Well, let me see. She is beautiful, young, but not too young," said Segundo. "What are you going to do about Constance McCoy?"

"I am going to enjoy her company until she wishes to leave," answered Diego without meeting Segundo's gaze.

"Her father, mother, and those two sergeants are going to head for California sometime," said Segundo. "Are you going to escort them? Do you think she will stay here with you?"

Diego DaVia had been thinking all manner of things concerning Constance. But now Segundo's good-natured questioning was beginning to irritate him. He did not have any good answers. But he could not be angry with his friend. So, Diego DaVia, this strong Dead Man Who Walks Away, quietly said, "Buenas noches." He then went to bed, only to toss and turn over that question most of the night.

———

Diego awoke from a fitful sleep. His breakfast was made worthwhile though by the lovely female company awaiting him. Mrs. McCoy, of course, and her husband, Captain McCoy, were already finishing when Diego joined them. Segundo, Socorra, and Constance McCoy had decided to wait to eat with Diego. "Please accept my apology for sleeping in," said Diego.

"You earned every minute of it," said Captain McCoy. "You performed a soldier's job rescuing us and escorting us safely here. I am most grateful to you."

With the fleetest of glances at Constance, Diego replied, "It was my great pleasure to be able to accomplish that."

Captain McCoy had, from the moment his party arrived at la Rancheria Fantasma, been taking in every detail. "I am most impressed!" he exclaimed. "I had heard many tales concerning your horses and your rancheria, and I had certainly seen your Vaqueros at their best; but I had no idea of anything like this." As he said that he could not help sweeping his arm out to accentuate his feeling of its magnitude. "Unbelievable! I must admit that I had thought it to be something of a large horse farm."

"I suppose it is," said Segundo. "But, if not for Don Diego, it would not even exist."

"But I know that you both are owners," said Captain McCoy.

"Yes, but that all came about due to very strange circumstances," began Segundo.

Don Diego interrupted. "That's dry business talk. Talk of the beauty of this San Rafael Valley."

"Let's do!" said Constance. "From where I am now sitting, I am looking at a huge valley of waving grass, rolling hills, the beginning of a river, and many, many horses grazing as far as I can see. All that is surrounded by beautiful mountains! I am amazed."

At that point Socorra spoke up. "Do not let these men fool you with their 'it is merely a peaceful horse operation' talk. They have had to fight just about everyone in this part of the world to acquire it and then to keep it."

Socorra's comments broke the ice concerning la Rancheria Fantasma. Socorra was determined to have her say regarding the history of la rancheria and of the courage and dedication of these two dons in making it happen. Socorra had enormous pride in Segundo, her father, and the Vaqueros. But, when she began to tell of whatever she knew of Don Diego, he raised his hand toward her and asked that she not speak any more of it.

"I would rather give our guests a tour of la Rancheria Fantasma and let la rancheria take their minds off the ordeal that they have survived," he said. However subtle was his manner in interrupting the direction of that conversation, his message was clear. It was certainly noted by Constance. Socorra also noticed the understanding in the eyes of Constance. As they walked around the area close to the hacienda and the various outbuildings close in, Socorra was also aware of Constance always being in close proximity to Diego. Now and then, because of this, a small smile came to her face.

After an hour of such inspection, the group began a slow ride, away from the buildings and out onto the huge, grassy expanse of the San Rafael Valley. The talk continued upon the horse operation but began to center on the need to protect la rancheria, and the whole San Rafael Valley for that matter, from enemies.

"What enemies? This place is so remote from any civilization, and so large, how and why would anyone attack you?" questioned the McCoy women.

Captain McCoy tried to answer. "From a military standpoint, I can see that your remoteness here is only one of many reasons for an enemy to try to take it over."

"I find that hard to believe!" exclaimed Constance.

The men did not wish to immediately respond to that, primarily because Constance and her mother had not been in the Southwest for but a short time. Once again, Socorra intervened to help the situation. "You see, Constance, this land is considered very valuable not only for raising horses, but its location makes it militarily worth controlling."

Don Diego and Don Segundo glanced at each other with eyebrows raised. Evidently Socorra had been paying more attention to la Rancheria Fantasma than they had thought. They both now would take more interest in her comments to Constance.

"The San Rafael Valley, la Rancheria Fantasma, is isolated, nearly surrounded by mountains. Yet, the southern portion of the valley crosses the border into Mexico. If any of the warring factions in the United States, Confederate states, or Mexico wished to do something drastic on either side of the border, it could easily be done from here," explained Socorra.

At this point, Don Diego thought it best to take control of the conversation. It had reached an area of concern that might leave their guests uneasy. Therefore, Diego casually said, "It is for many reasons that we have created a force of Vaqueros to care for our horses, yet also to become the best military unit in the Southwestern deserts. We have chosen to become a society unto ourselves. We have the ability to protect ourselves, all of our people here, and what is ours."

"How can you accomplish this?" asked Captain McCoy, who had been listening closely in silence. "Who are your enemies, and how can you anticipate their actions from this remote location?"

Don Diego replied, "I will tell you, but do not allow yourselves to become alarmed. We have controlled this San Rafael Valley for a long time now. Our enemies have been, at various times, the North Americans, the Mexicans . . . whatever government was in charge, the constant revolutionary forces at various times in Mexico, and, of course, the Apache. We have managed to handle each faction so far without excessive violence. Recently, well-vested individuals tried to attack us in force, but we routed them before they could cross into la Rancheria Fantasma. But it is only the Apache that are unpredictable."

Captain McCoy spoke again. "Don Diego, what about the non-battle of Tucson, as you called it?"

A barely detectable smile came to Don Diego as he replied, "That was a fortunate show of force put on by our Vaqueros."

"Well, it was certainly fortunate for Tucson!" exclaimed Captain McCoy.

"Yes, a battle in which no one was injured. I am sure that embarrassing subject has come up often around the campfires and wikiups of the Apache!" said Don Diego, chuckling.

The sweet voice of Constance was heard then. "I heard that the victory had more to do with someone the Apache called Dead Man Who Walks Away."

It was then that Constance and Socorra both noticed the iron eyes of Dead Man Who Walks Away. Then the look passed, and Diego said, "Who knows what makes the Apache do anything? It is late. We should rest before the evening meal. We should start back to the hacienda. I know the ladies of la Rancheria Fantasma are looking forward to fixing a real Vaquero supper for you. Vamonos!"

The ladies of la Rancheria Fantasma did not disappoint. They set forth a feast of the finest Sonoran style cuisine. Captain McCoy had been stationed in Tucson for quite a while, but Mrs. McCoy and the lovely Constance had been in the Southwest only a short time. They had not been exposed to the pleasures of Sonoran style cooking. They simply could not get enough. The Vaquero ladies were extremely pleased to see their work so enjoyed.

Later, on the ramada-styled porch of the hacienda, the talk turned to the possibility of the McCoys continuing to California.

"Capitán McCoy, I know that your position as capitán of the U.S. garrison at Tucson will not permit you to remain here for very long," stated Don Diego.

Captain McCoy was quick to clarify. "Unfortunately, Don Diego, my garrison has been rather forcibly replaced by Confederate forces. They are a ragtag bunch but have still taken over. I am afraid, until this rebellion is over, I must do my fighting from whatever units are in California."

"I understand that all too well, Capitán. And I understand your urgency to report to your unit and retake command. However, I am reluctant to see your wife and daughter subjected to resuming the journey you have experienced and, luckily, survived," said Diego.

"There was no luck involved. Had you not intervened, we all would be dead somewhere in the desert between Tucson and the Colorado River. I fear very much for the safety of my wife and Constance, but, as you are aware from your own military experience, I must return to carry out my orders," said the captain to Don Diego.

"Of course, Capitán, I agree. But is it necessary for your women to make that trek with you?" asked Don Diego. As he spoke, he glanced in the direction of Constance. At that point, Constance was giving Diego's words her full attention.

"What do you mean, Don Diego?" asked the captain. "I cannot just leave them."

"Hardly. However, both are welcome to remain here as our guests until the time comes when it will be safe to travel to wherever you may have to be," offered Don Diego.

"Yes. And I would love to have them both here at la Rancheria Fantasma. We'll get on famously!" exclaimed Socorra.

The captain began to offer some small disagreement but was loudly shouted down by Socorra, Constance, and, to a lesser degree, his wife. Not having the words to say without showing his emotion and relief, Captain McCoy rose to his feet and, standing at attention, delivered a most crisp salute to Don Diego. It had been a long time, but Don Diego, former capitán of dragoons, Mexican army, crisply returned that salute.

Don Diego assured, "Your wife and daughter will be under the protection of Don Ruiz, Socorra, the Vaqueros of la Rancheria Fantasma, and me personally upon my return, until it is safe for them to rejoin you, sir."

Captain McCoy did not miss the "upon my return" part of Don Diego's assurance. "What do you mean 'upon your return'?" he asked.

"I prefer to escort you and your sergeants safely to the banks of the Rio Colorado. Across the Rio Colorado you will be in California, under the control of the United States federal forces. You should be able to rejoin your command. We will be accompanied by a detachment of our own Vaqueros. There is safety in numbers . . . especially those numbers," stated Don Diego.

"But how will my family be able to rejoin me, Don Diego?" asked the worried Captain McCoy.

"I'm afraid we cannot follow the route used by Socorra and Segundo on their honeymoon trip to San Diego. You would be an American officer, unofficially in Mexico. This would never do. We must use some initiative in finding a northern route," explained Diego. "Two Vaqueros will remain with you until you are settled with your command in your new location. They will then return with that information. Then, once I am satisfied that it is safe to deliver your wife and Constance, I will do so, also with a contingent of Vaqueros. I would trust no others," instructed Don Diego. Diego saw the deep concern on the face of his guest and said, "Your wife and Constance will be delivered to you safely as soon as possible, amigo. This I swear."

"How can I ever repay you for all you have done and are doing still?" said Captain McCoy.

"'Favors are delivered back and forth between friends,' if I may quote another friend, amigo," said Diego, looking back at Segundo Ruiz.

"Then I should prepare to leave," said Captain McCoy.

"Prolonged farewells merely prolong the sadness of departure," said Diego. "You and I, with our escort, will leave tomorrow morning. Segundo, please make sure that we forget nothing."

"Your horses will be awaiting you at dawn," said Segundo.

"Don't get carried away. After breakfast will do!" said Diego, laughing.

All eyes were on the McCoy family as that discussion ended. Yet the eyes of Constance never left Don Diego.

———

The next day after breakfast, the travelers left for California. They were led by Don Diego and Captain McCoy. Captain McCoy's two sergeants and ten Rancheria Fantasma Vaqueros followed, in a column of twos. The Vaqueros were commanded by Enrique Murietta, who had reported directly to Socorra's father. The expedition presented a formidable image to anyone with mischief in mind.

Those left behind were sad to see the expedition leave, but, again, the sharp eyes of Socorra saw the tears in the eyes of Constance as she watched Don Diego ride off. Socorra smiled inwardly. She thought she understood. Yet . . .

25

Captain McCoy was on his way to rejoin his command . . . he hoped. Yet, even after the ride from la Rancheria Fantasma, he really did not understand how he would accomplish that. Don Diego thought he had a pretty good idea as to how that would work. Realistically, only Enrique Murietta knew for certain. Enrique Murietta was no stranger to this area. A very few years earlier, he had been a bandolero. He was one of the most proficient bandoleros in the area. He rode with sometimes as many as ten men, holding up and robbing stagecoaches and passengers. And then he met a girl. She had a brother. The brother beat the bandolero out of him! The brother was a Rancheria Fantasma Vaquero and helped him to become one, also. Enrique Murietta had become one of la Rancheria Fantasma's best Vaqueros. It was Enrique's plan that would be implemented to safely transfer Captain McCoy to California.

The first day of their ride was spent in almost total silence. The trail was difficult and required each man's undivided attention. It was nearly the trail rode by Don Diego and Segundo earlier to reach Tucson. This time they were trying to get some distance west of and avoiding Tucson. They were making their own trail through some very rough, rugged terrain. Yet, despite the difficulty, their first night's camp found them nearly a third of the way, according to Enrique Murietta anyway.

The hungry, tired men ate almost in silence. Eventually, Don Diego broke that silence. "What the hell! Enrique, where the hell are we going?"

"Do you not trust me, Patrón?" replied Enrique.

"Sí! I do. However, I am supposed to be in control of this hike. So, I want you to tell me what we are doing and then how we are going to do it!" demanded a somewhat exasperated Diego.

"Oh! I thought you knew!" exclaimed Enrique with the slightest bit of chuckle in his voice.

"All right! You both have my attention. You can quit fooling around. If I were any more involved, I would fall right into this campfire," said Captain McCoy. "What is going on?"

The grin no longer hidden on Diego's face, he said, "Enrique, tell us all now. What is your plan?"

"Sí, Patrón. I was seeing how long it would take before you asked me," said Enrique, with a grin as wide as all outdoors. "We are going northwest to eventually cut the trail of the old Butterfield Stagecoach Line. Ever since the Graycoats—Confederate forces—took over, there has been no stagecoach from Texas to California. People can get some personal mail only from a courier wagon operated by some locals in Tucson. They operate over the same old Butterfield Stage Line Road. We will intercept that courier stage wagon."

Captain McCoy then said, "But there could well be Confederate military on that stage!"

Enrique replied, "Sí, Capitán. The local Confederate garrison provides escort almost to the Rio Colorado as a courtesy for some Tucson residents. They get off the coach before they reach the Rio Colorado and await the return trip in camp in the desert. It is not comfortable, but they are paid well to do it. But now, that courier operating east of Tucson is well escorted by many graycoats. They must deal with the Chiricahua Apache there. But the courier west of Tucson to the Rio Colorado has only two—maybe three—guards. Not even the Apache want to do anything in that country. So, why load up on guards?" explained Enrique.

"Are we going to attack it?" asked Captain McCoy in wonder.

"Sí. Never fear. I know very well how to do that," said Enrique.

"Capitán, I must explain. Enrique was, some time ago, a bandolero—a bandito specializing in stagecoach robberies—and a quite successful one," explained Don Diego.

A wide-eyed Captain McCoy said, "Well that's reassuring! I'll sit back and listen then."

Enrique continued. "We will stop the stagecoach. If any guards defend it, they will be shot. We will change clothes to wear their uniforms if that slovenly bunch even wears them. I and some of our Vaqueros will wear those uniforms and act military. You will wear clothes that we have packed. You will look like a Mexican rancher. Travelling as such will draw less attention to you as a bonified traveler only . . . much safer than as a mounted rider. We will then proceed to the Rio Colorado at the village of Yuma. Some of our Vaqueros will ride a mile or so ahead to scout our way. Some of our Vaqueros will ride a mile or so behind to protect our rear. We may have to swim you over the river, but you will be in California after that. Once across into California we will escort you to the nearest Union army installation. Simple. No?"

"You realize that, if I am captured wearing civilian clothes, I could be shot as a spy!" stated Captain McCoy emphatically.

"Well, if that is all that is bothering you then we should get to sleep and get at it early," said Don Diego, laughing.

The men let what was left of their small fire die out and sought their blankets. Don Diego lay awake for another hour. He was thinking of the many, many things that could go wrong in that simple plan.

— - —

Three days later, Don Diego and his men crossed the old Butterfield Stage Line Road. It was not much of a road—wagon ruts mainly. It is one thing to know where a courier stagecoach operates but another to know exactly when it does it. It was possible that they might have to wait a week or more. The Fantasma riders decided that it would do no good to continue travel along the road waiting for the stagecoach. Whenever it would show up did not matter. They still needed the coach if the captain were to arrive safely at Yuma without discovery by Confederate patrols. It did not matter where they intercepted it. The riders could use some rest anyway. So, they made a small camp on a low rise, away from the roadway but out of sight of anyone on the road.

———

Two days later, their patience was rewarded. The courier stagecoach was seen on the desert road about a mile away. It was seemingly in no hurry. Two of the Fantasma Vaqueros were waiting in the roadway. One had made his horse lie down in the road. The coach could easily go around the horse and the men, but that would have required some initiative and suspicion that something threatening was about to happen. As it happened, the coachmen were more interested in taking a break anyway.

The stagecoach was manned by a driver, a guard riding shotgun next to the driver, and two riders, one on each side of the coach. These were supposed to be riding behind the coach, but the dust was too thick. Breathing in that dust was a problem. It was then that one of those little things that could go wrong, that Diego had worried about, did go wrong. There were two passengers in that coach: a man and a woman. Whatever Diego might have done about that could not have been done. One of the guards riding beside the coach recognized the uniforms of Diego's men and yelled, "Fantasma Vaqueros! Look out!" As he did so, he drew his rifle from its scabbard and aimed it at the two Vaqueros. At that point, Enrique Murietta ordered, "Fire!" Ten rifles cracked as one from the side of the road. The Confederate personnel were all dead in seconds. The two Vaqueros standing by the road did not even draw their weapons.

However, there were screams from inside the stagecoach. The man inside the coach was not hit by any bullet, but he was certainly dead. Evidently, the violence of the attack caused a fatal heart stoppage. The screaming came from a woman. She was unhurt but very vocal! She screamed until she was helped from the coach and was standing, looking at the attackers. It was then that she stopped making any kind of sound. She was looking at the Fantasma Vaqueros. She knew that Vaquero uniform. After taking a moment to catch her breath, she turned and looked into the iron eyes of Dead Man Who Walks Away. For some reason, her breath was not enough, and she fainted. Don Diego caught her before she fell to the ground and carried the unconscious Doña Monica Ruiz to some shade at the side of the road.

The Fantasma Vaqueros, at Enrique's command, began stuffing the dead men's uniforms into bags for possible further use.

"I want her bound, Sergeant! No 'ifs,' 'ands,' or 'buts' about it! Loosen her clothes to allow her to breathe better but keep her tied!" commanded Don Diego to the astonished sergeant. The sergeant had been trained all through his young life to treat women with some dignity and tenderness. This was anything but.

"I do not want this female to be loose, and I do not want her to be able to say anything! If she starts to say anything, anything at all, stuff your socks in her mouth! Do you understand?!" continued Don Diego, his eyes flashing. "You allow her any freedom at all, and you will immediately become infantry and walk to California!" Don Diego yelled.

Captain McCoy, having just witnessed men shot to death, finding a woman passenger in the stagecoach, and seeing Don Diego explode while ordering her captivity, was understandably perplexed by it all. Yet, not wishing to cause any more violent outbursts by Don Diego, McCoy quietly walked up to Don Diego and said, "There seems to be something going on here that I do not completely understand. When you calm down, perhaps you can clear this up for me."

Don Diego, still angry, turned away and paced back and forth a few times before he regained control of his demeanor. He stopped and, turning to Captain McCoy, said slowly and deliberately, trying to avoid sounding belligerent, "That woman . . . that bitch . . . is Doña Monica Ruiz . . . sister of Segundo. She is the one behind all the trouble for la Rancheria Fantasma and all of us. She should have been in Mexico," he said between clenched teeth.

"I recall," stated Captain McCoy, "that she was to be transferred to Mexico City to stand trial. She must have been released before she was even sent. How could that happen?"

"When I find out, someone may die!" swore the infuriated Don Diego.

"Who would dare to release someone like that?" asked Captain McCoy.

That question need never have been asked. Don Diego was already working on it. He paced and paced, back and forth, while the Vaqueros were making ready to get under way again.

"Who was that dead man in the coach?" asked Don Diego. Enrique Murietta was already searching the dead man's clothing and personal effects.

"Patrón, look at this," said Enrique, holding a folder containing papers. Don Diego took the folder and, together with Captain McCoy, began perusing them. Captain McCoy was very engrossed in one special paper. While Don Diego was looking at one page after another and returning them to the folder, Captain McCoy was closely scanning only one.

"Don Diego, you'll love this," said McCoy. Captain McCoy could read some Spanish but could never be as fluent as a native, Don Diego. However, he could read enough so that, when he handed the paper to Don Diego, he had a slight smirk on his face. As Don Diego read the document, he began to understand the smirk.

"How the . . . ?" began Diego, as he began reading. "This civilian is really a lieutenant in Major Sanchez's garrison. He is dressed in civilian clothes. He could have been shot as a 'spy.' This letter asks the commander of the Confederate forces in Tucson for safe passage through to California! A 'P.S.' addressed to the commander explains that this 'attractive' woman is a 'most agreeable' and 'personally accommodating' woman who could be counted upon to amply cover her fare to California . . . whatever that negotiated fare might be!"

"Interesting bit of correspondence, right, Diego?" said McCoy, again with that little smirk.

"This woman is extremely wealthy," said Diego. "But I know her better than to believe that she spent her money to get here. No, I think Major Sanchez, this lieutenant whoever he is, and the Tucson Confederate commander all were paid, in one way or another. I'm certain that we all know how she paid!"

Captain McCoy and Don Diego both turned to look at the stagecoach as Doña Monica was being loaded inside. Enrique Murietta was standing beside the coach door. Noting the looks by Captain McCoy and Don Diego, Enrique strongly asserted, "Do not even think it! If I touch this witch, it will be with my knife to slit her throat!"

At that assertion by Enrique Murietta, Doña Monica's eyes snapped open wide. It was a good thing that she was unable to speak past the old sock that was stuffed into her mouth.

The caravan then moved on . . . west.

The weather along the western part of what was then the territory of New Mexico, along the Rio Colorado, had been terrible for months. Weeks of rain had pummeled the entire West Coast from Alaska to Mexico and had caused extreme flooding of all waterways in that part of the country. That flooding played a large part in delaying the United States Cavalry in California from entering the Confederate-held part of that region. The "California column," as it was called, was then, finally, across the previously flooded Rio Colorado, intent on defeating the Confederates or, at the least, driving them back into Texas. That eastbound column of Regulars had met no resistance at all until they met the westbound Fantasma Vaqueros. The Fantasma Vaqueros, as ordered, formed up into a line, which crossed the road in front of the stagecoach, and halted. The U.S. Cavalry, seeing the very military presence of the Vaqueros, formed up in a line facing the Fantasma Vaqueros. For a tense long moment, the two units measured the merit of the other. Captain McCoy then intervened, shouting, "We are not Confederates! I am Captain McCoy, commander of the United States garrison of Tucson!"

The column of cavalry, once stopped, took advantage of the opportunity to rest themselves and their mounts. Captain McCoy took that opportunity to introduce himself, his rank, and his former position as the U.S. commander of Tucson. He was able then to change into his military uniform. He was again fully military. With this fortunate change in plans, Captain McCoy and the Fantasma Vaqueros joined the California column and proceeded back to Tucson. The Confederate forces in Tucson, having been made aware of the advancing U.S. cavalry, had been making a hasty forced march in retreat to escape across the territory of New Mexico toward Texas.

However, the matter of Doña Monica Ruiz still had to be administered in some way.

26

It had been another two days of travel in intense heat when the California column slowly entered the city of Tucson. The local citizens were not overjoyed to see them but did not offer resistance. They had been supporters of the Confederates over some preconceived sense of injustice, or over the fact that most were from Texas anyhow. However, having seen their Texan Confederates taking flight, rather than fight the unwinnable battle, these citizens did not cause any real trouble.

Part of the California column consisted of men from Captain McCoy's original garrison. He was, understandably, very selective in choosing which of his former command would stay to occupy Tucson or continue with the column further into the territory of New Mexico pursuing the Confederates. The Fantasma Vaquero unit, under the command of Don Diego DaVia, would leave Tucson and head directly back to la Rancheria Fantasma.

"Don Diego," began Captain McCoy, "what are your wishes for the disposition of Doña Monica Ruiz, sir?"

"It does not matter. You would not do it, anyway," replied Diego dryly.

"I am afraid that woman is your problem and must be attended to within your jurisdiction," said Captain McCoy. "I hate to do this to you. I feel as though I am giving you a snake."

Don Diego nodded.

Captain McCoy continued. "You are providing care and comfort and friendship to my wife and Constance, and yet I can officially do nothing for you in this matter."

"I am former military and fully understand, Capitán," said Diego. "I will take her to la Rancheria Fantasma. I officially promise you that I will not kill her, torture her, or molest her. But I unofficially promise you that this woman will never cause either of us further trouble."

"Don Diego, if any other man made such a promise to me, I would be terrified for this woman. However, I know you as a gentleman and an officer and know that you will justify my high opinion of you in this matter," said Captain McCoy. "Now, in the matter of my family, currently enjoying your hospitality at la Rancheria Fantasma, how and when can they be returned to me?"

"I have given that question much thought," said Diego. "As you may have noticed, I have been quite taken by Constance. I would prefer to continue her visit at Rancheria Fantasma while I can also be there."

"I have noticed that interest and honor you for it. I know that, for as long as she is in your care, she will come to no harm or discomfort," said Captain McCoy.

"Then, in that regard, realizing that it will be some time before you are actually secure from difficulty at this post," offered Don Diego, "she is welcome to stay until all are in agreement that she and your wife can safely be reunited with you here in Tucson."

"Although I miss them both terribly, thank you, Don Diego, for relieving me of a great burden at this time," agreed Captain McCoy.

"In that case, Capitán, my Vaqueros and I—and, unfortunately, my problem—will make ready to leave for Rancheria Fantasma without delay," said Don Diego.

"Good luck. Have a safe trip. Convey my love to both my ladies," said Captain McCoy.

"We will keep in touch by courier regarding the well-being of your ladies and the time of their eventual return to you. I promise," said Don Diego. "Vaqueros! That ugly coach is now ours. Secure that woman in it, and I mean secure. When you have done that . . . vamonos!"

Then, Don Diego DaVia, sitting straight in the saddle astride Hiero, with the small band of Vaqueros and their unwilling passenger, moved south.

During the long, hard ride over albeit now familiar trails, Don Diego DaVia had plenty of time to mull over the situation concerning the disposition of Doña Monica Ruiz. He remembered vividly the evening he had spent with her in the shadows of the pines at the edge of Meadow Valley, near the hacienda at la Rancheria Fantasma. He remembered her warm softness as their attraction moved toward the inevitable climax of their sexual encounter. He had known that she was baiting him, trying to wrest a way for her to gain her ambitions concerning la Rancheria Fantasma. He remembered her tantrums every time it became obvious to her that her attempts to turn Diego against Segundo were not taken seriously . . . at all! Oh, Diego certainly remembered his own pleasure while enjoying the warm sensations of her very lovely body. Unfortunately, Diego also remembered the vitriolic explosion when she realized that everyone knew her scheme and was impervious to it. Diego remembered her attempt, along with her useless brother Raoul, to attack and take by force what he and Segundo had worked so long and hard to create—la Rancheria Fantasma. All else he could forgive as the acts of a spoiled and vindictive female . . . all else but that act. The memory of that attempt to attack la Rancheria Fantasma promoted all manner of punishments for her. As he conjured up these horrible punishments for her, a smile would sometimes show itself. But, after a time, he was brought back to reality by remembering the words of Don Miguel Peralta concerning another female: "We are not barbarians!"

Well, at least those thoughts helped Diego pass the time.

Meadow Valley, at the very northern end of his San Rafael Valley, had come into view from one of the last hillsides on the trail when Don Diego DaVia pulled Hiero to a halt. He sat in the saddle for a moment, deep in thought. It had taken his entire five-day ride to see it. But he knew now how to handle the problem of Doña Monica Ruiz. He uttered a little laugh out loud as he started Hiero down the last remaining trail to la Rancheria Fantasma—home.

"Segundo! Hermano mio!" shouted Diego as Don Francisco Ruiz leapt from the long porch of the hacienda.

"Welcome, Diego!" shouted Segundo as he collided with Diego, who was trying to dismount.

Mrs. McCoy, who had been terribly worried about her husband, saw immediately the smiles and laughter of Don Diego and all the Vaqueros and knew that the trip had been successful. Captain McCoy surely was well.

Socorra was simply all over Diego, with Segundo, trying to embrace him. She was obviously sharing in the happiness and relief of her husband that his friend and partner had returned home safely.

Don Diego DaVia basked in this outpouring of welcome for a moment before letting his eyes search for someone else. Then he saw her. Constance McCoy was standing on the long porch of the hacienda, almost unnoticeably shaking with emotion, tears running down her cheeks. Don Diego DaVia slowly walked to her. As he neared the porch, Constance fell forward into his waiting arms. Diego, holding her tightly, kissed her. And Constance kissed him back! For a moment, the happy revelers in the yard became quiet, then broke into a volley of cheers at the happiness of the couple.

"You thought changes were coming another time you went away!" remembered Segundo.

Socorra added, "And this time, again, we all knew but you! Ha!"

It was some time before the joyous ones had settled down. Diego and Constance had not had a chance to even speak to each other, yet without words were still clinging to each other. At last, Diego found the words to speak. "Once again, there is much to be discussed. I knew I would be happy to be home, but I had no idea that I would be as happy as I now am. But there is more yet, Segundo. You and I have a problem. Capitán McCoy had no choice but to allow us, you and I, jurisdiction in this matter."

Looking in his direction, Don Diego shouted an order to Enrique Murietta: "Open the coach, Enrique!"

A short silence ensued, and then: "Are we bound by any limits, Diego?" yelled Segundo through clenched teeth.

Diego answered, "Only conscience, hermano mio, only conscience."

The silence was momentarily deafening. Then, from Segundo, "Enrique, select some of our Vaquero ladies to guard her, cleanse her, and make her look more human. She is to be fed and locked up until we decide what to do with her. Place guards to secure this arrangement."

The evening meal was served to a most happy group on the long veranda of the hacienda. Everyone at la Rancheria Fantasma seemed nearly
as happy for Don Diego and Constance as they were themselves. Even
the presence of Doña Monica, now residing within the walls of a room
secured just for her, could not dull the excitement of the occasion. Of
course, Constance and Diego arrived fashionably late, but to the applause of all present. Until that moment, nothing had been said between
Constance and Diego concerning any plans for their future. One can
only guess the conversation between them during the hour or so from the
arrival of Diego to la Rancheria Fantasma to the arrival at the dinner on
the veranda. However, as they were about to be seated, Don Diego DaVia
halted and, looking deeply into her bright-blue eyes, said, "Constance,
here, in front of my dearest friends, including hermano mio, my brother,
Segundo, I ask you to share my life and my love, and to be my wife."

One would have thought an explosion had occurred there on the
veranda! All were on their feet and cheering loudly!

"Wait! Wait! Por favor . . . please!" exclaimed Diego. "Constance has
yet to answer!" Turning again to the lovely, about to be tear-stained face
of Constance, Diego said to her, "Will you?"

"You know very well I will!" came the reply.

Then the explosion really happened. Those Vaqueros who happened
to be near the hacienda knew without any doubt what had occurred. It
seemed the entire Rancheria Fantasma knew, and the noise was deafening! The fact that Constance and Diego were then locked in a long
embrace certainly was convincing of that fact. All knew that another
marriage was about to happen on la Rancheria Fantasma.

However, it might not happen for a while. No doubt, the bride
and her prospective groom would have liked the wedding immediately.
Mrs. McCoy, due to her strict upbringing—and perhaps something
else—would have none of that. A proper waiting period—proper being
a few months—would be necessary. Constance argued loudly with her
mother over this. Diego could do nothing but act politely, roll his eyes
a bit perhaps, but, though inwardly angry, he managed to remain calm
through that whole ordeal. Diego agreed to the delay in order to have
Captain McCoy at the wedding; this was most important to all. For a

brief moment, noting the look on the face of Mrs. McCoy, Socorra felt some concern that something was shadowing the plans. That moment passed, and she shared in the joy of the celebration.

———

There were some good times during that waiting period. Constance and Diego were often gone from the hacienda taking frequent—very frequent—rides to the outlying areas of la Rancheria Fantasma. Those rides were never close to the hacienda, where prying eyes would be watching every action on their part. No, these two lovers were looking for seclusion. When they went riding, they always found that seclusion. Constance thought that Diego must have been a master at deception. It was much simpler than that. Diego had left stern orders that he and Constance were not to be disturbed at any time.

It was at those times that the wishes of Mrs. McCoy, and any other protocols concerning the lovers, were disregarded. Constance began wearing soft clothing containing very few buttons. That soft clothing became easily accessible and removable to provide Diego unrestricted access to the beautiful female body beneath. Diego certainly appreciated and took full advantage of that. Constance had the idea that no one knew what was happening. But Socorra knew and smiled often as she watched them come and go. Segundo knew. He also knew better than to say anything but would give Diego a subtle pat on the back upon their return to the hacienda. To be sure, every Vaquero and lady Vaquero knew and shared their secret. Diego always had been respected, but now they rejoiced in his happiness with the lovely Constance. The days went by, slowly for the couple, but rapidly for the rest of la Rancheria Fantasma.

There was one person at la Rancheria Fantasma who enjoyed none of it. La Doña Monica Ruiz was spending every waking hour hating everyone at la rancheria, including the new lovers and Segundo and Socorra. She made no pretense about it. She was under guard whenever she was allowed to leave her quarters. She was locked in those quarters whenever she was not performing chores assigned to her around la rancheria. Her hatred dominated all her thoughts.

The upcoming wedding had delayed any effort on the part of Diego and Segundo to develop a humane way of ending the problem Doña Monica presented. No matter what she had done, neither wanted to kill her. Somehow, she must be returned to Mexico to answer for her actions. If that happened, she would spend a long time in prison. This alone would be a very harsh punishment for her. Life in prison was not pleasant for women. Yet Diego and Segundo could see no other way to handle the matter. Realizing that Doña Monica had in all probability pleasured her way out of the control of Major Sanchez, Don Diego and Don Segundo both were looking forward to having words with him. They did not blame Major Sanchez for enjoying some pleasure, but they certainly blamed him for allowing that to gain Monica's freedom.

———

It had been quite a while since any real trouble had occurred near the San Rafael Valley. The Rancheria Fantasma Vaqueros were enjoying the lull in crises as much as anyone. The McCoy women were thoroughly enjoying the beauty and serenity of that wonderful valley. The wedding plans were being made, and everyone was looking forward to that great day.

Socorra and Constance had—it would seem—become fast friends and were spending much time with each other. Segundo and Diego joked about how they needed an appointment to interrupt the ladies' activities. "Who the hell is getting married around here anyway?" exclaimed Diego often, echoing the sentiments of Segundo. However, all five would manage to get together for lunch on the veranda of the hacienda. The talk was generally centered on the wedding plans. At one such luncheon, a cry of alert rang out that one of the Vaqueros was escorting someone through the pasture north of the hacienda. As they neared, Don Diego made out the uniform of a Union cavalryman.

"This soldado has a dispatch for the McCoys," announced the Vaquero. The soldado was, in fact, a lieutenant of cavalry.

Don Diego, sensing immediately what this visit by the Union lieutenant could be, stepped forward.

The exhausted lieutenant snapped to and was about to announce for whom the dispatch papers were intended when Don Diego interrupted.

"I will take those dispatches, Lieutenant. Stand at ease until I peruse them." The lieutenant, even though Don Diego was not in any kind of military uniform but had given him the order as if he were in command, handed the pouch to Don Diego.

Don Diego, after reading the short message, looked at the exhausted lieutenant and said, "Thank you, Lieutenant. I understand these orders and relieve you of your most unpleasant assignment." He then said to Pancho, who had just strolled by, "Take the lieutenant to guest quarters, allow him to refresh himself, and be sure he comes back here for some refreshment."

As the lieutenant was leaving, Diego said softly to Socorra and Segundo, "Please stay with me now. I will require your support."

He then turned toward Mrs. McCoy and Constance. As they looked at him with apprehension, Diego said, "I will skip the introductory words on this letter and will read to you the message only." With that said, Diego read, "As commander of the United States Cavalry column, headquartered at Tucson, New Mexico Territory, I regrettably must convey the following message: 'On or about fifteen June 1862, Captain Samuel McCoy, while accompanying units of the California cavalry column in pursuit of Confederate forces trying to escape to El Paso, was killed in ambush by Apache tribesmen at a place called Apache Pass. Captain McCoy was buried in the field with full military honors. He will be sorely missed. Yours, Sincerely, etc., etc., etc.'"

Socorra grasped the fainting Mrs. McCoy and guided her to a comfortable chair as Diego caught Constance as her knees were giving way. Constance and her mother were then taken by Socorra and some lady Vaqueros to their rooms. Segundo and Diego, after the first shock and unsuccessfully trying to comfort Mrs. McCoy and Constance, returned to the veranda. "The rest of the communication related the details," Diego said, "Evidently the column entered Apache Pass, near the Apache Springs, and was ambushed by a large force of Apaches. The Apaches were surprisingly dug in on both grassy hillsides. The Apaches had the upper hand until the cavalry began unloading cannon fire into the hillsides."

"That is something new . . . and frightening," said Segundo.

"It certainly is," agreed Diego. "What does this indicate to you?"

Segundo said, "The Apache have changed. They attacked a large military force . . . unafraid. They are becoming much bolder."

"Anything else?" asked Diego.

"What else?" asked Segundo.

"The Apache were dug in. This was not the old style of 'attack from the bushes and run' operation. They have learned a bit under this Cochise. And you are right, Segundo. They have become much bolder," said Diego. "I will be busy for a while with Constance and her mother," he continued. "Gather the Vaqueros together. Tell them what happened . . . all of it. I do not want them to run into any surprises. Bring the horses in closer and double the perimeter guard."

"It will be done," said Segundo. "Diego, I never knew Capitán McCoy's name was 'Samuel.'"

"Neither did I," said Diego. "No one ever spoke of it."

Don Diego spent many sad hours with Constance and her mother. They seemingly did not sleep for many nights. Socorra was invaluable in not only helping Constance in her own battle with grief but helping Constance with her mother also. However, Mrs. McCoy had been a military wife for many years, so that, when she was again in control of herself, she began seeing about what was necessary to be done. Constance showed her strength also.

The lieutenant had been asked to stay until decisions could be made. He had respected Captain McCoy greatly and was only too glad to stay longer at la Rancheria Fantasma for the captain's family. When the McCoys' decision came, it came swiftly. When relayed to Don Diego, he liked none of it. Mrs. McCoy had decided to return to Tucson with the lieutenant and a force of Vaqueros for protective escort. She would then be transported to San Diego, California. The part of her plan that greatly upset Diego was that she would require Constance to go with her. When they were settled in with a cousin and family, Diego could visit Constance there. Until then, the wedding must be delayed. Perhaps a wedding in San Diego could be planned.

In the presence of Constance, of course, Diego was sympathetic and supportive. When he was alone, his anger knew no bounds. The hurt and unhappiness brought to Constance and her mother was hard for him to bear without lashing out at someone. Segundo knew him well enough to know this. Socorra simply felt the emotion. However, Socorra's earlier feeling of concern now returned. Mrs. McCoy had, in her grief, made remarks relating to this remote, savage land and how she could never feel secure in the knowledge that her daughter would be living here. Socorra was very perceptive seeing the anger in Diego's iron eyes.

Yet nothing could forestall the day of departure. Constance, Mrs. McCoy, the lieutenant, and fifteen Fantasma Vaqueros hand-picked by Segundo Ruiz were mounted in front of the hacienda veranda. Constance and Diego embraced, and then, through tear-filled eyes, Diego helped her mount her horse. All having been said, Diego slapped Constance's mount, and the departing formation moved northward. Diego watched until the party disappeared into the distant mountain shadows. When his Constance could be seen no more, Diego turned and said in a growling tone to the man he called his hermano, "Apache!"

27

"Apache," said through clenched teeth and in a growling tone, was all Segundo needed to hear. "Pancho!" he ordered. "Twenty Vaqueros! All marksmen and fighters! Assemble them in the mess house in one hour." He then turned to Socorra, who still had tears in her eyes from the sadness of all that had happened. "Socorra, have the Vaquero ladies prepare jerky and other nonperishable, light food for ten days. *Ahora!* Now!"

Don Diego was already in the corral with Hiero, making sure his legs were firm and ready for the ordeal of a forced march through strange terrain. Segundo walked up to him, and the two stood in silence for a few moments while Diego gathered his thoughts. Diego looked toward his best friend, his "brother," and answered the question in Segundo's silence.

"We leave as soon as we are supplied and the Vaqueros ready," said Diego.

"Oh, they are ready! They are eager," answered Segundo.

The Yaqui nation had been under much pressure from the Mexican government and, in various places in Mexico, had been involved in a defensive war. Shooting had been reported in many areas. However, the Yaquis in that part of Sonora, just south of the border and the San Rafael Valley, were still on good terms with la Rancheria Fantasma and her Vaqueros. True . . . many Vaqueros were part Yaqui. So, it was not strange that information about the neighboring Apache bands was made available to la Rancheria Fantasma Vaqueros. The news of such Apache bands had been getting more threatening for some time. La Rancheria

Fantasma had not only to keep the unending revolutionary units from stealing horses, but now also had to be on constant alert against Apaches.

It had been many years since the Peralta massacre that resulted in the creation of the Dead Man Who Walks Away legend among the Apache. Many younger warriors either had not heard of him or simply did not give a damn. It had become apparent to Diego, and to Segundo, that the protective influence of that legend was probably wearing off. With the presence of Constance, her mother, and the promise of their wonderful wedding, Don Diego had been reluctant to handle the death of Captain McCoy in the manner that it would have required. All that now behind them, it was time to act.

The twenty Fantasma Vaqueros ready and mounted, Segundo awaited Diego. Socorra had already said her goodbye to Segundo. Her tears still made small rivulets on her lovely cheeks. When Diego DaVia strode out and off the veranda, silence prevailed. All were stunned to see him in his old dragoon cavalry uniform coat. All knew that, after all those years of trying to forget, Dead Man Who Walks Away was on his way back. Any Apache who had not heard of him, or had forgotten, would soon have that legend . . . right in his face.

Iron eyes focused straight ahead, Diego DaVia stepped up into the saddle on Hiero, the son of the big grey, and started forward. All knew then that Dead Man Who Walks Away was riding to the Apache . . . for revenge.

The Fantasma war party did not waste any time. Diego chose to take the same way he first wandered into the San Rafael Valley—through the mountain passes to the long, dry canyon and then down the Rio Babocamari. His plan was to reach the Rio San Pedro, cross that river, and hit the Apache somewhere south of the Rio Babocamari. This area was well known to be a main route of the Apache attacking in Sonora, returning to the sanctuary of the United States' side of the border. His old cavalry uniform, coupled with the uniform of the la Rancheria Fantasma Vaqueros, would clearly identify this war party.

It did.

After four days of tireless riding, the men were nearing the abandoned Babocamari village. "Diego do not be alarmed. It is Romero," said the Indian who had slowly moved his horse into the center of the very shallow rio.

"Buenas tardes, Romero," said Diego. "You remembered me. I am gratified and honored."

"Who else could you possibly be?" asked Romero. "The uniform of la Rancheria Fantasma Vaqueros is well known to us. The uniform you wear is known to me, also."

Diego said, remembering, "You are right, amigo. I was wearing it back then."

Romero then said, as he had once before, "Come to our village, eat, and rest. We will talk."

"Your invitation is most welcome, amigo," said Diego.

Diego then waved his Vaqueros to follow Romero out of the shallow Rio Babocamari and into the desert toward the Babocamari camp. They bypassed the ruins of the old Babocamari village in which Diego had tried to camp on his way many years before. The village that had welcomed him years before now offered the same again to la Rancheria Fantasma Vaqueros.

Diego, Segundo, and the Vaqueros ate a supper that guaranteed a good night's sleep. After the Vaqueros had eaten their fill of the food prepared by the women of the Babocamari village, Diego bade his Vaqueros to get some well-deserved sleep. They were sure to need all the rest they could get. After the Vaqueros had gone, Diego, Segundo, and Romero remained by the fire. Diego had been quiet for most of the meal and so chose this opportunity to speak. "Romero, you treated me well when we last met, and here we speak again. What is happening? I see in your eyes that you have something to tell."

"Sí," said Romero. "You look like a war party—ready to fight. Who is to receive all this 'attention'?"

"Apache!" answered Diego.

"Is this a private war? Did the Apache strike la Rancheria Fantasma?" Romero asked.

"In a way," spoke Diego, hesitant to recite his recent sadness. Segundo chose to answer in more detail. "Diego was to be married to a wonderful young woman. Her father was a capitán in the Union cavalry. The Apache attacked the column in what is called Apache Pass. El capitán was killed. Diego's woman and mother left to go to California. The wedding is delayed for . . . who knows how long."

Romero said, "I understand. *Lo siento,* amigo. I am sorry. Then, this is a revenge raid on the Apache?"

"It is," said Diego, his head lowered, gazing into the fire.

"We have far yet to go to reach the Apaches in the area near Apache Pass," said Segundo.

"No," said Romero. "You must return to la Rancheria Fantasma. You must leave as soon as your Vaqueros are ready in the morning."

Diego raised his head. The look in his eyes showed that he understood very well what Romero was saying.

Romero continued. "I did not see the reason before, but I believe the Apaches who passed here earlier today may be the ones you seek."

Diego and Segundo both had stood up, both fully understanding the words of Romero.

"The Apache are heading for la Rancheria Fantasma! Am I correct?" Diego stated more than asked.

Romero answered, "I thought nothing of their passing this morning, but now I believe that is so."

Diego looked at Segundo. "Give the Vaqueros four hours sleep. Then, we ride to Fantasma!"

In less than four hours, in the middle of the night, the war party of la Rancheria Fantasma was riding hard to get back to the rancheria before any tragedy could occur. Don Diego drove all unmercifully, but no one held back. Each felt the urgency. Each had loved ones at la rancheria. Each and all were getting there as fast as they could. The horses suffered most. Through cactus and thorns, creosote and chaparral, they charged.

———

Three days later, they saw smoke rising from the direction of la Rancheria Fantasma. As they neared the rancheria, they began to see horses scattered and running frightened in all directions. Then they saw the main structures of la Rancheria Fantasma. Their hearts fell as they saw the fires.

Nearly every structure was burning. Weapons drawn, they charged into the smoke and debris.

Segundo charged directly into the center of what had been the main yard, screaming out the name of his beloved: "Socorra! Socorra! Please, please answer!" The second time he made his circle, screaming her name, his lovely wife came running out of the root cellar.

"Segundo! Segundo! I am here!" she screamed.

Segundo simply flew off his horse and into her arms. Together they knelt in the dirt, holding tightly to each other, crying unashamedly.

Each Vaquero went on his own search for loved ones and friends. Some were successful. Some were not. Many Vaqueros and women had been killed. All had been fighting back at their attackers. Socorra and some of the women had gathered the children into the root cellar. To-gether, those women had fought off every attempt by the Apache to gain access. The women and children would have been a great prize to be taken back as slaves and to be traded. However, the Apache had come primarily for horses. Unfortunately, they were successful in that regard.

Don Diego DaVia remained in the saddle. Hiero was exhausted but continued to carry his rider slowly around and around the scene of de-struction. Diego was sickened by the sight. There were many Vaqueros lying dead on the ground where they had fallen and were draped over fences, wagon wheels, anything from which they had been fighting. The Apaches had carried off their dead, but there was evidence that there were a great many to carry. The Vaqueros of la Rancheria Fantasma who had stayed behind at the rancheria had, obviously, done a magnificent job of defending it and its people.

Diego had not seen anything like this since the Peralta massacre. He was sick to his stomach by the sight. He was sickened but proud of these people. How they must have fought! He dismounted and stood with Se-gundo and Socorra. He embraced them both together for many minutes. He looked into the eyes of Segundo. Through the joy of finding Socorra to be safe, and the pride he had in her, his eyes began to record the anger within him. Diego saw the same in the dark eyes of Socorra. He simply asked them, "Do we agree?"

"Yes!" loudly proclaimed Socorra. "Yes!" answered Segundo. The walking wounded who had managed to gather near them also gave Diego a resounding "Yes!"

Diego then said, "We will care for our wounded. See that la Rancheria Fantasma's loved ones and children are safe. Rest for as long as it takes to restore some semblance of order here. Then we will go hunting!"

Socorra spoke up, "They have been gone only a couple hours with a large part of our herd."

"We know how long it takes to drive a horse herd through this inhospitable country. We will catch them!" swore Diego.

"They went south, toward Mexico!" came a chorus of information.

"Yes. But they will try to reach the Chiricahua Mountains," said Diego. "Once out of our San Rafael Valley, the Apache will have to drive them east between the mountains to their north and the civilized area around Cananea to their south, and then up the Rio San Pedro."

"You know that country very well, do you not, Diego?" said Socorra. Once again, Diego realized that Socorra knew a lot more than he first thought.

"Yes. I know it better than I ever wanted to know it," he answered. "Let us see about our people now."

"Socorra," Segundo started to ask, "where is Monica?" He then added, "Where was she during the fight?"

Socorra replied, "Madre mia! She was cleaning in the cooking area. She was under guard, as usual. What happened when the Apaches attacked, I do not know."

Segundo said simply, "What is . . . is. She is my sister, but if anyone can fend for herself, it is Monica. We will care for our wounded and console our grieving people. If we find Monica, fine. If not, then not. She has pushed us so much that I no longer care."

"Pancho! Where is Pancho? Has anyone seen Pancho?" yelled Diego to anyone within earshot. "Is Pancho all right?"

"I am here, Patrón," came his very tired reply. Walking across the open area toward Don Diego was Pancho. He was bleeding slightly from a cut on one side of his head. However, he was still able to bring a small child under each arm, with another hanging on to his leg, as he walked toward them. Socorra ran to help him. As Socorra ran to help Pancho, she ordered, "Get organized. Do not just stand there! See who is hurt, dead, or able to fight with you against the Apache!"

Socorra's taking of command shocked Diego and Segundo into action. They looked at each other for a second in amazement. Then Segundo said, "See why I love her?"

"We both know very well why you love her, but today . . . this will do!" said Diego.

The inventory of la Rancheria Vaqueros and loved ones turned up some surprises, not the least of which was that, aside from the fourteen dead Vaqueros, only three of the remaining wounded were too badly injured to be able to fight. The bad news was that thirteen of the women of la rancheria were dead. No women were carried off by the Apache, none perhaps but la Doña Monica. No children were injured severely.

As much as everyone wanted, no retaliatory force would be going out that day. Perhaps, the next day. As wounds were being attended to, and the dead cleaned and cared for by loved ones, the question of Doña Monica was being asked. One person would ask another: "Have you seen what happened to la Doña Monica?" Eventually, one person, a boy about six years old, answered. "Sí. La Doña was throwing butcher knives and trying to slice the Apaches who were after her. She caused much blood. Three Apaches tied her in a blanket and rode away with her."

"She was alive when they rode away with her?" asked Segundo.

"I think so," said the boy. "There was much shooting, fire, and smoke. I could not see."

"Mañana!" sighed Diego, with Segundo echoing, "Mañana!"

28

"We will travel on water and jerky. We will leave all other food and supplies here for the care of our people. I told you valiant Vaqueros that we would be a country unto ourselves and protect ourselves and our Fantasma Vaqueros. I allowed us to be drawn away from la Rancheria Fantasma. I alone allowed this to happen; I opened Rancheria Fantasma to attack. This was my fault. But now we will be the attackers. The Apache believe that they have hurt us badly. They think we will stay home to lick our wounds. They are wrong. La Rancheria Fantasma Vaqueros will never tolerate being attacked, our loved ones hurt and killed. Never! Never! Never!" promised Don Diego DaVia to the thirty Vaqueros mounted in formation before him.

"Never! Never! Never!" voiced the Vaqueros.

Diego DaVia and Segundo wished all their Vaqueros to know exactly what they were planning to do. Diego continued. "The Apache, driving maybe two hundred of our horses, will probably try to take them to the area south and east of the Dragoon Mountains and west of the Chiricahua Mountains. They must drive them out the southeast side of our San Rafael Valley. They must drive them around the south end of the mountain range that forms the east side of our valley, then east, passing through the lowlands there. They must then turn north up the Rio San Pedro. Driving two hundred head of horses will slow their march."

Segundo continued. "La Rancheria Fantasma Vaqueros will go north and east to ride down the Rio Babocamari to the Rio San Pedro. We will then march southward to meet the Apache head on as they drive the herd north . . . straight into our guns!"

The Fantasma Vaqueros as one voice shouted, "Viva! Viva! Viva la Rancheria Fantasma Vaqueros!"

Then the thirty Fantasma Vaqueros turned, in formation, and followed Don Francisco Ruiz and Don Diego DaVia toward the north exit of la Rancheria Fantasma at a swift but easy lope.

———

The next three days held little of interest for the Fantasma Vaqueros except constant riding, at that swift lope, over mile after mile of high desert, gradually levelling out toward the Rio San Pedro. The ride down the Rio Babocamari held the possibility of ambush, but that never materialized.

A brief counsel with the Babocamari Romero merely confirmed Diego's assessment of the Apache plan. It was known by the Babocamari that the Apache had won a great victory over the Rancheria Fantasma Vaqueros and were indeed driving a large herd of stolen horses back toward their home grounds near the Chiricahua Mountains. The Rancheria Fantasma Vaqueros politely fumed over hearing that they had been defeated in the attack on la Rancheria Fantasma. But, having thanked Romero for his information and hurried hospitality, Diego DaVia and the Vaqueros resumed their march down the Rio San Pedro.

———

The fifth day of their march, the sixth day after the attack, Don Diego raised his hand to halt the formation. There had been no need to send out scouts to know they were nearing their quarry. The Vaqueros could hear the sounds of their horse herd for miles up the Rio San Pedro. The Apache were nearing the place where they would have to cross the Rio San Pedro and head east toward the southern end of the Dragoon Mountains. There was a pass there that, if the Apache were able to enter, they could probably keep the Fantasma Vaqueros from their attack.

The Apache were feeling highly confident of their success now that they were so close to their destination. They all knew their area very well.

They would shortly leave the Rio and be in the flat desert prior to entering the pass through the Dragoon Mountains.

Diego DaVia, on the other hand, had ordered skirmishers ahead as soon as the sounds of the herd and the dust of their movement were noted. The main body of Fantasma Vaqueros quickly followed. The Fantasma Vaqueros were positioned in the desert scrub and grass awaiting the arrival of the lead horses in the herd. They were scattered, hidden by the scrub trees and creosote bushes, in a half-circle. The open end of that half-circle faced the center of the horse herd. When most of the horses, and the Apaches, were within the wings of the half-circle and enveloped in the dust of the desert, Diego fired his Dragoon pistol and, waving his saber in the air, charged the leading Apache. The Apache warrior evidently had heard the legend of Dead Man Who Walks Away and, shocked motionless in fear, was killed by Diego DaVia's saber. The old cavalry uniform coat, Hiero—son of the big grey—and the uniformed Vaqueros riding hard to the charge sent most of the warriors into uncontrolled panic. Shouts of "Dead Man Who Walks Away" terrorized the warriors. They forgot their herding duties and, in terror of this Dead Man Who Walks Away, rode into each other, as well as into the accurate guns of the Vaqueros. The shouts of "Dead Man Who Walks Away" reverberated across the entire battlefield, causing increased chaos among the superstitious warriors. The warriors, trying frantically to escape the apparition of a man who should be dead—but was not—found themselves facing the gunfire of the Vaqueros. That gunfire was deadly.

The gunfire stopped. The dust began to clear. The Fantasma Vaqueros cautiously began to assess the damage to themselves and to the Apache. Diego and Segundo were slowly riding in ever widening circles to see who was alive or dead. Amazingly, no Fantasma Vaqueros were killed. Thirty Vaqueros answered when their names were called. An accurate count of the Apache dead was not made. They were scattered all over the area. The Fantasma Vaqueros had done their job.

Segundo looked over at Diego DaVia. What he saw made him hurry to Diego's side. Diego was still riding in tight little circles, his iron eyes seeing this massacre and, also, another—that awful other. Segundo saw him trembling in the saddle. He approached the trancelike Diego slowly and cautiously.

"Diego, it is over, hermano," he said.

Diego DaVia, who until that second had been, again, Cavalry Lieutenant and former Capitán of Dragoons Diego DaVia. When Segundo spoke slowly and deliberately, Diego raised his eyes to his friend and sighed. He let the breath come out of his lungs slowly until there could not be much more air in there.

"Are you again with us here, Diego?" Segundo said in a low voice.

Diego looked at his friend and nodded slowly.

"This time we have won, hermano," said Segundo.

Diego nodded. "This time."

Segundo, still not sure Diego was all right, asked him, "What shall we do next?"

Diego's eyes regained their iron. "We round up as many horses as we can, as quick as we can, and get the hell out of here! Those damn dead Apaches aren't the only ones around here."

Segundo reaffirmed, shouting, "Vamonos, Vaqueros! Get our horses and ride for home!"

Segundo need not have given that order. The Fantasma Vaqueros had already seen the need and were rounding up as many horses as they could find. Within minutes, an actual herd had begun to form. Horses that had been scattered by the gunfire and the chaos were returning, on their own, to the instinctive safety of the herd. The Vaqueros would return with a smaller herd than before, but it would have to do.

It did not matter what time of day it was. The herd was being driven home by la Rancheria Fantasma Vaqueros. The Vaqueros were all full of the excitement that follows a great battle—which they had won. However, each Vaquero was well aware of how fleeting life can be, victory or not. Not all Apaches had been killed. Many had escaped, wounded or not, to tell the tale. There was no way to tell how that news would be received by the Apache chieftains. The Apache would probably return. This herd had been important to them. They had lost it. They had suffered greatly. And it had been done by the hand of Dead Man Who Walks Away. Would their need for the horses, the humiliation of having lost the herd in battle, or the fear originating from a decision made a long time ago to allow Dead Man Who Walks Away to live unmolested dominate their thinking? The Vaqueros did not know. But they were not about to hang around to see. They were, to a man, "getting the hell out of there!"

Any retaliatory raid by the Apache would come soon after the new day, after they had time to discuss this battle in their councils. But Don Diego, Don Segundo, and the Vaqueros were not waiting to see what would happen. It had become night, but the herd was moving toward la Rancheria Fantasma. It was moving fast through the moonlight. Everyone was riding hard to keep the herd moving. It seemed that nothing would slow it down. Then one of the Fantasma Vaqueros, who had been riding in the advance, was seen riding hard toward Segundo. He reined his horse to a dust-scattering stop. He removed his hat and said, "Don Ruiz, please forgive me. I do not have the proper words to tell you!"

The Fantasma Vaquero was nervously shaking, with tears in his eyes, as he said, "We have found a woman. We think she is la Doña Monica. It grieves me to tell you this, Patrón. She is dead."

"Diego!" shouted Segundo. "Vamonos! Pronto!"

Diego was already riding toward Segundo when he saw the rider approach. He spurred Hiero and fairly shot forward.

"They have found a dead woman!" yelled Segundo. "He thinks it is Monica!"

"Vamos, Vaquero!" ordered Diego. "Show us!"

Riding out ahead of the herd, the same trail taken by the herd as they were driven by the Apache was not hard to follow. The moonlight seemed to show every obstacle in bold, silvery relief. The Fantasma Vaquero scout who had brought his news rode a few yards ahead. About a mile ahead of the herd, he raised his hand to signal a halt. Fifty yards ahead, two other scouts were standing by their horses maintaining a sort of vigil over something on the ground. Diego and Segundo slowly approached. Neither man really wanted to see what was there. A pile of branches and scrub vegetation had been covering something on the ground. When the men had come to a stop overlooking the pile of branches, both men hesitated to move or say anything. After a deep breath, Segundo spoke. "Vaquero, lift the branches."

The Vaquero carefully lifted the mantle of foliage. The moonlight, with its cold, silvery light, showed clearly what had been hidden. Diego had to grasp Segundo's shoulders to keep him from sinking to the ground. "*Dios mio* . . . my God!" exclaimed Segundo softly.

"*Lo siento,*" said Diego as he, too, saw what had been brought into view.

"I never wanted this," whispered Segundo toward the form that had once been his sister.

"I know," said Diego. "You could not possibly have imagined it would come to this."

Segundo looked for only a moment at the body of Monica. Then, emotionally spent, he turned away, slowly sinking to the ground. Diego realized that there was no reason to keep his friend standing upright. His grief at what he was witnessing was too much. Segundo was suffering, even though he knew Monica had brought this on herself. Her greed for la Rancheria Fantasma, coupled with her jealousy of Segundo and his ownership of it, compelled her to do the horrible things she did. Yet Monica was still his sister. Whatever tender feelings Segundo had had for her in their youth were manifest again now.

Diego could well understand and empathize with Segundo. Monica had been a physically beautiful woman, capable of the best of womanly feelings. Diego had enjoyed the physical dalliance he had had with Monica. He had felt no love for her. He had known at the time that she was merely playing him, trying to take advantage to steal la Rancheria Fantasma from Segundo and, unknown to her, from Diego himself. He felt the natural regret that they had to fight off her treachery. Yet, even he, Diego DaVia, Dead Man Who Walks Away, could not help feeling the sorrow felt by his friend at seeing what had once been la Doña Monica Ruiz. The body of Monica Ruiz had been tossed into the brush and nearly covered by random scrub bushes. She was naked, bruised, and covered by cuts and dried blood associated with those wounds. She had obviously been repeatedly raped over the time of her capture. No one at that scene could possibly blame Segundo for the wracking sobs of his grief.

After what had seemed hours but had only been a few heart-wrenching minutes, Segundo stood up, controlled his emotions, and said, "I have a shirt in my saddlebags. I will try to clean her up a bit." Then, addressing the three Vaqueros: "Gracias, amigos mios, for watching over her. I have my bedroll on the saddle. Please get it so I can wrap her in it."

Diego then added, "Vaqueros, we will find some poles to make up a travois. We will place Doña Monica on that to take her home."

It did not take long. The most time-consuming job was the cleansing of Doña Monica. Once all was in readiness, the body was placed on the travois, and they began the sad journey to la Rancheria Fantasma.

Segundo remained riding alongside the travois. Diego had no choice but to lead the Fantasma Vaqueros and la mañada de fantasma home. This was still not a cake walk. The Apache could always be planning a retaliatory raid to get the herd back. He took it upon himself to be constantly on alert, riding around and around the herd, talking to the Vaqueros, keeping everyone vigilant. He had been involved in forced marches before through dangerous territory. There must not be a moment's laxity in vigilance. Diego had put in place a plan, should the Apache attack while the herd was moving. Depending upon where the attack might occur, every second Vaquero in formation would ride directly at the leaders of the attackers.

Thus, la mañada de fantasma was driven, day and night, the Vaqueros pausing only to snatch a short nap, toward their la Rancheria Fantasma home.

———

The returning Vaqueros were already moving northward on the open grassland of la Rancheria Fantasma when the attack came. A large war party of Apache warriors attacked at full gallop from behind the tired herd. Waving blankets to stampede the horses and shouting, they charged the weary Vaqueros. Diego's plan was almost automatically put into action. Every second Fantasma Vaquero turned and, firing their Dragoons, charged the Apache leaders. The Apaches were stunned! This strategy was a complete surprise. They had expected the Vaqueros to chase the stampeding horses and be picked off as they fled. Instead, they had to face an unstoppable charge of hate-filled Vaqueros, firing at point-blank range. Those Apaches who were not instantly killed turned around in panic to ride away, back from where they came.

It was then that the unbelievable occurred for the Apaches. The crack of rifle fire was heard from all directions as they tried to retreat. An unseen force of riflemen had opened fire on them from the high grass and scrub bushes. Nearly all the attacking Apaches were killed. Those who survived to tell the tale told of the man clad in an old Mexican cavalry coat, charging with his saber, killing any Apache in front of the big grey horse he rode. The council fires of each band would proclaim that Dead Man Who Walks Away was not to be challenged. His medicine was too powerful.

Diego DaVia had more than his medicine working for him in that battle. He had his own Fantasma Vaqueros, the ones that had remained behind to mind la Rancheria Fantasma, waiting in the grassland for the returning weary Vaqueros. But even Diego could not believe what had occurred. When the Fantasma Vaqueros and la mañada de fantasma returned to the hacienda area, he was informed that, in the absence of himself and Segundo, Socorra had assumed command of the home forces. It was Socorra who realized that trouble might follow the returning Fantasma Vaqueros, and, knowing from where the herd would be coming, it was Socorra who placed the riflemen in that tall grass.

If there was anything that could bring Segundo out from his sorrow for his sister, that did it! Never was a man so overjoyed to see his wife. Don Diego DaVia later toasted: "Never was a man so blessed as to have a woman such as Socorra, and never was la Rancheria Fantasma so blessed because of her!"

The Apache threat to la Rancheria Fantasma would be gone for a long time, thanks to their fear of Dead Man Who Walks Away. But that fight was won because everyone at la Rancheria Fantasma belonged to it and fought as if they were a country unto themselves and protected everyone in it.

The burial of la Doña Monica Ruiz was short but well attended. Out of respect and love for Don Segundo Ruiz, all who could attend, did attend.

A time of peaceful ranching prevailed as la Rancheria Fantasma returned to quasi normal. After all, the Apache threat had been thwarted. All they had to deal with then were the revolucionarios fighting against the recently invading army of France.

29

Don Diego DaVia, former capitán of dragoons, Mexican army, sitting on his comfortable veranda, pondered the predicament of his people in Mexico. He had no trouble coming to the realization that, in no way, at no time could—or would—he ever have fought to allow forces of the French army of Napoleon Bonaparte to rule Mexico. Yet from that veranda, there was nothing he could do about it. He wanted to do plenty, but all he could do was watch. He did manage to sell quantities of excellent horses to the anti-French fighters. Yet he honored his word to his people at la Rancheria Fantasma that he would treat all potential buyers even-handedly. It was not his fault that the pro-French supporters did not choose to approach him for horses.

So, time went by peacefully and profitably for la Rancheria Fantasma. Well over a year had passed since the rout of the Apache. Everyone at la rancheria seemed to be doing well and was happy . . . all but one. And the very perceptive Socorra saw it. Socorra saw the iron eyes dim with sadness and longing for the one who was not there for him. He had not heard from Constance McCoy for a long time. He had sent letters to be posted in Tucson but had no replies. Socorra had watched Diego and Constance closely while Constance was at la Rancheria Fantasma. She had seen the outward adoration of Constance for Diego. She had seen the joy in Diego's face when Constance was nearby. Now she could only imagine what was going on in Diego's mind. So, Socorra took the matter to its source.

"Diego DaVia!" Socorra's sudden call of his name shocked his feet from the low table on which they had been propped. He found himself quickly standing up to see what prompted that interruption.

"Que pasa?" he questioned.

Socorra, never one to mince words said, "You are pathetic!"

"What?" asked Diego again.

"How long has it been since you heard from Constance? Huh? A month? Three months? More? Much more? How long?" Socorra jabbed.

"Too damn long!" Diego retorted, trying to defend himself.

"Well, what the hell are you going to do about it? Sit there waiting for a pigeon to bring you some news? Come on, big Patrón, what about it?" Socorra continued jabbing. She was going to get a rise out of him no matter what.

"What are you saying, Socorra?" asked Diego, plainly on the defensive.

"I am your best friend's wife, your almost sister-in-law. You think I do not see what is eating you up. Get up off your dead butt and go find her! Bring her back here or not. But settle it. Or are you going to continue sulking around here like a lovesick yearling colt?" Socorra seemingly had had it with Diego's sadness. She was going to pull him out of it, as she had heard him say, "no ifs, ands, or buts."

For only a brief moment of silence, Diego did not know how to react. But looking into Socorra's concerned yet seemingly angry face cleared up everything.

"Socorra. Have Segundo, Pancho, Pancho's grandmother, or anyone else put together provisions for a five-day ride to Tucson. I will catch a coach to California. I will return . . . when I return!" said Diego with passion. With that he turned and walked, with his old, determined step, to the stable to check on Hiero.

"Bueno!" loudly yelled Socorra at the now-smiling face of Diego. *Whatever happens, the matter will be settled,* she thought.

And so, it was done.

The next morning, everyone available at la Rancheria Fantasma was there to wish Diego godspeed on his journey. Segundo said, "I think we can get along without your grouchy face for a while here. Get it done, Hermano!"

Socorra added, as she clasped Diego's hand tightly, "Go with all the love we can give you."

Pancho said, "My grandmother could not be here, but even she wishes you well!"

That caused Diego to laugh. "Adiós, Fantasmas mios!"

Hiero did not wait for a spur. His first leap forward nearly unseated Diego. Amid laughter and cheers, Diego DaVia left la Rancheria Fantasma on his quest.

The cheers had not quite died down as Hiero charged away from the hacienda with Diego DaVia holding on to remain in the saddle. Diego's loud commands to "slow down" began to work on Hiero. "You, too, you crazy acting horse? You'll have us both killed before we leave our valley!" Hiero was crossing into the woodland north of the San Rafael Valley when he slowed to an easy lope. After months of moping around, this sudden activity was definitely needed to clear Diego's head. He realized that he had been wasting valuable time feeling sorry for himself. He knew that he wanted Constance again. That was all that mattered to him now. How he would manage to accomplish that, he had no idea. But he was on his way, albeit, thanks to Hiero, a bit faster than planned.

He knew that a stop in Tucson would be necessary to ascertain if any messages were there from Constance. He wished to find out if anything had happened that he should have known about.

———

Four days later, a very tired Diego rode into Tucson, on a prancing Hiero. Diego shook his head. Even Hiero's sire, the big grey, would have at least walked, not pranced. "Damned show-off!"

There was an address in San Diego that the postmaster said was to be used to forward any mail. Never having been to San Diego himself, Diego had no idea where that address was in that town. However, after a good night's sleep he would be on his way. Before he could leave, he had to see to Hiero. Diego would be taking a stagecoach to San Diego, but Hiero would have to be boarded somewhere in Tucson. He would visit Judge Morales. After all the chaos within the military in Tucson, he would very much prefer to ask Judge Morales about a trustworthy place to leave Hiero.

Diego found Judge Morales in the hallway outside his official chambers at the courthouse. Judge Morales instantly recognized Diego DaVia standing there waiting for him. The judge rushed over to greet him.

"Don Diego, what a pleasant surprise to see you here. Are you here because of some problem or a social visit?" asked the judge.

"Buenas dias, Your Honor," replied Diego. "I need to ask you a favor, amigo."

"If the favor is legal, I will be happy to oblige," joked Judge Morales, smiling broadly.

"It is legal but very important, at least to me," said Diego, his smile turning to a serious look.

"Ask it, my friend," said the judge.

"I must travel to San Diego, and who knows where else, until I find someone," began Diego. "And I must find a place to board my horse, Hiero, until I return. Hiero means much to me. I must be certain of his care and that he will be here when I return. Can you help me?"

"Diego, I will keep Hiero at my home. He will be well cared for and guarded at all times. He will be here for you whenever you return," assured Judge Morales. "No, Diego. Do not even ask. Hiero will be my guest until you return."

"Gracias, amigo! I could ask for no greater assurance," said Diego and added, "I will bring him to you shortly. I plan to ride the stagecoach to San Diego tomorrow."

"May I ask the beneficiary, or perhaps the victim, of your search?" inquired the judge.

"The wedding, to which you were invited some time ago, has been delayed for too long. I go to find Constance and bring her home to la Rancheria Fantasma," proclaimed Diego.

"Ha! Then when you arrive here with your Constance, I will present you with a fine mare for her to ride with you to la Rancheria Fantasma, as a wedding present," promised Judge Morales in return.

"Gracias, Your Honor," said Diego.

"Buena suerte!" added the judge.

Diego DaVia saw no reason to delay delivering Hiero to the judge at his fine home on the outskirts of Tucson and did so immediately. He then spent a quiet evening awaiting the morning to board the stagecoach west to San Diego. He could not help wishing that he could simply ride Hiero. But he had no idea exactly where in California he would have to go to find Constance. Diego DaVia boarded the stagecoach for San Diego with high hopes for the future, a future shared with the lovely, blonde-haired Constance McCoy. It would be a long, dusty stagecoach ride to San Diego. Never having been there, he had no idea what he would find. But he hoped to find his Constance.

—–—

Long dusty ride? Unbelievable! Diego DaVia, by the time that stagecoach topped the last hill—mountain—and he saw the Pacific Ocean in the far distance, was sure that he should have simply ridden Hiero all the way. He would have been more comfortable and enjoyed better company . . . none! He would have been more able to focus on some plan of action. Merely sitting in a drafty, dusty, spring-less conveyance left him sleepy most of the time, hour after hour.

When he was able to leave the building that doubled as coach depot, freight office, and general information center for wandering travelers having an urgent need to spend their money, he made his way to one of the recommended hotels, checked in, and, throwing his limited gear on the floor, flopped on the bed that, surprisingly, turned out to be quite comfortable. He was exhausted from the long trip. He managed to get himself downstairs for a dinner he considered way overpriced and then went outside for a walking tour of the city. He found several things he did not particularly like, but for the most part he was favorably impressed. He did not have far to walk to have seen the whole "downtown" area and so located the local postal facility. He planned to visit that first thing the next morning.

—–—

The next day Diego did just that. He arrived at the local U.S. mail office early. He, not unexpectedly, had to wait a while for the postmaster to make himself available to meet. When that meeting eventually occurred, Diego was impressed with his manner and the knowledge he possessed. The postmaster, when asked about the address of the widow McCoy and her daughter, Constance, did remember them. The address Diego had been sending his correspondence to had always been a general delivery mailbox number. However, the postmaster looked up the forwarding address, which proved to be a house high on a hill overlooking the ocean to the west. Diego copied all the information he could, thanked the postmaster for his assistance, and left with the intent to get there as fast as he could. That meant renting a horse at the local livery stable.

Once mounted, and armed with directions to the house, Diego wasted no time in finding it. Prior to dismounting, Diego sat in the saddle and looked at the house. He thought, *how could a capitán of cavalry afford such a home?* The view of the ocean, from either of the two verandas, had to have been awesome. The home was Spanish in architecture, with its double verandas, stone arches, and overall stucco exterior. Diego dismounted, tied his horse to the ornate iron rings made for such a purpose, and ascended the long stairway to the front veranda. Once at the double-width doorway, he paused, caught his breath, and pulled the chain to ring the doorbell.

After a moment, the door was opened by a very well-dressed male servant of some sort. The man asked Diego, "May I help you, sir?"

"I am calling on Señorita Constance McCoy. Is she available to see an old friend?" said Diego, not yet wishing to tell him that they were engaged to be married.

The servant replied, "Miss Constance is away now. May I tell her who was calling on her?"

Diego, disappointed, chose not to ruin the surprise.

He merely said, "No. Thank you."

Then, turning to leave, he caught sight of Mrs. McCoy, who had evidently walked past behind the servant. He saw her suddenly put her hand to her face and step hastily out of sight. Having seen her, Diego turned back and asked the servant, "Is the widow McCoy available?"

The servant hesitated. "Why?" came the curt reply.

"I am acquainted with both Señorita Constance and her mother. I would enjoy visiting with both ladies," said Diego, maintaining his composure.

The servant, with no hesitation, said, "Mrs. McCoy is also unavailable. Good day."

"Buenas tardes," replied Diego. If the servant noticed the iron in Diego's eyes, he did not show it, as Diego DaVia slowly turned and descended the stairs to his horse.

It had been many, many years since Diego DaVia had been dismissed by anyone, and never by someone telling an outright lie, as that haughty servant had just done. He had seen Mrs. McCoy, seen her rush from his view and evidently signal the servant to tell him she was not there. He could not understand it. It was not as if he were there to sell her something. After all, she and her family had been his guests at la Rancheria Fantasma for many weeks, under some very unforgettable circumstances. What's more, if Capitán McCoy had not been killed at the battle of Apache Pass, Diego would now be her son-in-law. His thoughts continued as he rode slowly away. *What the hell's going on?*

Diego DaVia was never one to let a question like that go unanswered. He turned his horse around a corner, found an area of trees and shrubbery, and waited. It was a nice area of the city, but it was a city. It had become boring to him. He was getting hungry sitting there on his rented horse. Now and then a fancy coach would pass by, drawn by a very well-cared for horse. But for a very few minutes, no one of interest passed. Then, he saw a very stylish black surrey pass by moving quickly. Normally, Diego would have paid it no mind, except this surrey was driven by that haughty, nervous looking servant. Diego decided that surrey was worth following.

Keeping to one side of the road, and well back, he was able to keep the surrey in sight without himself being seen. The road twisted and turned inevitably downhill and toward the ocean, with the expected row of homes set back from the water. The surrey was halted in front of a large home with a spacious veranda facing the ocean. The veranda held approximately thirty young men and women. There was music playing in the background. Some couples were dancing. Some were merely standing, with their drinks in hand, laughing and talking.

Diego decided that he would be less conspicuous not mounted. He walked his horse a few hundred yards down the beach from the party. He tied the horse to a rail for that purpose. He then walked a bit closer to the party and sat down on a bench, not far from some other people who were simply enjoying the view of the Pacific Ocean.

This time he did not have long to wait. He could see the veranda very well from his seaside bench. His eyes had been immediately drawn to some familiar locks of blonde hair. The servant also had been drawn to that blonde-haired woman. He stepped up to her as she was dancing with a very well-dressed young man. The servant spoke a few words to her. Her reaction was electric! Her young dance partner was nearly knocked off his feet by her response. She rushed off the veranda and raced to the surrey with the servant. The surrey lurched into action as the driver used his whip. Diego had no chance to escape being seen by Constance as the surrey, throwing sand behind it, flew by him. He did see her, for only a moment, hide her face in her hands, as the surrey careened past. He had been seen. He knew it. She had been seen. She knew that, too.

Diego, rather than charge after her, decided to allow her to go home without pursuit. He chose to do some research and investigating. Leaving his horse, he nonchalantly walked up the beach to the beach house veranda. The party goers had noticed the hurried departure of one of their lovelier guests and were standing in some amazement. As Diego approached, he showed his most appealing smile and asked in some wonderment, "What just happened?" He said laughingly that, "Being nearly run down by a surrey on the beach does not happen to me every day."

A very pretty, dark-haired woman, still wide-eyed by the experience, answered without thinking as to whom this stranger might be, "I do not know. Constance was dancing with her fiancé, when something was told to her by her servant, and she just exploded away!"

"Well!" said Diego, somewhat startled. "One would think he would have gone with her. Are they newly engaged or something?"

"Wait. Who are you anyway?" the woman asked Diego.

"Evidently, I am an escapee from a dangerous woman!" Diego laughed. "Do you know this blonde woman well?" he asked.

"Why yes! Her fiancé is my brother," she replied. The dark-haired woman asked very politely, "Are you a stranger to San Diego?"

Diego thought for a moment, as he studied her serious, dark eyes. He then said, "I am a stranger nearly everywhere. I will always be a stranger here."

The young woman had begun to show some serious concern for what was happening and said, "Where is your home? Do you know Constance McCoy?"

Diego, without hesitation said, "You will no doubt see her soon. Tell her that you saw a man from the San Rafael Valley. Tell her that, when you saw him, he was again walking away."

Don Diego DaVia left the beach area with as dignified a walk as possible. He knew the woman to whom he had spoken would no doubt be watching. He was smarting from the knowledge that his Constance was now engaged to another man. He was hurt and beginning to boil inside with anger. *How could she do this to me!* he asked inwardly. He walked toward where he had left his rental horse, paying attention to nothing but his inner hurt.

A voice from behind suddenly asked him, in a tone bordering on an order, to stop and turn around. He turned, ready for anything, and faced the man who had been dancing with Constance. Seeing the anger in the iron eyes, the man backed a few steps away.

"I must ask you, sir," the young man demanded. "Who are you, and how do you know Constance McCoy?"

Diego was swiftly losing his gentlemanly pretense for leaving the party area.

"Having been asked for this information much more politely by your sister, I feel you should ask her," replied Diego. His gentlemanly manner was beginning to be replaced by the old, combative Diego.

"I am engaged to marry Constance and so demand an explanation! Now!" the young man demanded haughtily.

Don Diego had been exposed to haughty individuals aplenty as he grew up in Spain among his own Italian nobility and those of Spanish descent. Their haughtiness usually gained them a flattened nose delivered by a young Diego DaVia. Diego was now making a valiant effort to restrain himself from delivering the same to this young man.

"I am certain that we can both be spared a most unpleasant afternoon by you merely asking that question of Constance herself," said Diego as calmly as he could.

"I would not insult her with such a question. I would rather settle this between you and me!" said the naïve young man, evidently looking for a duel of sorts.

"If you are seriously planning to marry Constance, or any other woman, you'd better be able to talk to her. It would probably save you a whole barrel of trouble," said Diego, having had enough of this young man.

"I am going to marry Constance, and I will have none of yo—" he tried to say.

Diego, becoming angrier at this young upstart, interrupted. "There seems to be a line forming to accomplish that!"

At that remark, the young man tore off his dainty leather glove and prepared to throw it at Diego's feet in challenge. Don Diego DaVia caught the glove in midair and promptly smacked him in the face with it, knocking him off his feet in the sand.

"Do not misunderstand the meaning of that smack, young man. It is not a challenge. Consider it merely a slight spanking!" snapped Diego.

The young man's friends had been listening and watching and had gathered around their young friend.

"You'll pay for this! I promise!" threatened the now sandy fiancé.

Diego, slowly walking away, answered, "If you still desire that after speaking to Constance, I will oblige. I will be easy for her to find. Tell her I prefer to simply walk away."

With that, turning his back on the men in obvious disdain, he slowly walked away.

—•—

Within a few short hours, Diego had returned the rental horse. He made the necessary arrangements to return to Tucson and then retired to the hotel to await the next day's coach. Once again, Diego had great difficulty sleeping, but certainly not because of the threats of Constance's fiancé and his friends. He could not believe what he had seen after having travelled all the way from la Rancheria Fantasma to retrieve Constance and marry her. He could not reconcile, after all they had supposedly been to each other, that she would so quickly marry another.

—⚊—

The morning came early for Diego DaVia. Breakfast was short and, as before, overpriced. Diego had entered the stagecoach for the return trip to Tucson, but before it could depart, two friends of Constance's fiancé tore open the door and dragged Diego out of the coach. They said they were acting as "seconds" to the fiancé and were there to arrange the date and time of the duel. That did it for Diego. He leaned a bit forward, as if to bow to their proposal, and reached out and cracked their heads together. As they lay there moaning Diego said, "Tell Constance, and her silly little friend, that this is something new for me. After all, I've never even cracked the heads of Apaches together like that!" Having said that, Diego reboarded the coach and ordered the driver to "drive on."

30

After the long, grueling stagecoach ride to Tucson, a dusty, dog-tired Diego DaVia stepped down from the creaky stagecoach. It was late, so Diego did not wish to bother Judge Morales about his grey horse, Hiero. He had all he could do to find a room for the night. He slept until after sunup and, after cleaning up a bit, went to see Judge Morales. He found Judge Morales sitting quietly at his large desk in his chambers.

Upon hearing Diego knock once at the door, he raised his head and motioned him inside the office. Diego saw that the judge's smile of welcome was genuine but saw that something was troubling him as well.

"Don Diego, pull the door closed and sit down," he said.

They shook hands, and Diego asked, "What is it, Your Honor?"

"Did anyone see you and recognize you as yet?" asked Judge Morales.

"I do not think so. Why do you ask?" Diego replied.

"I received this a few minutes ago," the judge said, handing Diego a piece of paper.

"What is this?" Diego asked.

"This is a telegram from the authorities in San Diego, California. It instructs me to have you detained on charges stemming from an altercation concerning you and two young men in San Diego. Was there a fight or something?" asked the judge.

"I have a greater fight every morning just getting my boots on over my feet," responded Diego.

"Well, you are being charged with assault and battery by a man named Atherton on behalf of two of his friends, whom you supposedly knocked out as you were leaving San Diego," asserted Judge Morales.

"Ha! I reached out and, in one motion, cracked their heads together," said Diego, laughing.

"Diego, if you were anyone else, I would not be able to even speak to you of it before your trial. I would be forced to have you arrested. Even now, talking to you about it is breaking the law. What the hell happened?" asked the judge. "And be quick about it. There is not much time."

"I went to find Constance McCoy. The widow McCoy avoided me, even though she saw me. I then followed her servant to the beach and saw Constance dancing with a young man. She saw me as she was whisked away in her coach by her servant. The sister of the young man with whom Constance was dancing had told me that he was her fiancé! Did you say his name was 'Atherton,' Your Honor? I told her to tell Constance that the man from the San Rafael Valley was going to just walk away. The fiancé then threatened me, so I walked away from him and his friends. His two friends pulled me from the stagecoach as I was leaving, trying to frighten me by demanding to set up a duel. Ha!"

"Then what?" asked Judge Morales.

"I reached out and cracked their heads together," Diego said, laughing.

"Did you injure them?" asked the judge.

"I have slapped horses on the rear harder than that!" asserted Diego.

"San Diego's upper-crust society boys, evidently. I've seen that type before," said Judge Morales.

"What should I do, Your Honor?" asked Diego, becoming concerned. Up until then it had seemed a trifle silly to him.

"You put a bandana around your head and walk inconspicuously out the door to my place. Get Hiero and ride slowly out of Tucson. I will swear I have not seen you."

"Where should I go?" asked Diego.

"Anywhere except la Rancheria Fantasma for a while. You must hide out for a time. Wait a few weeks before you try to contact me, at night. Now go!" said the very unhappy and concerned Judge Morales.

Diego DaVia was not one to waste time when there was not much time to waste. He tied his neck bandana around his head as though he were a laborer going off to work. He carried his short waistcoat over his arm and, with head lowered, walked toward the judge's residence slowly shaking his head. He could not believe this was happening to him. Because Constance, for whatever reason, chose to marry some little pipsqueak in California. Making his way around the back of Judge Morales's residence, he saw Hiero in the small barn. He had to hold Hiero's head to keep him quiet when he recognized Diego. Once he had saddled Hiero, Diego chose to walk him away from the main area of homes. He looked as though he were a servant merely exercising the horse for Judge Morales. However, once out in the open, Diego stepped in the saddle and rode swiftly east from Tucson.

A few miles east of Tucson, Diego DaVia slowed his horse to a walk. He had no idea what he was going to do, or where he was going to do it. It seemed to him that all the cards were stacked against him. He was wanted by the Americans for an insignificant matter and known, hated, and feared by the Apache. There were those in Mexico who would love to see him dead as well. "Whoa, Hiero! What the hell am I doing? I am riding straight into the land of the Chiricahua Apache!" Diego found a secluded place under some trees off the road and dismounted. "I will not be driven from my life by those city pansies!" He kept asking himself, *where would no one think to look for me?*

He was tired and somewhat sore. The ride by stagecoach had certainly taken its toll on him. He needed a short rest, so he propped himself up against a tree trunk and dozed for a few necessary minutes.

He awoke, noting that Hiero was nervously gazing westward, toward Tucson, from whence he had come. *Well, I've trusted in "horse sense" before,* he thought, and mounting, turned back and rode west, directly toward Tucson. Before he neared the town, however, Diego placed his coat and other articles that would identify him as a prosperous man in the saddlebags. He was in shirtsleeves and sweat as he rode through town. No one paid him any attention. A quick stop to purchase a supply of food, and he was on his way. West of town, he asked Hiero for some more speed. "You are supposed to be tired, Hiero," he said as the big horse accelerated.

Tired or not, a cold camp was made many miles west of Tucson, a few hundred yards off the trail. Even without a fire, Diego's thoughts ran on and on. With the decision made, he fell asleep. The morning found

Diego, a broad smile on his face, again heading west. *I wonder what those little nitwits will do after chasing me, as I catch them!* he wondered.

———

Many, many days later, Don Diego DaVia, astride Hiero, gazed upon the Pacific Ocean from a hilltop east of San Diego.

This time, Diego chose not to get a room near the bustling center of San Diego, as he had the previous visit. This time he chose an unlikely area, high on the bluff, near the old mission. He planned to maintain a low profile at first and see what happened around that city. Constance was located not too far away from his new residence, but he had no plans to visit her in any manner. He did plan, someday, to visit her fiancé and his mouthy friends.

Diego found that he was able to cross the border into Tijuana, Mexico, and back any time he wished. The authorities in Mexico would have no record of any trivial matters happening on the United States side, so he felt free enough to open a bank relationship in Tijuana. Once established, he set up communications with the bank in Hermosillo to contact Don Segundo. Segundo was surprised and delighted to hear from the bank that Don Diego was alive. He forwarded money from his account to Diego in Tijuana so that Diego could have funds during his stay.

Segundo had no knowledge of what was going on, but "authorities" had visited la Rancheria Fantasma looking for Diego. Segundo had spoken very civilly with them while they were at la rancheria and during anytime Socorra was with him. However, as they were preparing to leave, Segundo leaned forward and said quietly, "Be it known to you, if you ever return to la Rancheria Fantasma, I . . . will . . . kill . . . you." The ten steely-eyed Fantasma Vaqueros standing beside Segundo made certain the men understood. After they were out of sight, Socorra asked Segundo, "Did you say what I think you said to them?"

Segundo looked at her very innocently and said, "Sí".

Socorra threw her arms around him and said, "Bueno!"

———

There was still much work to do to rebuild la Rancheria Fantasma due to that awful raid by the Apache. But it was getting done. Everyone was sad that Don Diego was not there to be a part of it. They had heard only the authorities' side as to why they were looking for him. Obviously, Constance would not be back. The thought was that if Constance had done what they thought she had to Diego, then she was not wanted there. Socorra remembered the times when she thought something was wrong concerning Constance. She had pushed such thoughts aside. Now, she realized that either Constance had been only playing or that the widow McCoy had swayed her against coming back to Diego. At any rate, Socorra thought it stunk!

Diego had enough cash to enjoy life as a visiting Mexican-American gentleman. The money was used to purchase clothing that was fashionable at the time in San Diego, the kind one would hate to smudge or get the least bit dirty. Diego looked like an older version of those prissy-looking young brats. *Yuck!* he thought. Up until that moment, Diego had always been clean-shaven. Now he began to grow a very fashionable mustache, well-trimmed, of course. Don Diego DaVia now began to look more like his actual heritage—Italian.

So, Don Diego DaVia began visiting the places in San Diego where he might accidently run into the arrogant friends of Constance's fiancé. Diego had no knowledge of the visit to la rancheria by the so-called "authorities." Diego would have been searching for these people for a serious meeting. If he had investigated who these so-called authorities were, he would have found out that they were merely private security employees. That would have been the last trip they ever made. As it was, Diego had made up his mind to make himself available for whatever developed. He had no intention of meeting Constance, or killing off her young fiancé, Atherton. But he wanted to permanently end their pursuit of him.

Many days went by. Diego was enjoying the mild southern California climate but had no contact with the men he was pursuing. He decided he had wasted enough time. He began paying attention to local newspaper articles concerning upcoming social events. His research paid off.

A large ball was to be held some distance from the commercial, bawdy downtown. It was a short distance from the beach, not far from Diego's temporary residence. As a former officer in the Mexican cavalry, Diego DaVia had attended many such gatherings. He would attend this one. He polished up his best military manners and made his plans to attend. He had no invitation, but he had walked into other such events with merely a smile to the lady at the door.

There was a well-guarded area for the coaches of arriving guests and an enclosed stable for horses of guests who chose to ride to the festivities. Diego rode Hiero and placed him in that stable. Always alert for the possibility of trouble, he placed Hiero in a stall near the rear exit. With no plan in mind, he secured the cavalry saber on the far side of Hiero's saddle, covered with a coat normally used for inclement weather. Then, straightening his garments, he walked to the entrance of the grand pavilion. This was an outdoor event with the dance area under a magnificent pavilion with windows unshuttered and open to catch the breeze from the Pacific Ocean.

Diego was right. The lady at the door merely blushed as Diego smiled, winked at her, and walked on inside. Once inside, Diego saw that most of the guests probably had already arrived. There were many people milling around, socializing, waiting for the music and dancing to begin. His eyes were everywhere, looking for Constance, but only because he knew her young Atherton and his friends would be nearby. He watched, from his position near a side exit, for nearly an hour. He saw many very pretty, young women with their silly, pretty, young men escorting them. Diego began wondering if Constance and her little entourage would show up.

Then, after the dancing had been going for about half an hour, Diego saw the flash of familiar blonde hair. She was waltzing with her Atherton and danced right past Diego as he watched without expression. He watched her as the couple moved around the dance floor. As Constance neared Diego's position again, she saw him. Diego saw her eyes widen. She nearly tripped her fiancé as she turned her head violently around as she danced past Diego. Diego heard Atherton's cry of "What the . . . ?" after they had danced past him. Diego gathered his composure for the meeting that he knew was about to take place.

Within half a minute, Constance, her fiancé, and the two so-called friends of his were moving toward him.

Constance said nervously, "Diego, I never thought you would be here!"

Diego started to ask, "Why not?" but his words were drowned out by the loud insults by her gentleman fiancé, Atherton.

Constance now had to yell loudly to be heard. "Diego, I was told that you had 'walked away'!"

The noise quieted as Diego replied, "Constance, you know very well I have walked away from a massacre and other disasters, but I never have walked away from a fight."

Constance's Atherton now screamed, "Here is a fight you will not walk away from! Choose your weapon, old man!"

Now a look of terror filled Constance's eyes, yet she could not speak. Other men had formed quite a crowd. Some of them loudly proclaimed "Duel!"

Diego's answer was even-toned and cold. "Sabers," he said.

The upstarts around Constance began yelling, "Get us some sabers!" Some of the men in the pavilion agreed to go to the stable to get sabers.

Diego calmly said, "My saber is in the stable, also. Shall we all retire to the stable and pursue whatever will be?"

Diego DaVia, to everyone's surprise—except for Constance's—because he was outnumbered, coolly and deliberately led the raucous dandies out to the stable. He walked deliberately to Hiero and slowly pulled the veteran saber from its scabbard. The sport of the crowd was being erased by the seriousness of Diego and what was obviously a military, not social, weapon. However, the reckless young men—the fiancé and his smart-mouthed friends—continued their advance. Diego had had his back to these adventurers as he had drawn the saber. When he turned to face them, the young smart-mouths found themselves looking into the iron eyes of a cavalry Capitán of Dragoons, Mexican army. In only an instant, the "old man" looked extremely formidable.

A well-dressed man, near Diego's age, tried to make some semblance of an actual duel out of that three-to-one supposed mismatch. As Diego slowly raised his saber upright in front of him and assumed the stance of a man ready to fight to kill, Constance screamed, "Stop, you fools! Diego has killed many, many men! The Apache fear him as no other!"

She had hoped to dissuade her Atherton and his friends. They took her warning as a challenge. They attacked!

As they put their social swordsmanship to the test, Diego, in short order, disarmed the two men who had accosted him at the stagecoach. He forced them to lie face down in the straw of the stable, under his promise to kill them if they did not. Then he faced Atherton who, in his rage at seeing his friends humiliated and lying on the floor, rushed forward swinging his saber wildly at Diego. Atherton's saber slash passed Diego's side, and, as it did, Diego, with a backward slash, snapped Atherton's saber in two. Atherton's hand, stinging in pain, dropped the abbreviated blade to the straw. In one quick motion, Diego placed the point of his saber against the throat of Constance's fiancé.

Constance screamed, "No, Diego. No! Please, no!"

Atherton found himself holding a very painful right hand with his left, looking into the iron eyes of Diego DaVia. Diego's saber had not moved an inch from its place against Atherton's throat. Atherton's face was white with fear.

Diego said, as much to the crowd as to Atherton, "I once cared for your Constance. It is because of her that you are still alive, you young whelp! If you ever pursue me again, in any way, with or without your paid police, I . . . will . . . kill . . . you! Do you understand?"

Atherton could barely get the word out. "Yes."

"Yes, what?" yelled DaVia, inches from Atherton's face.

"Yes, sir!" whined Atherton.

Removing his saber from the throat of Atherton, Diego looked at Constance as she slowly came forward.

"I am so sorry," she said to Diego.

"You certainly are," said Diego as he stepped into the saddle on Hiero. As he rode past her, the astonished crowd again heard, "You certainly are."

31

Diego DaVia rode slowly away from the gathering of social misfits calling themselves the "elite" of San Diego. He did not look back, for there was nothing there that he particularly wanted to remember. A short stop at the residence where he had his few things nearly packed, and he was on his way. It would be a long ride to la Rancheria Fantasma, but he did not care. He was going home. He felt as though a very painful thorn had been removed from his side. His wounded heart had healed some time back, but the insult had remained. Now, even that had been avenged. Don Diego DaVia was going home.

He headed somewhat due east from the city of San Diego. He crossed the mountain range between San Diego and the Rio Colorado. There he purchased two fair-sized, lightweight wooden water casks. These fit by a sturdy leather strap on each side of Hiero behind the saddle. Two more waterproof leather water bags were added to the casks. Thus, Diego figured he would be able to cross the desert that lay before him. He would ration the water, primarily for Hiero, the rest for himself. Jerky would be his mainstay. He then turned southeast into Mexico.

There was a trail that sort of followed the newly-created border of the United States and Mexico. It was not the route followed by Segundo and Socorra on their honeymoon trip to San Diego. It was new and obviously sparsely travelled. Once again, Diego DaVia was travelling with the intent to avoid other people for a time. His route took him always a few miles into Mexico. He would follow that trail as long as it took him closer to the San Rafael Valley and home. He expected this route to get him home after about fifteen days of unhurried riding. Diego had no intention of putting any undue hardship on Hiero.

———

The days and nights slowly passed. One desert hill or ravine looked pretty much like another as on and on he moved eastward. After ten days on that sort of trail, looking for a place to camp for the night, Diego saw a small stand of juniper trees. It wasn't much, but it looked like all the shelter from the hot wind he would find. He guided Hiero toward it. His attention, concentrated on the stand of trees, failed to detect a movement to his right as he passed. He heard the click of a weapon being cocked, along with a sharp command to "Halt!" Realizing he was at a distinct disadvantage, he halted.

Diego sat perfectly still in the saddle, his iron eyes looking directly ahead.

"Who are you?" came the voice from the scrub brush behind him.

"You will never find out by standing behind me," challenged Diego. He was very much aware that a weapon was cocked and pointed at his back.

"Drop your *pistola,* señor!" the unidentified voice demanded.

"You see my hands are raised. Come in front of me and take it," said Diego, his voice firm and unwavering.

"I will take it from your corpse!" said the voice as the person started to move forward.

"Halt, Ernesto!" came a very commanding order. Diego noted that the new voice had a distinctly feminine tone. "I believe I know who this caballero is."

"Señor, I must ask you before all hell breaks loose here. Do you know a woman named 'Socorra'?" asked the definitely feminine voice.

"Sí. I do," answered Diego and added, "So what?"

"So, I believe I know of you," answered the feminine voice.

"That is very nice, but we are wasting time . . . mine," said Diego.

"Knowing who you are, I would not do that. But we must talk. Keep your *pistola* and get down from that beautiful grey stallion," said the woman in a commanding, yet softer tone.

Diego dismounted and turned to see the person who was giving orders in that thicket. He had already figured that he was a prisoner of one of the "Juarista" fighters. These militia fighters were fighting in the name of Benito Juarez against the French invaders of Mexico. What he saw took him back for a moment. He had expected a rough-clad, dirty, part-time soldier, female or not. He found himself looking into the eyes of the most attractive soldier he had ever seen.

"And just who do you believe I am?" asked Diego.

"I believe you are Don Diego DaVia of la Rancheria Fantasma," the woman replied.

"And if I am . . . ?" started Diego.

"You are, and, therefore, you are in no danger from us," she answered.

"You have me at somewhat of a disadvantage. You have identified me, but I do not know of you. You are obviously in command here, but in command of what? What military unit and a part of what army?" questioned Don Diego.

"Normally, I would not give you that information, but, knowing you, I feel confident that no harm will come from it. I am JoAnna D'Artiaga, first lieutenant in the army of el Presidente Benito Juarez," she said proudly.

"That is not much on which to place one's confidence, Señorita D'Artiaga. What makes you feel that you can place any trust in me at all?" asked Diego.

"Because my cousin Socorra would not lie to me!" said JoAnna D'Artiaga, laughing.

"Cousin!" exclaimed Diego, suddenly smiling. He laughed out loud when JoAnna D'Artiaga added, "Do you not remember me? I was at Socorra and Segundo's wedding . . . at la Rancheria Fantasma. You paid me no attention whatsoever!"

"I must have been plagued by problems with my vision," proclaimed Diego, "to not have noticed so lovely a guest!"

At that, Lieutenant D'Artiaga turned and addressed her comrades. "Compadres, this gentleman is Don Diego DaVia, half owner of la Rancheria Fantasma . . . of the San Rafael Valley."

To Don Diego, she said, "Stay the night, share our supper, and tell my compadres of la Rancheria Fantasma . . . and of the Fantasma Vaqueros."

Diego replied, "That would please me greatly. Thank you."

After the meal was done, guards relieved, and it was quiet, Diego asked, "Do you prefer to be addressed as 'Señorita' or 'Lieutenant'?"

"When not performing my military duties, 'Señorita' would please me very much. My military rank is something of necessity, to maintain some semblance of order in this small detachment," answered Lieutenant D'Artiaga.

"Then I will refer to you as 'Lieutenant' until such time as does not seem necessary. You do seem to have a good measure of control over those men assigned to you. I understand these things. Your men have promptly obeyed everything you have mandated to them, thus far. This shows respect for you . . . not just the rank. Orders can be followed willingly or grudgingly. I have noticed that they take your orders willingly. I am impressed," said Don Diego.

"Coming from you, Don Diego, I accept that as a compliment. Were it not for this firelight, you would probably see me blushing," said Lieutenant D'Artiaga.

Then, leaning slightly forward, Diego asked, "Lieutenant D'Artiaga, why are you here? Why are you leading soldiers at all, but especially, why here in this stark desert?"

"You do not know of the invasion of our Mexico by soldiers of France?" the lieutenant asked incredulously. "Do you not know of the 'puppet' of Napoleon, the Austrian duke Maximilian, who is proclaimed 'emperor' of Mexico?"

"Dios mio!" exclaimed Diego. "I had heard of the invasion by the French. I knew Mexican patriots were fighting against them under Benito Juarez, but I did not know of this 'Maximilian'!"

"That is why we are here. That is why I am a lieutenant in our army!" the lieutenant proclaimed.

"How many men . . . soldiers . . . are here in this desert?" asked Diego.

"In this bleak area, we have but fifty men," answered Lieutenant D'Artiaga. "Today I lead merely a patrol of fifteen soldiers."

"Are there French forces in this area? Have you seen any fighting?" Diego asked.

"We have skirmished against mixed forces of French and of Mexicans integrated into their army, mostly French cavalry and conscripted infantry. They have been very cruel to the villagers," offered Lieutenant D'Artiaga.

"Are the French operating in strength—large numbers of men—or are they sparse—hit and run units?" asked Diego, his military background clearly taking control.

Lieutenant D'Artiaga answered, "They try to force a direct fight, whether a dug-in or frontal attack kind of thing. They avoid taking any prisoners. Do you understand?"

"Yes. The only prisoners they would take are the crippled who could be further tortured for information and then killed," replied Don Diego. "Yes. I have seen that before."

"It is difficult," stated Lieutenant D'Artiaga. "How do we fight that kind of battle?"

"I know. It is hard. It requires some painfully difficult decisions when there is no more honor in battle," said Diego.

"What kind of decisions, Don Diego? I have heard you have much experience in these matters. My rank did not come from schooling or even experience. And, after all, I am a woman. It was given to me out of necessity. There was no one else around willing to make any kind of decision. I started yelling to people what I thought they should do," admitted Lieutenant D'Artiaga somewhat emotionally.

"I have some experience," Diego relayed.

"I know something of Dead Man Who Walks Away from Socorra. I do not pretend to understand," said Lieutenant D'Artiaga.

"Then, perhaps I can refer to you as Señorita JoAnna for the rest of tonight. We can speak of war . . . mañana," offered Don Diego.

A short time later, Don Diego DaVia and Señorita JoAnna D'Artiaga rolled out their blankets. Both tried to sleep. Both were troubled. Neither was certain whether the troubled thoughts were of the war, or of each other.

The next day, surprisingly, found Don Diego DaVia slowly riding further south into Mexico. He had not planned it that way, but Lieutenant

D'Artiaga needed to move her camp a few miles deeper into an area of dry washes and ravines. She did not want to be encamped anywhere in that open desert. Her comment was that French patrols had been known to use local sympathizers to attempt ambushes. Also, as she told Diego that morning, "I am hoping we can spend some time conversing with each other."

Diego's response was, "Am I now speaking to la Señorita or Lieutenant D'Artiaga?"

A quick smile and a "Both!" and he had decided to ride along.

———

Less than one full day's ride south, amid a small creosote forest, the small detachment of Mexican fighters and one semi-displaced Don Diego Da-Via found themselves in a seeming maze of dry ravines. Those ravines, dry at the time, had not been created by wind. Many times, during the stormy monsoon season, those ravines had flowed bank-full of raging water. If no storms occurred in the mountains upstream, the small party would stay dry and safe. However, anyone trying to survive in that maze of dry ravines in the desert heat must have a supply of water. The small Juarista party was no exception. It became obvious to Diego that a one-day supply was all the Juaristas had.

Because no running stream or spring seemed likely to be found, Diego knew that there had to be a well somewhere in the area. If so, did it belong to someone sympathetic to the Juarista cause? Diego rode quietly in the procession and waited to see what Lieutenant JoAnna D'Artiaga had planned. Wisely, Diego made sure that Hiero had his share of the rationed water, then took a small drink of what he had allocated to himself. He did not like operating with barely enough water.

He also did not like the spot chosen for their campsite. Lieutenant JoAnna D'Artiaga called a halt for the night on the top of a small hill, surrounded by the maze of rugged ravines. Lieutenant D'Artiaga had chosen this site because she felt that it could be defended in case of attack. Diego DaVia quietly asked to speak to her away from the ranks of her detachment.

"Lieutenant," he began.

"Oops! It is 'Lieutenant' tonight. I must still be on duty," she quipped.

"You tell me," replied Diego. "Are you sure you want to camp here? Would you mind some friendly advice?"

"More than just friendly would be nice. But go on," said Lieutenant D'Artiaga.

"As you wish," said Diego. "This spot, if attacked, could be a trap for us. If we were not to destroy all the attackers in the first wave, we would have no avenue of retreat. These ravines could be blocked off by the enemy, leaving us to be picked off at will."

"Where would you camp, Señor DaVia?" Lieutenant D'Artiaga asked with a hint of irritation in her voice.

"I would proceed further out into the open area, find a low spot, and camp there. We could see an enemy coming. We could make a good decision to stay and fight, retreat to another area, or attack the enemy instead," replied Diego. "At the worst, we would control our own destiny."

Lieutenant D'Artiaga did not reply for a moment. She then said, "You are right. I did not think of that."

Wheeling her horse around, she ordered, "Remount! We will find a better campsite! Vamonos!"

"Feel better, Don DaVia?" Lieutenant D'Artiaga asked.

"So far, but I'll sleep better if we find a low, open area," returned Diego.

"I would not want you to lose any sleep . . . not over that anyway," laughed JoAnna D'Artiaga.

With that, the detachment moved slowly out of the ravines and into more open country. In less than a mile, the detachment slipped into a small depression, surrounded only by small sage and creosote bushes. There they camped, unseen, until morning.

———

Morning came, and with it the usual doldrums of a small unit having to get active out in the wilderness, away from anything seemingly important. A small, nearly smokeless fire had been burning for about half an hour, when a young soldier came up to JoAnna D'Artiaga. He whispered, "There is movement in those creosote bushes north of us."

Lieutenant D'Artiaga looked at Diego. "Did you hear?" she asked.

"I heard," Diego replied. "Select two men to walk their horses a short distance to our east. Everyone else, on my signal mount and charge directly at the bushes to our north. Start now."

As the two men seemed to be leaving the encampment to the east, the bushes north of camp seemed to be moving as if to follow their movements. At that point, Diego fired his Dragoon once and, swinging into the saddle, charged the bushes. Shots rang out in panic as the enemy soldiers fired at the charging Diego, wildly missing him. By that time Lieutenant D'Artiaga was charging with the remainder of her detachment. Firing point-blank at the stricken enemy, D'Artiaga's men killed twelve of the enemy and sent the others, who had been able to mount their horses, in a frantic attempt to escape. Most of them did manage to escape. Of the twelve dead, it was noted that three were uniformed as French cavalry.

"I want two sharpshooters with me," said Diego.

"Why?" asked Lieutenant D'Artiaga.

"We need to see what we are up against . . . not just to wait around to be attacked," answered Diego. "Besides, we need water. I bet they know where to get some."

"You are going after them?" asked D'Artiaga somewhat incredulously.

"Sí. They will not expect to be followed by a small force. There are not many. Our sharpshooters will give us the edge. The remaining French will be looking for a place to lick their wounds . . . near water," explained Diego.

"Socorra was right. You do know what you are doing . . . in war," said Lieutenant JoAnna D'Artiaga, sounding more like Señorita JoAnna.

What the hell did she mean by that? thought Diego, as he and two seemingly very young Juaristas rode carefully after the escaping French soldiers.

JoAnna D'Artiaga watched Diego DaVia and her two young marksmen ride off after the escaped French cavalry; and as she watched she was not sure whether she was watching as Lieutenant D'Artiaga or Señorita JoAnna D'Artiaga. But, after a moment's introspection, Lieutenant JoAnna set about reorganizing her remaining detachment. Diego DaVia had not given any directive, but she took it on her own to carefully follow his tracks. After all, she was in command of these men, not Diego DaVia. She would have her detachment follow at a distance to be ready to assist him, if needed, or take advantage of any water he might find in his pursuit.

Diego DaVia, leading the two selected sharpshooters, had no trouble following the French cavalry, who probably thought they had escaped the disaster behind them. They had no idea that they were being trailed by an avenging force. DaVia needed only to look ahead of him to see their direction. The sun was up and hot, and the dry desert was giving a clear dust trail to follow. Realizing that his little party could also be seen giving off the same indication of his location, Diego chose to follow in a semi-zigzag pattern, trying to keep in the creosote and chaparral as much as possible.

After riding for nearly two hours, Diego saw the dust cloud ahead of him dissipate. He called his sharpshooters to a halt, ordering them to dismount and proceed on foot. Shortly, they neared a small grove of scrub trees. On the far side of the trees, a small adobe building could be seen. But what caught Diego's eye was the small, primitive windmill, which indicated a well and water. The French cavalry had watered their horses, tied them outside the building, and gone inside. Diego counted nine horses tied outside.

The two sharpshooters circled around the rear of the building and returned to Diego. The rear of the building had one small broken window and a door, which did not look as though it had been opened in some time. Diego stationed one of his sharpshooters in the brush behind the building. The other sharpshooter he stationed to the east of the front of the building. Diego positioned himself west of the front of the building.

Diego said, loud enough for all in the building to hear, "Compadres! You have guests outside. Please demonstrate your friendliness by greeting us with your hands up . . . outside!"

Diego received the greeting he had expected: gunshots from inside. *How foolish and obviously panic-stricken these French were*, thought Diego. They were firing blindly at an enemy they could not see. Diego had given orders that the sharpshooters hold their fire unless the French made a charge out the door. For a while, the French seemed quite content to occupy the building. Diego was not feeling particularly murderous but had a very pronounced need for the water in that well. He could not get any water for himself, his men, or their mounts with the French able to fire upon the area surrounding the well. Diego motioned for the sharpshooter behind the building. After a few tries, the sharpshooter smiled his understanding of what Don Diego wished. Within a few minutes, the sharpshooter approached the building from a side angle, unseen by those inside. He carried a large flaming bouquet of dry weeds, which he shoved in the window at the rear of the building. Whatever that bouquet landed upon immediately caught fire and burned with intense smoke.

The French cavalry burst through the front door, firing straight ahead in an attempt to panic or kill whoever was out there. Unfortunately for them, Diego and his sharpshooters were not in front of them, but on both sides. They were caught in a merciless crossfire that ended their flight in seconds. Diego cautiously walked among the bodies. One man, an officer, was still alive.

It was then that Lieutenant JoAnna D'Artiaga arrived with the remainder of her detachment. Dismounting on the run, she ran to Diego and the fallen French officer. What was said between them, Diego could not make out. The officer's last words were ended when Lieutenant D'Artiaga blew the top of his head off with a shot from her Dragoon pistol.

"What the hell?!" shouted Diego DaVia. "We could have gotten information from him!"

"Not him!" snapped Lieutenant D'Artiaga in return. "I know him. He would have never told us anything. He was the second in command at the French outpost at Calera. It was at his orders that most of the Indian villagers around the mission were murdered."

"Damn!" said Diego. "I would have obtained some information from him. How many are under the French command at this . . . Calera?"

"I do not know . . . maybe sixty," responded Lieutenant D'Artiaga.

"We need to know that!" spat out Diego. "Where the hell is Calera anyway?"

"About a three days' ride to the southeast," said D'Artiaga.

"This man was in command of a twenty-man unit way out here, where nothing of military importance exists, to attack your detachment?" said Diego, his military mind working. "Why?"

Lieutenant D'Artiaga was slow in answering.

"He was looking for me," admitted JoAnna.

"Again! Why?" angrily demanded Diego. "Why? Damn it!"

With muted breath, JoAnna D'Artiaga replied, "I would not have him, but he wanted me anyway."

Don Diego DaVia took a breath, stepped back a few steps, and looked at JoAnna D'Artiaga from head to toe. "That's the first thing that has made any sense in the past two days. That, I can understand."

JoAnna D'Artiaga was not sure how to respond to that. While she was trying to read his actual meaning, Diego said, "What was his complement of men before we killed these men?"

"I said sixty . . . perhaps," answered the lieutenant.

"Where are the rest of your forces?" asked DaVia, trying to remain calm.

"I do not actually know," said Lieutenant D'Artiaga.

"Wonderful! Somewhere in the western part of the great Sonoran Desert are thirty-five soldados, which we need but will never find in time!" exclaimed Diego.

"In time for what?" questioned D'Artiaga.

"In time to attack the forces at Calera," responded Diego.

"Wha-a-t? Why?" questioned D'Artiaga.

"Because a third of their forces are dead, and they do not know it. Because we cannot just stand here acting military and do nothing. Because they would never expect or be on guard against it," expounded Diego DaVia. "Order your 'army' to water these horses. Take the French horses. Pack as much water on those horses as we possibly can. When that is done, we march on Calera!"

Lieutenant JoAnna D'Artiaga had no time to give the order. She was still standing in awe of what Diego had ordered, but her detachment had heard. They gave a shout and hurried to implement that order.

Within the hour, led by Dead Man Who Walks Away, a small but determined Juarista Mexican cavalry was on its way to Calera.

32

As the little band of Juaristas rode toward the small village known as Calera, Don Diego DaVia said little, much to the dismay of Lieutenant JoAnna D'Artiaga. She would have taken advantage of the long ride to speak with Diego. She would have asked about military things, of course. But she would have used the time to get better acquainted with this man. He was a few years older than she, but JoAnna found that singularly attractive. She had felt that way at Socorra's wedding at la Rancheria Fantasma. Don Diego DaVia had not been able to find the time for an acquaintance with a young woman. When it was time to leave, she had barely been able to say a proper, thankful "adiós." But as she accompanied him on this long ride to Calera, she realized that she had thought of him many times since the wedding. Now, with the urgency of the raid on Calera, he still had his mind . . . elsewhere.

Don Diego DaVia could not help thinking about other things, most prominently Calera. The further they marched into Mexico, the more Diego questioned the motive for any military action here . . . at all. Calera, from what he could gather, seemed to be nothing more than a mission settlement to the north of the much larger town of Caborca. He had committed himself to this raid out of regard for Lieutenant D'Artiaga, and what he had already seen of the French occupation, but he would need to have more serious talks with D'Artiaga. Later that afternoon, as they rode side by side, Diego made time to speak to Lieutenant JoAnna D'Artiaga.

"Lieutenant," he began, "what else can you tell me about this 'Calera'?"

"Calera was once a place where villagers could come to worship in the little mission, get married, be buried in the Mission cemetery, live the quiet life of most Mexican peasants. It was a good life, a good life that was ended by the French," Lieutenant D'Artiaga said.

"The French soldados did not do this without orders!" said Diego, somewhat exasperated by this whole situation. "Why the hell did a French commander order his soldados to try to annihilate a whole village? Surely, they were no threat to his command."

Lieutenant D'Artiaga hesitated before saying, "They had been hiding me."

"Were you already a 'Juarista' at that time?" asked Diego.

"No," came the one-word answer.

"So, you were hiding from the French commander in this little mission!" said Diego, his voice slightly elevated.

"No. The villagers, and then the priest, had hidden me, but they had taken me out in the desert to evade him. He could not find me," D'Artiaga answered, her voice wavering.

"Are you saying that the French commander did this deed in retaliation for the help given you by the priest and his villagers?" asked Diego.

"Yes," came her answer.

"And is this detachment of yours a real Juarista fighting unit, or only a group of the remaining villagers from Calera?" asked Don Diego.

"These men are Juaristas. Some of these men are from Calera," D'Artiaga replied.

"Now I begin to understand the enthusiasm they showed for the decision to attack Calera," said Diego.

"These men hate the French in Calera!" exclaimed D'Artiaga.

"What about the larger town next door to Calera, Caborca?" asked Diego. "Are the French not occupying that town, also?"

"They control it out of fear, but they are quartered in the mission at Calera," said D'Artiaga.

"This information will help formulate a plan of attack," said Diego. "However, I need to hear one thing more."

"What?" asked Lieutenant D'Artiaga.

"I wish to know the name of the French commander at Calera," stated Diego DaVia.

"Why do you care?" asked JoAnna D'Artiaga.

"What is it?" restated DaVia.

"It is Boucher," answered JoAnna D'Artiaga. "He pronounces it *boo—shay*. Damn him!"

Diego's answer stunned her. Diego DaVia said, "French for 'butcher.' Now it is personal for me." With that, Don Diego DaVia turned his attention back to the trackless ride to Calera. He rode in silence with Lieutenant JoAnna D'Artiaga riding alongside. The miles: hot, miserable miles, spent in a most inhospitable desert, marched by. They had taken no break for a noon meal, so, by the time they at last made camp in a chaparral clearing, one third of the distance to Calera had been crossed. They were careful to create a small, smokeless fire. After they ate the rations brought with them from the cabin where they had replenished their water supply from the well, Diego motioned D'Artiaga away from the fire.

"Señorita JoAnna," he began.

"Oh, now I am 'Señorita!'" JoAnna exclaimed, venting her resentment at the very business-like interrogation he had given her earlier.

"Señorita JoAnna," continued Diego unperturbed, "please tell me more about you. You are right; I know almost nothing about you. I like what I see. You are a beautiful woman. The uniform you wear cannot conceal that fact. Long, dark hair with a hint of red that shows in the sunlight; soft, dark eyes that seem to see right through me; a smile that makes me feel that I was, indeed, blind not to have noticed you at la Rancheria Fantasma. I am impressed by what you have accomplished with these men. I only have a small picture of why you have done all that you have. I want to know where you have lived. I want to know if you have ever been married. I want to know Señorita JoAnna D'Artiaga. I have a strong feeling that I missed a golden opportunity during the wedding of Segundo and his lovely Socorra."

Señorita JoAnna D'Artiaga was stunned by this sudden change in Don Diego DaVia. He had become less military and single minded than before. She had thought, all day, that he had turned away from her as a woman. Now, the opposite seemed true. All she could say was, "What do you want me to tell you?"

"Everything. Do you come from this Calera?" said DaVia.

"No. I come from Arizpe, Sonora," she said.

"Arizpe?" said Diego, feigning ignorance of the region. He was hoping that no connection was made of Arizpe being the home of Don Miguel Peralta and the embarkation place for the ill-fated Peralta expedition of which DaVia was the lone survivor. Diego felt a sudden twinge at the possibility of this beautiful young woman having knowledge of that fact.

"When did you leave Arizpe?" asked Diego somewhat casually.

"I left as a little girl. I was, perhaps, only twelve years old. My father had a cousin who had a small rancho outside of the village of Fronteras. I grew up there," said JoAnna.

"What kind of rancho was it?" asked Diego, with some small measure of relief.

"My father helped his cousin raise the cattle. I, too, worked with him taking care of the herd," she said.

"I suppose you tired of that and wished to leave the rancho as you grew up," speculated Diego.

"Oh, no! I loved working with the cattle, and the horses as well. That is where I learned to ride," she added.

"Well, you do ride well. You certainly look good doing it, too," Diego added.

"Well! It is about time you noticed!" exclaimed JoAnna.

"If we were not preoccupied with this so-called military operation, I would investigate that subject more closely," stated Diego.

"And after our mission . . . ?" JoAnna boldly asked.

"I have plans for you," confessed Diego.

JoAnna tried to look demurely surprised, but it did not work.

"You will not need that sort of uniform," assured Diego. What Diego had been thinking, he had been thinking for days, and nights. JoAnna was a very feminine female. He would do all he could to get her out of this military role in which she found herself. He wanted to know more about her family and what placed her in a Juarista uniform.

"Are your father, and the father of Socorra, brothers?" Diego asked.

"Questions again!" rebuked JoAnna. "No. Socorra's father is my mother's brother."

"Why did you leave Arizpe?" again Diego asked.

"My mother and father were killed when the Apache raided Arizpe during their war a few years ago," related JoAnna. "I lived with Socorra's family, then went to school in Hermosillo." Diego thought she seemed reluctant to tell her history.

"And then . . . ?" queried Diego.

"One day the French entered the school and took many students away. Yes, they took me, too!" she said, becoming a bit agitated and defensive.

"And . . . ?" slowly asked Diego.

Again, a hesitation. "And, like most of the other girls . . . I was raped! Do you need to hear all the details?" said JoAnna in a loud whisper.

Then it was Diego's turn to hesitate. But when he spoke, it was in a low voice filled with concern for her feelings. "I will speak of that no more. I assume that you escaped."

After a moment to gather her composure, JoAnna replied, "I sneaked away at night, following the road that ran northward. I let my tracks mix with those of a cattle herd for a while. After a long time, I found myself in Calera, nearly starving. The people were so kind to me. They allowed me to help with their small cattle herd and provided me a place to stay."

"Until the French came to Caborca and then to Calera?" continued Diego.

"Yes," said JoAnna.

"And then came Boucher?" prompted DaVia.

"One day he saw me in the pasture. He made his attempts. I refused him forcefully. Then he threatened the family who had given me shelter. He was so arrogant! He sent his men away so that he could force me to . . . you know. I shot him! God forgive me for not killing him when I could have! I fled into the desert. The next day, one at a time, these young men began to find me. They were also fleeing this Boucher. He had begun going house to house hurting and killing anyone he thought had helped me escape. He killed many. Some of these young men had already joined the Juarista cause. They needed a leader. In their hatred and anger, they joined me." Thus, JoAnna related her tale to Don Diego DaVia.

At that point, Don Diego DaVia stood and lifted JoAnna to stand in front of him. He placed her sobbing face against his chest, and the two stood in long embrace, ignoring the understanding looks of the rest of her Juaristas.

At first glance, Calera was a sleepy little village that sat at some distance northwest of the larger village of Caborca. Calera boasted a small mission church, admittedly in need of some ongoing repairs, but still able to serve its small congregation.

However, the only activity in this sad little village had to be associated with that cavalry unit wearing French uniforms and bustling with the dreariness of soldiers stationed where they did not wish to be. There were recreational facilities to suit their desires in the larger village of Caborca nearby. But, due to the recent events in Calera, evidently the few officers of this French cavalry were allowing only themselves to take advantage of them. Caborca was off limits to enlisted troops. All this had become obvious to the observers on the hillside west of the village of Calera. It was after sunset when Diego, JoAnna, and her Juaristas positioned themselves on that hillside.

"Tonight, we watch. Tomorrow, we evaluate and plan. Once we have decided upon a plan, we will execute it. We will not go off half-cocked and ruin what can be a decisive victory here at Calera," were the words of Don Diego DaVia to his Juaristas, including one very pretty JoAnna. "We want them all dead. We want ourselves all alive. Nothing else will define a successful military mission. To this end, we all agree. To this end, we will follow the decided upon plan . . . to the letter. All in agreement . . . ?"

All heads nodded the affirmative.

"Now, Lieutenant D'Artiaga, and two to assist her, will maintain the first observation watch over the village of Calera. The rest will get a good night's sleep. After all activity ceases in Calera, everyone will get their ration of well-deserved sleep," directed Diego DaVia, clearly in command.

Lieutenant JoAnna D'Artiaga then asked, "And what will Diego DaVia be doing?"

The answer was: "Diego DaVia is going to slip into Caborca to see what the French officers are doing to entertain themselves. This will help us make the annihilation unanimous when we execute it. Please do not shoot me when I return. Lieutenant D'Artiaga should see to that small request. Buenas noches, all."

It was not much later when Diego DaVia made his way slowly along the wooden walkways of Caborca. It was not a large village. However, it boasted a few establishments where soldiers and officers could get drunk, gamble, and take advantage of entertainment by professional ladies in those establishments. Yet it was large enough that an average-dressed stranger would not be noticed as anyone of suspicion. Diego took note of said establishments, each in turn, as he passed them on the unpaved streets. He had finished his reconnoitering, noting where he saw French officers enjoying themselves, when he set about another, more personal mission. Diego had not spent his life in a gunny sack, so he had a good idea as to the proper size of clothes to fit JoAnna D'Artiaga. After all, he had spent these past days—and nights—studying her every curve. So, when he arrived back at the Juarista camp, there were a couple of soft packages in the saddlebags.

The next morning, Diego DaVia related his plan of attack to JoAnna and her Juaristas.

"There is no need to delay. We will make our attack tonight," said Diego.

All heads nodded. All faces held the appropriate grins.

"We will accomplish this in two actions. The first action will be for me to lead six men into Caborca. We will establish who our victims will be. These will be the French officers enjoying themselves in the various 'playpens' in town. Not all will be in the same playpen, so we will selectively stalk each victim. In each case, when the time is right, during their movements throughout the night, we will strike. We will kill each one, quietly . . . by knife. There must be no noise. No shooting of *pistolas*! Because I do not know which men are talented in such matters as this, Lieutenant D'Artiaga will select my six assassins," related Diego.

JoAnna then asked, "What of the thirty-five or so left in Calera?"

Diego finished. "That is the second action. After the French officers have been eliminated in Caborca, we will return to join you in a, hopefully, silent attack upon the rest of the enemy. They should all be sleeping in their quarters, which, unfortunately, are the rooms within the mission itself now. In the hours between three o'clock and dawn, the guards will probably be nearly asleep. We will use our knives on them also, quietly. We will then move into the mission and use our knives until some awaken, then use our *pistolas*. There must be no prisoners!"

JoAnna again questioned, "What about the bodies? When they are found, there will be more retaliation on the villagers."

"The bodies, even those we bring you from Caborca, will be brought here and leave with us, tied across the saddles. North of the village, we will dump them in a ravine. We will cover them with boulders and gravel. It will be long before they are found, too long. Their horses will go north with us. At that point we will make another decision that will affect us all. Get some sleep. We'll need it," ended the conversation by Diego.

Napping during the day was nothing new for a people who siesta to pass the heat of the day. However, when it is merely to pass the time until taking part in an attack of retaliation, it becomes more difficult. Each Juarista rolled out his blanket nearby, keeping a small distance from anyone else. Diego and JoAnna realized this fact. However, they found a small, secluded area and spread their bedrolls together. The horses were shaded in a small ravine, and so there was comparative stillness. Talking, with the planned night's activity before them, would have been most difficult. They simply lay there, sharing a closeness made even more precious by the actions and danger planned. Yet, in those moments, they shared an unspoken bond that both hoped would be consummated later.

The hours went by, seemingly ever so slowly. But finally, the hour had come. No one had had any appetite for food, and a meal had been passed over. But it did not matter. The entire Juarista party was focusing on their mission, a mission more personal and retaliatory than militarily justified.

The six men selected by Lieutenant JoAnna D'Artiaga were standing tall and ready when Diego DaVia walked up to them. Each had a steadfast look of determination, so that Diego had no qualms about Lieutenant D'Artiaga's choices. Each had a small utility knife, such as any farmer would carry. No one would think twice about its presence. Each also had, concealed in a sling under his plain, loose-fitting white cotton shirt . . . a machete.

"Compadres," addressed Diego DaVia. "The French officers we seek will, as they have before, depart to Caborca to pleasure themselves in the local cantinas and brothels. They will take the road from the mission at Calera and enter Caborca through the main thoroughfare. We must leave now to be there as they enter the village. Each of us will select a target and follow him to his destination. After darkness falls, we will wait until he can be stopped, alone, hopefully out of sight. Most of these places have rear entrances. We will wait and strike as each officer attempts to either rejoin his fellows or tries to return to the mission alone. We must make our 'kill' before he can rejoin his fellows. Hide the body in the shadows of bushes until we can load them up to return to Calera. *Comprende?* Understand?"

They all understood. Each had repeatedly gone over the plan in his mind all day.

"One more thing," said DaVia. "Boucher . . . is mine!"

The shadows were getting longer. It was time. Each of the Juaristas moved off casually, at intervals, inconspicuously toward Caborca. Diego had borrowed a horse, not wishing to have Hiero drawing attention. As he was about to leave, JoAnna appeared at his side. He put his hand down to touch her cheek. As his hand touched her cheek, JoAnna caught it and held it for a moment. Nothing was said. Diego DaVia turned his mount and casually rode toward Caborca.

Diego had been gone barely ten minutes when the group of French officers also rode by on their way to Caborca. Diego was nearing the entrance to the village when the French officers nearly ran him off the roadway. Diego made note of the ranking officer of the group. Looking ahead, he could see them tying their horses in front of one of the cantinas. He was able to discern his Juaristas casually lounging about as if they were part of the local men of Caborca. Each Juarista was waiting for his target to separate from his compadres.

It seemed to be taking a long time for each French officer to leave the others to seek his own private entertainment. Diego sat as if napping on a stool in the shadows across the street from the cantina where the French officers had begun their evening partying. However, after getting suitably drunk, each officer left the cantina. Diego saw that, within a moment, each French officer had a shadowy figure following a short way behind. Each Juarista would be sure to allow his quarry to become as intoxicated as possible before attacking in the dark, shadowy walkways near each destination. Each destination was a brothel, and the back door of each was dark and shadowy. The individual attack would be accomplished in those shadows.

The last French officer to leave the cantina, the French commander, stumbled toward the brothel closest to the cantina. He was so drunk that Diego thought he might not make it to the brothel. Diego did not want to have to kill him in the street. However, the officer made it to the brothel and entered. More anxious waiting. No telling when that officer would leave. But evidently the professional ladies wanted nothing to do with a man as drunk as him and, so, escorted him out the door. Then they slammed the door. Diego could not help a chuckle at the officer's embarrassment. But that left the French officer out on the street. This presented a problem for Diego. He could not kill the officer in full view of any passerby.

While considering whatever options he had, Diego became aware of a young girl walking on the board walkway. She was very young, barely in her teens. She was evidently on some errand and carrying a parcel of some sort. She was having a bit of difficulty carrying the parcel and did not notice the drunken officer standing quietly in the shadows until she was grabbed, a hand roughly placed over her mouth, and dragged back into the shadows. The young girl was unable to even scream as the officer's hand clamped her mouth shut. His free hand was already tearing at her cotton clothing.

Diego saw his opportunity. He rapidly crossed the street. He struck the French officer's head with the hilt of his machete, rendering him momentarily senseless. In the same motion he ordered the girl to run. "Vaya! Go! Do not make a sound! Do not look back!"

The terrified young girl, realizing she had been freed from her assailant, did just that and, at top speed, ran away toward her home, never looking back.

Diego struck his victim again for good measure, draped him over his back, and carried him between the buildings and a back alley to a ditch where the Juaristas were to rendezvous. Diego was the last to arrive. As he arrived, he dropped the French commander to the ground and, in the same motion, slit his throat. To everyone's surprise, Diego shoved his knife inside the dead man's belt and sliced off the man's trousers. He rolled the trousers in a ball and waited with the others.

Shortly, a farmer's two-wheel cart arrived. The bodies were thrown in, and the Juaristas were on their way out of town, slowly and inconspicuously. Nearing the mission at Calera, Diego and his party were met by Lieutenant D'Artiaga. "We must move this wagon of the dead to a place behind the shed around the other side of the mission," said Diego.

"How many—?" she started to ask.

"Seven French officers . . . seven dead," came the reply.

"There are three doors that enter the mission," Lieutenant D'Artiaga said. "The French soldados are sleeping in the rooms along the outer hallway, not in the sanctuary of the mission. We will send one team through the sanctuary to get to the rooms near the center of the hallway. The other two teams will enter from the front and rear. Get in position. Starting now, count to two hundred; then slowly and quietly enter the building. Immediately tend to business! Count, now!"

Each team entered the mission within a couple seconds of each other. They did immediately tend to business. All the French soldados died by the knife. Those few who awakened had a hand jammed over their mouths and were killed by another Juarista.

Another few minutes were spent making certain all were dead. Then Lieutenant D'Artiaga gave the word to move the bodies outside. The bodies were tied, each one on a horse. Once that was accomplished, the macabre procession made its way northward. It was only three o'clock. Two Juaristas stayed behind for a while to erase most of the tracks of the procession. They soon rejoined the escapees.

It was after dawn when the party crossed the crest of the low mountain range north of Calera. There they rested themselves and the horses. From the crags, the scouts could see more than one ravine that would do to conceal the dead French. By mid-morning, the party had already begun placing the dead in the ravine. The floor of the ravine was strewn with boulders, a foot or two in size. The sides of the ravine were made up of loose gravel-like rocks that, with a little effort, were rolled down on the dead bodies. It would be a long time before anyone found them . . . if ever.

"All right! Tell me why the French commander is the only one with no trousers!" demanded Lieutenant D'Artiaga.

Diego then related the story of how he found the French commander with the young girl and then added, "He did not deserve to be buried with his pants on. He will face eternity with his bare butt sticking up to the sky!"

It was a symbolic gesture, yet each person hoped that, in this case, it would be true.

At that point, a meeting had to be held.

"Compadres, it has been an honor to have served with you in your cause to rout the forces of the French, and the so-called 'Emperor' Maximilian," began Diego. "You are not trained soldados, yet each of you fought as the best of those. Salud!"

"Now what?" chimed in Lieutenant JoAnna D'Artiaga.

"Now it is over," again spoke Diego DaVia. "I question whether those French buried in that ravine were even regular soldados. They seemed more like brigands. But whether they were or not, the battle for Mexico will not be won or lost here in this stark, sparsely populated desert. It will occur in the more heavily populated areas of Mexico."

"What are we to do?" asked many of the Juaristas.

"If you wish to continue your fight, you will have to make your way to the main Juarista army. You may wish to pick up your lives in a new place. I do not recommend that you return to Calera or Caborca until after this war is over," stated Diego.

"What about you, Diego? What will you do now?" some of the soldados asked.

"I will go back to my home at la Rancheria Fantasma. I have been gone too long. There is much I must accomplish there," replied Diego.

Lieutenant JoAnna D'Artiaga had been listening without speaking at all. But, when Diego DaVia added, "I will be taking JoAnna D'Artiaga with me . . . if she will have me," she exclaimed, "Oh, really! What makes you think that I—"

Diego interrupted. "Segundo has Socorra at his side. I want you, JoAnna D'Artiaga, at my side, to rebuild la Rancheria Fantasma as you remember it!"

"We-e-ll . . . I truly love that rancheria. So, I suppose I'll have to go with you!" said JoAnna with a smile on her face and a tear in her eye.

At that, the Juaristas cheered, throwing their sombreros into the air.

After a much-delayed kiss and a long hug, Diego DaVia and JoAnna D'Artiaga turned northeastward toward la Rancheria Fantasma.

The Juaristas slowly scattered, as suggested by Don Diego DaVia, to take up their interrupted lives.

34

When Diego DaVia decided to ride Hiero to San Diego, he had no idea that his ride would take him to where it did. The miles had been long and difficult. Yet Hiero seemed to thrive on them. The ride from Calera to the San Rafael Valley and la Rancheria Fantasma was more of the same: many difficult miles. But the way Hiero performed, he thought it only a walk in the park. For some reason, the horse ridden by JoAnna D'Artiaga followed Hiero's example. The miles seemed to fly by. New mountains, new valleys, new canyons, new albeit mostly dry stream beds—all seemed to lead from one campsite to another as time passed by.

Diego DaVia had found a new interest. That new interest was a most lovely young woman. Dark-brown hair with a tinge of red to catch the sun and dark, expressive eyes that seemed to follow him everywhere, made it hard for Diego to keep his eyes off her. Diego had been smitten before. He had loved a woman before. He had been betrayed. He had survived that, too. He had felt the pain. JoAnna D'Artiaga had proven herself beyond betrayal. These miles had given Diego an insight into JoAnna's character that went beyond her trustworthiness as a soldier of the Juaristas.

It seemed that, now alone on the improvised trail, they had grown more knowledgeable and intimate than even Diego could have imagined. They had been separated from the rest of JoAnna's Juaristas by a few miles when Diego reined Hiero into a protected grove of trees. There, Diego asked her to remove her Juarista clothing. To Diego's surprise, JoAnna simply looked up at him and, never taking her dark eyes off him, did just that. Diego gasped at her natural beauty. Then, Diego explained that he had purchased clothing more fitting for a woman of quality, and she was to put the new clothes on. However, JoAnna approached him, pressed her body against him, and merely said, "Later, Diego."

From that point on, the trip became nothing less than a joyful adventure. Diego DaVia and JoAnna D'Artiaga enjoyed the closeness that only two people loving and dedicated to each other could have. Day after beautiful day, and night after memorable night, these two pressed on toward the San Rafael Valley and la Rancheria Fantasma.

A short way south of the Mexico/United States border, Diego called a halt. The couple was silently looking at the very point where the Fantasma Vaqueros ended the incursion of Doña Monica Ruiz and Don Raoul Ruiz. Diego had mixed memories about this place but felt the need to stop, even for a few moments, to remember it. The fact that men had died there weighed heavily upon Diego. However, those bitter memories were offset by the pride he felt that the deaths were all on the other side. His Fantasma Vaqueros had proven themselves to be what he had trained them to be: the best fighting cavalry in the desert southwest. News carries fast, even in sparsely populated areas, so the fact that JoAnna had heard of that battle came as no surprise to Diego. The look in JoAnna's eyes told Diego that she fully understood what he was feeling. A few miles later, they moved on into the San Rafael Valley, the United States, and la Rancheria Fantasma.

As they rode northward toward the main hacienda area of la Rancheria, Diego was somewhat disappointed not to see more grazing horses than he did. Perhaps the great herd, la mañada fantasma, had not yet recovered in numbers from the devastation of the Apache raid. Don Diego DaVia had, some time back, changed into his Fantasma Vaquero uniform. The first Vaqueros to see him thought at first that he was merely another Vaquero. What really caught their eye was that he was with an extremely beautiful woman. Diego and JoAnna approached them with wide smiles.

One Vaquero shouted, "Patrón! Don Diego! At last, you have returned to us!" At that the other Vaquero waved, turned his horse toward the hacienda, and rode off at top speed to inform la Rancheria Fantasma that Don Diego had returned.

Don Diego and JoAnna had barely entered the area of outbuildings when it seemed the whole population of la Rancheria Fantasma came running from all directions to greet them. Everyone at la Rancheria Fantasma rushed to yell their greetings. Don Segundo was the first, pulling Diego off Hiero to be hugged unmercifully.

"A—a—ay—y—yyyy!" Came a sudden scream from Socorra. "Diego! You have JoAnna! Diego and JoAnna! I do not believe it! Is it true? Can this be?"

Diego hardly had time to nod in affirmation when Socorra had pulled JoAnna from her horse, and the two cousins were embracing and whirling around and around to the surprise and amazement of all. Segundo was still jumping up and down yelling and whacking Diego on the back as they made their way to the long porch.

Diego joined the yelling, "Give us a chance to breathe! We will tell you all about what happened when we are properly 'wet down!'" At that, refreshments were on the way.

It seemed an extraordinarily long time for the initial celebrating to settle down. Socorra had already requested the lady Vaqueros to prepare a festive dinner for that night. That request was unnecessary because the lady Vaqueros were already planning that anyway.

During the rest of the afternoon, Diego DaVia, with his JoAnna beside him, related most of his story to Segundo, Socorra, Pancho, and, because so many others were lounging around that porch, probably Pancho's grandmother. He left out some of the more intimate facets of his experience in San Diego concerning Constance herself. He did tell of his settlement of the issue with Constance's fiancé and his two would-be duelists. Segundo was nearly "on the floor" as that story was relayed. Things quieted somewhat as Diego told of finding his JoAnna. He told how speedily he had become enamored of her. He told how true she was to everything she did. He told how often she could have betrayed those men who counted upon her but did not. He told how she did what she had to do, as a Juarista, but hated doing it. He told how they had come to know, love, and trust one another.

It was then that he told all in attendance that, when they left Calera, the decision was made that JoAnna would not return to Mexico; she would stay at la Rancheria Fantasma. After a short pause, Diego said that JoAnna D'Artiaga would become JoAnna DaVia as soon as family and friends could be gathered. Socorra again let out that scream of joy at that news. She had known it the moment that she had seen JoAnna with Diego. To Socorra, that was so perfect. The love Socorra and JoAnna had for each other as cousins would be the greatest life for them together at la Rancheria Fantasma. Socorra, having known JoAnna for most of their lives, had thought JoAnna would be perfect for Diego and even wondered out loud why she and Diego had not gotten together at Socorra's wedding. How fate had managed to throw JoAnna and Diego together, to Socorra, was an act of God. Socorra loved her husband, Segundo, with all her heart but cared very much for the happiness of his best friend, his hermano. Her life at la Rancheria Fantasma had been wonderful, even having had to live through the Apache raid. But now, she would be part of the overall happiness of her own cousin and Diego, together.

There was much to do. Wisely, Diego and Segundo backed away and gave full rein to Socorra and JoAnna. It was a good thing that they did. Those two women began planning a party that would make the previous ones look like practice.

Segundo, trying hard to stay calm after the surprise return of his hermano, let Diego know that there was still a Rancheria Fantasma to operate. Diego mentioned that he had not seen as many horses grazing as he would have thought. "What is going on, Segundo? Is there some sort of problem?"

"Sí, Diego," said Segundo. "We never have returned our mañada to its size before the Apache raid. We are not obtaining horses at the rate we used to. I am not sure why, but I think it has to do with the war against Maximilian. There never was much fighting near our border, but we had supplied some horses. I think the war is being fought way farther south into Mexico."

"I have seen firsthand that what you say is true. The war against Maximilian will be won or lost much farther south into Mexico . . . closer to the large population centers, perhaps in Mexico City itself," agreed Diego. "What about the Apache? We both gained and lost horses to the Apache."

Segundo responded, "The Apache, under their war chief Cochise, have concentrated their war in the Chiricahua Mountains south into eastern Sonora and western Chihuahua. According to some Yaqui reports, Cochise sees no gain for them in action in our region."

"Understandable," said Diego. "So, our herd is smaller because we no longer have the market for them that we used to have." He said that as much as a statement of fact as a question to Segundo. "What do you think we should do about it?"

"I do not really know for certain," replied Segundo. "But we have had to raise cattle for our own use to feed ourselves and our Vaqueros. I have heard that cattle bring a high price at the railroad in Tucson."

"How strange things work out as times change," observed Diego. "JoAnna told me once how much she loved helping her father with the cattle herds he was working. She seems to know quite a bit about it."

"That could be a great help to us if we decided to add cattle to our Rancheria Fantasma," said Segundo. "I remember when we were recruiting Vaqueros for our Rancheria Fantasma; many had been vaqueros working with cattle herds. They often had to fight the Texicans who made raids into Mexico to steal cattle."

"It is a difficult decision," said Diego.

"Do you think that we can make it work?" asked Segundo. "I mean, a cattle and horse rancheria? Together?"

"Well. Now we have more than we started with before. We have you, me, Pancho . . . and his grandmother. We also have Socorra and JoAnna," said Diego.

"Sí! How can we lose?" said Segundo.

"That damn Apache raid hurt us mucho, hermano," said Diego. "The cost of rebuilding, without our former large market for our horses, drained us of cash flow. We need to find out how much cash we still have and compare that to what we will need to stake us to this new venture."

"New venture? You mean new adventure! Don't you?" chided Segundo.

"Segundo, while we are planning our wedding party, we need to be investigating the cost of cattle, getting them here, raising them, and marketing them. If, as you say, there should be a market in Tucson, using the new railroad, we'll have to drive the marketable herd to Tucson," suggested Diego.

"Daunting, isn't it?" said Segundo.

"Mucho!" exclaimed Diego. "But we have some time. We are not destitute . . . yet."

Segundo said, "That means poor . . . right? I have been trying not to use that word."

"Segundo: we have two beautiful women who are expecting us to lavish them with attention tonight. Let us be at it!" invited Diego.

And lavish with attention they did. Having two beautiful women who loved the dons of la Rancheria Fantasma almost made the concerns of operating la rancheria fade away . . . almost. Correspondence from Judge Morales in Tucson seemed to confirm what the two dons had originally surmised: that marketing cattle, especially at this time and for the immediate future, was a good enterprise. Tucson was growing and needed beef. Tombstone had come into existence and would be needing beef. The new railroad would be shipping cattle to markets all over the western states. Judge Morales had gone so far as to have some personal acquaintances research potential costs for such a venture. This work was still in progress. However, because Diego had not overlooked his earlier promise to invite Judge Morales to la Rancheria Fantasma, and to his wedding, the judge would be bringing the results of his research to la Rancheria Fantasma.

The efforts of Socorra and JoAnna to make the upcoming wedding and fiesta the grandest ever had certainly not been wasted. The same relatives and friends of Socorra and JoAnna would be arriving and bringing with them the same festive prospects. Neither woman had seen these guests since the wedding of Socorra and Segundo, so every hour of every day was a grand reunion. The priest who had married Socorra and Segundo evidently had forgotten the previous, bumpy ride. Judge Morales arrived the day before the ceremony. Don Diego DaVia and Don Segundo Ruiz welcomed him as if he were visiting royalty. He was overwhelmed. Judge Morales was awestruck by the sight of la Rancheria Fantasma as well. He stood on the porch overlooking the San Rafael Valley, unable to do more than shake his head in disbelief.

"All that I had heard about this rancheria, and this San Rafael Valley, did not do it justice," he spoke in awe. "I have seen ranches set in beautiful locales before, but la Rancheria Fantasma in the San Rafael Valley is as close to paradise as I have ever seen with these eyes." And, as he spoke those words, conversation had stopped to give added reverence to his observation. For it seemed true. The mountains surrounding the lush, grassy valley—with the beginning of the Rio Santa Cruz flowing southward amid herds of grazing horses—the rebuilt buildings, and that evening's array of beautiful people in their beautiful finery eclipsed his previous expectations.

"Diego and Segundo, had I seen this valley twenty years ago, I would have fought anyone and anything to keep it. And you have kept the natural beauty here. I cannot praise you enough. Thank you for allowing me the honor of seeing it."

"Gracias, Your Honor," quietly said both dons in gratitude for his kind words.

"Gentlemen, I have the estimates you requested. The figures are high; I am sure you knew they would be. But I believe you can accomplish your goal. Shall we sit somewhere and go over them?" asked Judge Morales.

"Your Honor," said Segundo, "Don Diego and his JoAnna have decided to postpone their honeymoon trip until a later date. They have not decided where they wish to visit. Socorra and I visited San Diego and had a wonderful time. However, as Diego will relate to you details of his recent adventures at that lovely city later, he prefers not to visit it again." This brought gales of laughter from the judge and all around them, except Diego. However, even his frown was somewhat exaggerated.

"Judge Morales, once you see the fiesta that will begin soon enough, I'm sure you will agree that the 'financials' can wait until such time as we can concentrate our attention upon them," explained Diego.

The wedding fiesta began that same night before the wedding. Guitars and singing went on and on into the night. The food was amazing. "I used to have gentlemanly manners," said Judge Morales. "But I have never had food such as this. I am making a pig of myself!" All that did was invite the lady Vaqueros to offer him some more.

The wedding ceremony was held the next afternoon in the grassy area between the main hacienda and the home built by Segundo for Socorra. It was not a long ceremony, but to Diego it was extremely fast. He had expected it to take longer. Segundo told him that it was the exact ceremony that married Socorra and himself. Diego was focused so intently on it that it seemed to fly by.

And then it was over. Don Diego DaVia, former Capitán of Dragoons, Mexican cavalry, had taken unto himself JoAnna D'Artiaga, the beautiful love of his life. He could hardly believe it. However, JoAnna DaVia spent all that night, and many more, convincing him that it was true.

And what a fiesta came after the wedding! It did not seem to end. The Vaqueros of la Rancheria Fantasma had, in their love for Diego, been waiting for this happiness for him for so long. They let it rip! The men had come to celebrate, and they certainly did. As for the women . . . well, they were on their own! There was many a foot race that night.

———

The next morning's porch breakfast came a little later than usual, closer to lunch. But no one cared. They had celebrated a wonderful night. The bride and the groom certainly looked loving. However, a party is a party, and Socorra and Segundo looked equally loving. The sight of Judge Morales seemed to bring everyone back to reality. But whether he had interesting financial figures or not, nothing was going to delay that breakfast.

Yet, those figures had to be scrutinized sooner or later. So, when Diego and Segundo began asking some questions about cattle, Socorra said, "JoAnna and I both know what is going to happen, even if you do not. So, we are going for a ride with the herd for a while. Adiós! For a while!"

So, then it was time to spread out the papers the judge had brought with him. The eyes of Diego and Segundo seemed to open wider with every entry. Expansion into the cattle business along with the horse operation would require a substantial capital investment. There were long periods of silence. During one of the silent periods, Judge Morales offered, "You are aware that not all of this must be your own cash. Business loans are available at one of our banks in Tucson. It is but one option for you to make the transaction as painless as possible. Another is to sell off part of your herd for cash. Another is to take out a mortgage on your property here in the San Rafael Valley. These are all various ways to handle this matter. You do not have to do anything now. You can think about it. When you are ready to make such a move, of any kind, I will be glad to assist you."

Seeing the look on both dons' faces, Judge Morales added, "I know this looks like a terribly difficult thing to have to do, but it is done all the time. This information is merely to help you decide what, if anything, you want to do. Of course, if you had a stash of money buried away, that would make it all easier."

The judge had said that in a light-hearted manner meant to relieve some of the tension he saw in both men. But that quip caused Diego to miss a breath!

Diego then said, "We will think over all that you have said. But, my good friend, I would like for you to stay here in our valley for as long as you enjoy it. We are honored to have you here. Your being here at my wedding has meant much to me."

"I have been honored to be here, my friends," said the judge. "And I have been honored to provide you with these options. I consider it a privilege to do a small favor for the men who saved Tucson in the non-battle of that little presidio."

Diego responded, "The favors that you have been doing for me are a little one sided now. I am certain that I will be seeing you in Tucson in the next few weeks. As Segundo told me once, 'Favors are delivered back and forth between friends,' so, it will be my turn."

After Judge Morales had left the breakfast table, Segundo looked at Diego and asked, "What are we going to do? Any ideas?"

Diego replied slowly, "I do not like mortgages. I understand them, but I do not wish to use that method of obtaining cash."

Segundo added, "Selling off our herd to obtain cash is like shooting one foot in favor of the other."

"Hermano, I must remain here for at least a few weeks. I am just married, and I cannot just up and leave. I owe this time to JoAnna," asserted Diego.

"I'll say you do!" agreed Segundo. "But . . . then what?"

"Then I must go to where I can obtain money," flatly stated Diego.

"Do you mean money . . . or gold?" asked Segundo, perceiving Diego's intent.

"Gold," said Diego.

"There is danger?" asked Segundo.

"Yes, probably," again asserted Diego.

"I could go with you," volunteered Segundo.

"Not this time, hermano. I must do this alone," slowly asserted Diego again. Then he said, "I need you to keep this rancheria safe. I need you to keep my JoAnna and your Socorra safe. Everyone and everything I love is here. I will need to know in my heart that you are all safe here."

"When?" asked Segundo.

"I will wait three, maybe four weeks," stated Diego.

"JoAnna will understand, Diego," assured Segundo.

35

JoAnna DaVia was awake early. She sat on the large ramada-style porch of the hacienda. Drinking coffee and watching the sunrise was only one of the daily pleasures she loved at la Rancheria Fantasma. She was a woman who had found and won the man she had had in her thoughts for a long time. Her happiness was nearly complete . . . nearly. Like her cousin Socorra, JoAnna was very perceptive. She had seen the look of concern on the faces of both Segundo and Diego. Something was bothering them.

Diego was not long in following his JoAnna to the porch. It made him smile inwardly to see his beautiful JoAnna waiting for him in the glow of the sunrise. Their "good mornings" and the accompanying kisses started his day off right. Breakfast would be along soon. Segundo and Socorra would probably join them on the porch as usual. Until then, the happy newlyweds enjoyed being with each other as they welcomed the sun.

A few moments after Socorra and Segundo joined them, while drinking their coffee, JoAnna asked Socorra, "Will it be you or me?"

Socorra replied, "You do it today."

Before anyone could do it, Diego asked, "Do what?"

JoAnna did not hesitate. "Diego, you and Segundo are quietly concerned about something. Socorra and I wish to know what is bothering the two of you."

"Segundo," started Diego, "the Apache, when he does not wish to show his true feeling about one thing or another, makes his face a 'mask.' We must practice that, hermano."

"Won't do any good, Diego," said Segundo. "Socorra sees through me every time, no matter what I do."

Diego thought for a minute then said, "I suppose it is about time anyway."

At that, both JoAnna and Socorra exclaimed, "About time for what?!"

Diego said, "I'll tell you." Then, looking directly at JoAnna, Diego said, "La Rancheria Fantasma, thanks to a changing market and a tragic Apache raid, is thinking about raising cattle, as well as our horses."

Socorra let JoAnna continue.

"And this is a problem because . . . ?" asked JoAnna.

"Because, for the first time in a very long time, we do not have the cash to do what we need to do," answered Diego.

"And I'll bet you will have to go someplace to get it, because there is not much of it lying around here," guessed JoAnna. JoAnna looked at Socorra, who said, "You are doing great, JoAnna. Continue."

"Never mind, you two; I'll tell you," said Diego. "La Rancheria Fantasma was founded primarily with a rather large amount of gold that I brought here many years ago. This gold was part of an even larger amount of gold, part of which was stashed in an old mine. It was thought that it would be recovered a short time later, but that was not to be."

Socorra could not help uttering, "Dios mio! The massacre!"

Diego looked directly at Socorra and then at JoAnna and said, "Yes, the massacre."

JoAnna then spoke very softly. "I do not like this. I am suddenly feeling very frightened."

Diego spoke to her also in soft tones. "I believe the danger has passed. It was a long time ago. What happened then cannot happen again. I believe I am the only man alive who knows where this gold is stashed, because I helped stash it there."

Segundo, never having heard this part of the massacre story, asked, "Is there as much as you had when you came to this valley?"

"Yes, and much, much more," said Diego. "I will not be able to carry it all out; but what I will be able to carry will make us all extremely wealthy for the rest of our lives."

JoAnna was quick to say, "I do not like it! We just found each other. I want to keep you . . . alive!" The beginnings of sobs were making their appearance. Diego stood up and held JoAnna close.

"We all love this rancheria. We all love this San Rafael Valley. We all love our way of life, and our Vaqueros, and their families. We have fought long and hard against powerful enemies to make it, and to keep it," said Diego.

"But why must you go alone?" JoAnna asked between sobs.

"I am the only one who knows where the gold was stashed. No one else knows. I am the lone survivor. More than one would possibly call attention to what I am doing. I am safer doing this alone."

"When?" asked JoAnna.

Diego replied, "Now that you know, the sooner, the better."

JoAnna began to cry in earnest. Socorra had tears in her eyes, too.

Diego looked deeply into her, now tear-filled eyes and said, "As I love you, and as I love you all . . . I will return."

Three days later, Diego DaVia pointed Hiero northward and began the return he had thought he would never make: back to the Sombrero mines. Diego had hoped never to see that scenery again. He feared seeing it again. He feared the memories and the nightmares that would surely return. Memories of Don Miguel Peralta, a man he respected; Capitán Antonio Garces, an excellent officer in command of the cavalry assigned to the Peralta expedition; Manuel Peralta, the son of Don Miguel, who took command of the expedition after Don Miguel had to leave for California; U Day Ah, the Yavapai girl, whose mixed feelings of friendship for the Peraltas battled the loyalty to her Yavapai nation; O hi Cama, the fierce warrior of the Yavapai, who guided the Yavapai to success in the massacre of the Peralta expedition and impressed Diego; Nanni-Chaddi, the Yavapai chieftain who, in spite of his hatred, honored his vow to allow time for the Peraltas to leave safely. The horror of the running battle into the canyon, the screams of wounded and dying men and animals as they were slaughtered by the massive force of Yavapai and Apache warriors, renewed the fear of remembering—the pain of remembering. The anticipation of seeing that countryside again occupied his every thought as Hiero took him southwest of Tucson to the mission of San Xavier del Bac. There he would rest, take on water, and gather his resolve. There he hoped that he would gain some semblance of peace to take forward on his journey. The padres there certainly did their best to that end.

———

It took two days and numerous visits with the padres, but Diego DaVia guided Hiero again northward, with new steadfast feelings and dedication, toward the Sombrero mines. Doing his best to avoid the area of Superstition Mountain, especially the northwest side—Massacre Ground—Diego veered west of Tucson, intending to come up to the mine directly from the south. He camped in the desert three times before he came upon the Rio Gila. He was considerably farther west along this river than when the Peralta expedition crossed on their northward trek. He was well west of where he had crossed as he wandered out of the canyon now called "Massacre Ground."

But as he pressed northward, he became aware that some small settlements had sprung up over the recent years. The only one of any significance at all was along the Rio Salado and directly between him and the Sombrero mines. It certainly was not there at the time of the Peralta expedition. It was not much of a town. Primitive would be a polite word for it. Situated about five miles east of the later downtown of Phoenix, it had been named "Phoenix." It was late when Diego DaVia rode into Phoenix on Hiero.

Riding slowly from the south, Diego knew he would not be sleeping in that hell hole. The buildings were ramshackle at best. Most structures were saloons or would-be saloons—these offering gambling, whiskey, and women, but not necessarily in that order. He took a long look and decided to make a cold camp a short way north of town. But first he would see what this town was all about. He then rode back into the "sprawling metropolis" of Phoenix.

He had noticed a saloon that looked, perhaps, a small cut above the rest in town. He wisely tied Hiero a distance from the saloons. His intention was to have a drink at the bar, not attract any attention, and pick up any information about the area that could be of help to him.

The existence of this town, where there had been no town before, gave him some measure of apprehension. This excursion to retrieve gold might not be the inconspicuous ride up to a desolate hidden mine as he had first thought.

Diego stood at the bar for a few moments listening to whatever conversations were happening around him. These were mostly miners, with a double handful of outlaw types thrown in. Evidently, some silver had been discovered in the area as well as some small amounts of gold. No great surprise to Diego. The conversation nearby was becoming a bit loud and boisterous and was turning into an argument over the possibility of gold in the rocky local mountains. One miner was exceptionally loud, proclaiming that there were once Spanish and then Mexican diggings in those mountains. Diego's attention piqued.

"The Mexicans tell of a large operation by the Peralta family of Sonora," one miner insisted.

"I never saw any Mexicans walking around with gold, from here or anywhere!" said another, laughing.

"Well, I believe it is true," insisted the first miner.

"Any Mexican flashing gold must be one of those 'Peraltas'!" he said laughing, mocking the other miner.

The bartender had asked Diego what he wanted to drink. Diego answered, "Tequila, por favor."

"I'll see your money first," said the bartender.

Diego reached into his pocket for his money. He had momentary difficulty getting it out. When he did, a gold nugget, which he had been carrying for a long time for luck, flipped out onto the bar with his money. The bartender tried to take the nugget as payment for the drink. Diego reached to retrieve it. But the damage was done. There was much smoke in the saloon, but the miners saw the nugget. As Diego tried to replace the nugget in his pocket, two very rough men had sprung forward to take the nugget. They soon found out that this was one Mexican who fought back. Diego knocked each man down. One man pulled a knife. The other man yelled something about "damn Peralta!" The one with the knife made a slashing motion and successfully slashed Diego across his side.

To the surprise of everyone, especially Diego, no sooner had the man said "damn Peralta" than a man was lunging across the room at them. The one with the knife fell to the floor when a bottle, swung by a man called Jacob Waltz, crashed across his face. The second brave attacker fled out the door.

Jacob Waltz was a cantankerous old prospector, well past middle age for the time, probably in his fifties. He irritated and aggravated many by his curt, abrupt manner and attitude. He spoke with a German or "Deutche" accent and, therefore, was called the "Dutchman." Jacob Weiser was less disagreeable, but, because of the common background between them, he was partnered with the Dutchman.

Jacob Waltz was not always known to be so charitable in matters such as this, but he, as an experienced miner, was more familiar with the name *Peralta*. He and his friend, Jacob Weiser, quickly escorted the Mexican, Diego DaVia, out of the saloon. Watching furtively over their shoulders, they made their way down the shadowy walkway to the room where Jacob Waltz had his bunk. Diego was not too seriously injured. But he did receive some whiskey. Some of it was poured over his wound in advance of a bandage, and some of it was poured into the Mexican, Diego DaVia.

"Rest, my friend," said Jacob Waltz. "We will talk in the morning."

"No," said Jacob Weiser. "We were getting some nasty looks as we left the saloon. Those drunks might start something. We need to get this man out of here. It is dark, and we should make camp outside of town a way."

"Sí! Por favor, amigos. My horse is outside. Get me out of here," directed the Mexican.

It did not take long to secure their Mexican guest next to a wash north of town. There they made a cold camp and spent the night. The dawn had broken when the two Jacobs became aware that their Mexican guest was already awake. They made a semi-smokeless fire so as not to attract attention and cooked a light breakfast, mostly coffee.

"My thanks to you both for saving my life back there in the saloon and getting me the hell out of there!" said Diego.

"You are welcome," said Jacob Waltz. "But what caused that ruckus anyway?"

"It has happened before in different places," volunteered Diego. "Sometimes these gringos like to pick on a lone Mexican. Usually, I can handle it myself. This is the first time one came up with a knife, though."

"There had to be something more to start that last night," said Jacob Weiser. "I think it was the gold nugget you flashed to pay your bill."

"Perhaps," said Diego. "I have not had to use one before. Usually, I use whatever cash I have on me. Last night I had cash but had to dig for it."

"So, you pulled out a nugget big enough to choke the bartender! Ha!" exclaimed Jacob Waltz. "Where did you get that big thing anyhow?"

Diego DaVia said nothing in response to the question.

"Aah! Relax. If we were going to rob you of it, we could have done it last night," said Waltz. "We've been doing our share of prospecting for some time now but haven't come up with anything like that."

"Gold is of great importance to you?" questioned DaVia.

"Never having had the privilege of owning very much of it . . . yah," answered Jacob Weiser.

"If not for the gold, why did you help me in that saloon?" asked Diego. "You are the only ones who made a move to help me."

The two Jacobs looked at each other for only a moment.

"I will tell you honestly," offered Jacob Waltz, pouring another cup of coffee. "The combination of seeing that gold nugget and hearing that trash cuss the name *Peralta* did it."

"Why would you care about the Peralta name?" asked DaVia. "I do not even understand why he said it." However, Diego was not looking directly at either Jacob Waltz or Jacob Weiser when he made the statement. The Dutchman saw the aversion of the Mexican's glance.

"Not everyone around these parts knows about the Peralta. But anyone who knows about gold mines in Sonora knows about that name," replied Jacob Waltz. "He, the old don or his family, pretty much ran the whole gold mining show for a couple decades in Sonora, and some say around here someplace."

"Most people, especially gringos, think they know more than they actually do," ventured the Mexican. The coffee was making him feel much better now. The conversation had become more than a little interesting.

"What do you know about them? Are you a Peralta?" asked Jacob Weiser.

"That depends on what you call a Peralta. I will not say that I am. But what if I were?" answered Diego.

"Relax, amigo. It does not matter to us," reassured Jacob Waltz. "We are not the most popular people in Phoenix, but that is by our choice. Finding a little gold and living a little higher on the hog would be nice, though."

"Yah! I'd like to give that a try sometime!" chimed in Jacob Weiser.

Diego DaVia stood up and slowly paced back and forth by the campfire for a few minutes. He was obviously thinking deeply about something. *That damn gold!* he thought. Finally, he turned, looking at the two Jacobs in turn, eye-to-eye. When he returned to his seat by the fire, they knew he would have something to discuss. They were not disappointed.

"Amigos, you know by the nugget you saw last night that I have some gold. You also believe that I have some connection to the 'Peraltas.' You are right. But you did me a good turn last night. I also know that you did not have to do it. I am sure that you did not act because you have a special love for Mexicans. I believe that a little gold flows through the veins of all three of us," said Diego DaVia.

"Ha! Not just a little!" laughed Jacob Weiser.

"We agree," said Diego. "Gold makes brothers of us all." With a flick of his hand, Diego DaVia flipped the gold nugget from the fracas the night before to the two prospectors. Jacob Waltz caught it in midair. "It is yours," stated Diego.

"There's a hook coming! I feel it," said Jacob Waltz suspiciously.

"No hook. A proposition to make you both wealthy men," said Diego.

The two prospectors sat silently and waited.

"I give you that nugget. It is yours. If you will wait for me for five days, you can be rich men. My connection to the Peraltas is no one's business. I have spent years trying to forget it. Maybe what I do now will help me forget. However, in five days, I will return to show you 'Peralta' gold. You must trust me for five days."

"What do we have to put up for this?" questioned Jacob Waltz warily.

"You have already paid for the privilege by saving my life last night. That is all," flatly stated Diego DaVia. "But you must trust me to meet you, and only you, here in five days. You must stay sober! You must tell no one! To do so could get us all killed. Are we agreed?"

"Considering that you are such a smooth talker, and that we have nothing at all better to do . . . yes," said Jacob Waltz. "Well, Weiser, give him your *yes*, too."

"Yah," said Jacob Weiser.

"Bueno!" said Diego DaVia as he shook the hands of both Jacobs. "I will see you here, in this place, five mornings from now. Provision yourselves for a few days camp."

Then, mounting Hiero, Diego rode away northward, into the palo verde, mesquite, and creosote bush-filled desert.

The two prospectors stood watching the Mexican disappear.

"What just happened? Is this really happening?" they asked, one to the other.

After but a moment's thought, Jacob Waltz said, "We've got nothing to lose, so we'll meet him here, if he shows up that is. Hell, we don't even know his name."

"Who cares? I like the look and feel of that nugget, so I guess we'll wait," said Weiser.

"We'd better prepare a stash of some digging equipment around here, in case he actually shows up and we have to do some exploratory digging," said Jacob Waltz.

36

On the night of the fourth day, the two prospectors, unnoticed by anyone, left town and made their way to the campsite where the Mexican
had promised to meet them. Once again, they kept a cold camp with no
fire to give away their presence to nosy strangers. These two men enjoyed
sleeping past the dawn on most mornings, but that morning dawn found
them wide awake. They had begun to get a little fidgety by the first hour
after morning light. But, not long after that, the Mexican, Diego DaVia,
rode slowly into their camp.

Diego did not directly ride into their camp. He had been watching
their camp for hours to make sure that these two men were, in fact,
alone. Satisfied, he had then ridden into their camp. He did not dismount but told the two Jacobs to quietly move the camp a couple miles
farther from Phoenix. He wanted some coffee but did not want to invite
any neighbors. A short while later, Diego DaVia had his coffee.

"Amigos, we have about a day and a half's ride ahead of us. We must
be extremely careful not to attract attention. We must be wary of everyone. No one we see will be our friend. Thieving miners from town,
Apaches, and Yavapai are all in the area. If you are brave, and quiet,
within two days you will be rich men."

Diego led them generally toward the northeast. They slowly rode
and sometimes walked their horses through the rough underbrush. They
were meticulously careful not to make any kind of noise, or to ride where
their silhouette would show too high over the brush and low trees. They
made a cold camp along a wash that emptied a little southwest of Blue

Mountain. They were exhausted, so they slept well, at least when not taking a turn on guard duty. They noticed the Mexican seemed to be a little nervous. Thoughts and memories of that place were playing uncontrollably in Diego's mind. But he allowed nothing to disturb the desert quiet.

The next morning, while trying to calm the two prospectors' excitement, Diego deliberately took his time getting started. He made sure the prospectors had proper digging equipment, which would enable them to dig past or remove some comparatively large rocks. The two Jacobs peppered their new friend with one question after another. They could not understand why they were not rushing forward to find their gold. Diego did not wish to tell them that in the bright light of the early morning sun, they would be extremely vulnerable to discovery and even attack. Fears, years old, still lingered in his mind.

Diego delayed their departure until just before noon. When they made their move, Diego DaVia, now noticeably wearing a holstered Dragoon pistol and carrying a rifle, led the two prospectors overland from Blue Mountain to a point where they could make their way up Blue Wash. Blue Wash would lead the men to a point south of the Rock in the Shape of a Man's Head.

They continued from there to the canyon leading to the Peralta stone cabin and mine. As they slowly rode up the canyon pathway, Jacob Waltz was beside himself with excitement. He had been striving for years to make a gold strike, but to no avail. DaVia had to nearly block the way with his horse to slow him down.

Then they saw and passed the spring, which, at some time, obviously had been chopped out to facilitate dipping buckets into it.

Fifty yards farther they came upon the ruin of the Peralta two-room stone cabin. The roof was gone, but some of the walls were still intact.

The debris field, above and behind the cabin ruin coming down from the upper shaft of the mine, held each prospector's rapt attention. At the top of this debris field, they would find the old stone ramp, which was constructed by either the Peraltas or the Spanish before them. They all dismounted. Diego let them make their own assessment of what had once been the mining operation in that place. When Jacob Waltz saw the arrastra, still intact, on the curve of the wash around the hill, he ran to see what gold residue might still be in the circle. Diego, dismounting his horse, then said, "Gentlemen," and pointing to the base of the hillside, "there is why you are here. That innocent-looking pile of rocks hides the lower, horizontal shaft of the mine."

"Let's get in there!" shouted both prospectors, thinking that they were going to have to dig the gold from the mine.

"Halt!" directed Diego DaVia. "Hear my words! What you find in there will probably astound you. It will be an awesome sight. I want none of it. It will all belong to you. Plan well what you will do with what you find in that hole," he cautioned. "Realize that men will try to kill you for it. Move that gold and hide it somewhere else—where no miner will ever find it. Defend yourselves well. Buena suerte, amigos!" he added.

The prospectors indicated that they had heard his words, but by then they were frantically ripping the rocks from the seemingly sealed entrance to the lower mineshaft. They paid no attention whatsoever to the Mexican who had guided them to what would become the most famous gold treasure in the southwestern United States—the "Lost Dutchman Mine." Because of this, the Mexican was able to mount his horse and, carefully choosing his way, ascend unnoticed the slope on the south wall of the canyon, the very spot from which O hi Cama had discovered the "new hole," which triggered the attack on the Peraltas.

Looking down on them, it was obvious to Diego DaVia that neither Jacob Weiser nor Jacob Waltz, the Dutchman, had noticed that part of the stony obstruction had recently been removed and replaced. He smiled inwardly, as well as outwardly. Then Don Diego DaVia dismounted, picked up two large, heavy leather saddlebags from under the ironwood shrub, where he had left them three days earlier. These two nondescript leather saddlebags contained more gold than he could spend in his entire lifetime. These he secured to his saddle, one on either side of Hiero. Then, before remounting, he looked with pride at the handle of the saber resting firmly in the saddle scabbard. The worn emblem, embossed on the saber handle and on the scabbard, seemed to leap out at him: the brass and leather insignia of a capitán of dragoons!

Then, on the ridge, silhouetted against the setting sun, that wry smile still in place, Don Diego DaVia, Dead Man Who Walks Away, rode into the lengthening shadows, toward the southeast, avoiding Superstition Mountain, carrying his share of "massacre" gold to la Rancheria Fantasma . . . and to those he loved.

Thus completes the Legend of the Origin of the Lost Dutchman's Gold.

About the Author

Herbert Dean Ely, educated primarily in Illinois and East Tennessee, spent time with the U.S. Air Force, which included being stationed within the Strategic Air Command—Underground. After the military, he served in management and executive positions in the cement and armored car/ATM industries.

Ely has resided for the past forty years in Arizona near Superstition Mountain. This has resulted in a keen interest in the legends of the Southwest, including the Lost Dutchman Mine and the Peralta Massacre. He was certainly not the first, but was one of the very few, who had located and visited the Lost Dutchman Mine.